PRAISE FOR

SEAL's Honor

"Megan Crane's mix of tortured ex–special ops heroes, their dangerous missions, and the rugged Alaskan wilderness is a sexy, breathtaking ride!"

—*New York Times* bestselling author Karen Rose

Also by Megan Crane

SEAL'S HONOR

SNIPER's
Pride

AN ALASKA FORCE NOVEL

MEGAN CRANE

JOVE
New York

A JOVE BOOK
Published by Berkley
An imprint of Penguin Random House LLC
1745 Broadway, New York, NY 10019

ISBN: 9780451491510

First Edition: May 2019

Printed in the United States of America
1 3 5 7 9 10 8 6 4 2

Cover photo by Claudio Marinesco
Cover design by Sarah Oberrender
Book design by Tiffany Estreicher

For Private Johnson

Acknowledgments

Thanks to Kerry Donovan for making my stories sing, and to everyone else at Berkley. It's such a pleasure to work with you! And I can never thank Holly Root enough.

Thanks as ever to Nicole Helm and Maisey Yates for being my first readers—and for keeping me from jumping off that proverbial cliff halfway through, when I'd forgotten what on earth I was doing. And to Lisa Hendrix for once again giving me an "Alaska read." Any remaining mistakes are all mine. Let's hope they serve the story!

Thank you, thank you, thank you to Lucianne Crenshaw and Shantell Dayton for teaching me, among too many other things to name here, how to fight. And to Kendall Coe and Brenda Kizzire for teaching me how to fight dirty.

And to Jeff, who still makes me giddy when he walks into a room.

One

After the second time her husband tried to kill her, Mariah McKenna decided she needed to get out of Atlanta.

The first time could have been an accident. That night she had gone to yet another strained charity dinner where everyone smiled sweetly, blessed her heart, and made it perfectly, politely clear they wouldn't be taking her side in the divorce. And even though Mariah knew better than to touch shellfish, it was always possible that there could have been cross-contamination in the food. Especially in a hotel banquet situation with complicated hors d'oeuvres passed around on gleaming silver trays by bored college students.

Mariah knew it was entirely possible that she'd tossed back what she'd thought was a little cheese puff pastry when it was actually cleverly concealed shrimp. She'd been too busy pretending not to notice the speculative, not particularly friendly looks being thrown her way to taste a thing.

It could easily have been an unfortunate accident. Or her own fault for not paying attention.

But she was pretty sure it was David.

He had gone out of his way to get nasty with her only the day before.

"You can't divorce me," he'd snarled, getting much too close to her in the sunny parking lot of the Publix in her new neighborhood. That had been her fault, too, for not paying closer attention to her surroundings. She should have seen David's overly polished Escalade. She shouldn't have imagined for a single second that he'd allow her to go about without permission, having a normal life like a regular person. "*You* can't divorce *me*."

That was why, when her throat had started to close up, the first thing in her head was the way his face had twisted like that, out there in a parking lot in the Atlanta spring sunshine for anyone to see. When David got mad, his accent—what Mariah's mother had always called *high Georgia*—changed. It became clipped and mean. Then there was the red face, the bulging eyes, that vein on his forehead, and the way he bared his teeth. None of that was pleasant, surely.

But for some reason the fact that he sounded less Georgia old money and more cruelly staccato when he was mad was what got to her the most. Because she'd worked so hard to get the redneck out of her own decidedly low-brow accent and she never, ever let it slip. Never.

Still, accidents happened. That was what the doctors told Mariah when she could breathe again. It was certainly what the hotel hastened to tell her, in the form of half their legal team crammed into her makeshift cubicle in the emergency room.

And despite the overly exposed feeling that stuck with

her every time she flashed back to that ugly parking lot confrontation, Mariah accepted the idea that it was an accident. She wasn't living in a gothic novel. Her divorce was ugly, but what divorce wasn't? There was no need to make everything worse by imagining that David was *actually* trying to kill her.

But the second time she found herself in the hospital, she stopped kidding herself.

There had been no banquet with questionable puff pastries that night. She'd been at home, delighted that she was now pointedly excluded from social invitations as word got around that David Abernathy Lanier and his jumped-up, white trash wife weren't simply in the throes of one of those trial separations that always ended up with a tight-lipped decision to stay together for the sake of the family fortune. David was divorcing her—Mariah knew that was how the story would make the rounds, no matter that she'd been the one to leave him—and Atlanta society was sensibly siding with the old money that made them all who they were.

Mariah had been all alone in the cute Midtown apartment she'd moved into when she'd fled David's showcase of a home in tony Buckhead. Her cozy one-bedroom was a mere seven miles away, but located in an entirely different world than the one where David and people like him lived. And it was the only place that she'd ever lived alone. She had gone straight from her mother's house to her husband's, where she couldn't say she'd lived with him so much as near him, surrounded at all times by the loyal staff who might have pitied David's poor, unsuspecting wife but were too well paid to intervene. Or even treat her kindly if David didn't wish it.

For a long time she'd measured her life against that

falling-down farmhouse in rural Two Oaks, Georgia, where there were more boarded-up buildings than people and where her family continued to live out of sheer stubbornness. While nothing in Mariah's life had turned out the way she'd been so sure it would when she'd been a foolish twenty-year-old looking to be rescued by a handsome man in a fancy car, she couldn't deny that there was a certain pleasure in having her own space at last.

No matter how she'd come by it.

It was while she lay there in another hospital room, cordoned off from the rest of the emergency room by a depressing blue curtain—staring up at the fluorescent lights, waiting for her EpiPen to finish letting her breathe, wondering if she'd have the dreaded biphasic second reaction—that she finally understood.

There was no safe space. Not for her.

David shouldn't have been able to get into her apartment, but he had. She was still trying to breathe, feeling like there was a hand wrapped tightly around her throat. She didn't bother telling herself any comforting stories this time. David had broken in or hired someone to break in for him. The latter scenario was more likely, because David was not a man who did anything that he could hire someone else to do for him. She felt a sick sensation roll through her, adding to the panic. It felt a lot like shame.

Or worse—fear.

Because David or some faceless minion had been in her pretty furnished apartment with its pastel walls and view over Piedmont Park. They had touched her few personal items. Rifled through her clothes. Sat on the furniture she'd started thinking of as hers. And at some point, tampered with her food to make sure she ended up right back in the emergency room with a far worse reaction than before.

They'd defiled the one place she had ever considered hers, then she'd put their poison in her own body, and she hadn't even known it. She hadn't sensed it. She hadn't *felt* any of it. She'd gone about her life as if everything were normal when it was actually a trap.

The sheer violation was almost harder to take than her near-fatal allergic reaction.

Again.

"You need to be very, very careful, Mrs. Lanier," the doctor said, scowling at her as if she'd thought *to hell with this potentially lethal allergy* and had treated herself to a big old lobster dinner.

"I'm always careful," she replied when she could speak. "And it's Ms. McKenna, not Mrs. Lanier. My name change hasn't gone through yet."

"Two anaphylaxis episodes in one month isn't being careful, ma'am."

And what could Mariah say? *My husband would rather kill me than suffer through a divorce, as a matter of fact. I think he snuck into my new apartment and doctored my food so this would happen.* Even if the impatient doctor hadn't already been scowling at her, she wouldn't have risked it.

David's family had a wing named after them in this hospital. In every hospital in Atlanta, if she remembered her father-in-law's genial bragging correctly. The last thing she wanted to do was find herself remanded to the psych ward, where a man whose name was all over the hospital could access her as he pleased. Possibly kill her at his leisure. Right out in the open, no incognito shrimp required.

"I'll be more careful," she murmured.

But she decided there was no longer any choice. If she wanted to live, she needed to run.

The only question was how to do it. If David had people jimmying locks and dosing food to kill her with her own allergy, she could hardly expect that a change of address would do the trick. She'd already tried that when she'd left that cold, bitter house of his.

She decided she couldn't call anyone she knew. She couldn't trust any of the friends she'd made since David had swept her straight off her feet and out of that tiny nowhere town in backwoods Georgia. She also couldn't go back there, no matter how many times she woke in the night with tears on her face, a deep longing for her mother's coarse smoker's laugh, and the scent of wild honeysuckle in her nose. Because David had found her there all those years ago, and it would be the first place he'd look.

Mariah was tough, but David was vindictive. And vicious in the way only a very rich man could be. His family had been proud residents of this city since they'd come in with the railroads, and he had allies everywhere. All his Southern captain of industry friends and their wide-ranging, overlapping networks of influence and threat. Police. Government. Charities. Media. Name it, and some person who supported David had a finger in it. Or three.

And he had already tried to kill her twice.

By the time she was released from the hospital, she'd tried to talk herself out of it a hundred times. After all, accidents really did happen. It was entirely possible that these were freak occurrences and she was letting David get to her. Letting him win without him having to do much more than say a few ugly words to her in a super-market parking lot.

Imagining that he has this kind of power is giving him exactly what he wants, she lectured herself in the back of the taxi that took her home from the hospital. She gazed out at another spring morning, bright and sweet, filled with flowers and lush green trees and good things that had nothing to do with David Abernathy Lanier. *He would love nothing more than thinking you were* this *scared of him.*

It was all in her head. She was sure of it. She needed to pay closer attention to the ingredients in the things she ate, that was all. Hadn't she heard allergies got worse as people got older? She needed to be more careful, just as the exasperated doctor had suggested, and she'd be fine.

But when she let herself back in to her cute apartment and stood there, looking around at the cheerful rooms that had brought her such pleasure only last night, she knew better.

David wasn't going to stop.

Because David didn't have to stop.

He had determined that he would rather be widowed than divorced. It would be better for the political career he'd informed her he was plotting, since he planned to run on wholesome family values—none of which, she'd pointed out at the time, he actually possessed.

"And whose fault is it I don't have a family?" he'd asked her, his blue eyes glittering, never dropping that soft drawl that sounded the way old gold would if it could speak.

And if Mariah had learned anything over the course of their ten years together, it was that what David wanted, David got. Her wishes and feelings were utterly unimportant to him. He had picked her because she was a good story he got to tell. She got to play Cinderella games, sure, but he was the benevolent Prince Charming in that scenario.

David really liked playing Prince Charming.

And when playing roles no longer worked to keep her in line? He'd showed her what was behind the mask. Threats. Contempt. Maybe even outright loathing.

What Mariah had to live with now was why she'd seen the truth and *stayed*. For much longer than she should have. And worse, why she hadn't seen these things lurking in David from the beginning, the way her mother had.

Mariah sat on the edge of the bed in the charming bedroom she doubted she would ever sleep in again and forced herself to think. To really, truly *think* with all the desperate clarity brought on by two near-death experiences.

Anaphylaxis got worse, not better. She had to assume that all the food in her house was tainted. That anything she touched could have been doctored and likely was. And that if she ingested shellfish even once more, it could kill her. Especially if she ran out of EpiPens.

She also had to assume she had no friends or allies in Atlanta. There was no one she'd met here who didn't have ties to David in some way. That meant none of them were safe. And she couldn't head home, no matter how much she wanted to slam through the old screen door into the farmhouse kitchen, let the dogs bark at her, and sit at the table with a slice of her great aunt's sweet potato pie until she felt like herself again.

Whoever *that* was.

Mariah blew out a shaky breath. She could always just . . . go on the run and plan to live that way. But that seemed inefficient at best. She would have to take excruciating care in covering her tracks, always knowing that one tiny slip could be the end of her. Every book she'd ever read or movie she'd ever seen about someone going on the run ended the same way. They slipped up and were found. Or they were caught by whoever was after them no matter what they did. Or they couldn't handle the isolation and outed themselves, one way or another.

Whatever the reason, life on the run never seemed to work out all that well for anyone.

If David was prepared to kill her—really and truly kill her—going on the run would only make it easier for him. And Mariah had no intention of dying in an out-of-the-way horror show of a motel somewhere, on the requisite dark and rainy night, with some pitiless henchmen of David's choking the life out of her.

She had no intention of dying at all. Not now.

Not when she'd finally gotten herself free of the lie she'd been living all these years.

If David succeeded in killing her the way he'd told her he would, he won. And if he won, nothing would change. He would go right on being the smiling monster she'd married because she'd wanted so desperately to believe that Cinderella stories could be real. Even more hilarious, she'd convinced herself that a white trash girl from those no-account McKennas out in Two Oaks could wake up one morning and find herself starring in a fairy tale.

If she died, David would tell her story however he liked, and no one would know any different.

But if she lived, Mariah could change everything.

She could go back home and see her mother at last. She could try to figure out which one of them had caused this distance between them. She had nieces and nephews she'd never met, and she was sure her network of cousins had some things to say to her after all these years. She could repair those bridges before they burned up altogether.

If Mariah lived, she could do what she wanted with her life. She wouldn't have to wait tables in her uncle's dinky roadside diner in the middle of nowhere the way she'd been doing when David found her on that fateful hunting trip. And she wouldn't have to play the society princess role she'd never quite managed to pull off to anyone's satisfaction in David's snooty circles, where everyone's great-grandparents had known each other and they all had clear opinions about uppity backwoods tramps like her.

If Mariah lived, she could find out who the hell Mariah McKenna really was.

Assuming, of course, that there was anyone in there, locked away behind all her bad decisions.

You told me not to marry him, Mama, she acknowledged inside her head. It was the only way she talked to her mother these days. Another scar she carried around and pretended wasn't there. *You begged me to think twice, but I was sure I knew better.*

If her mother were here now, Mariah knew what she would say in that smoker's voice Mariah had always secretly thought sounded like velvet. *Think, baby girl. You didn't use much of your brain hopping into this mess, but you sure could use it to get yourself out.*

Panic kicked at her, and for a minute she couldn't tell if it was another anaphylactic episode. Mariah laid her hand against her throat and told herself that she was fine. That she was alive and could breathe. She told herself that a few times, then a few more, until her heart rate slowed down again.

She decided it was nervous energy, and she would deal with it the only way she could. By *doing* something. She pulled one of her bags from under the bed, settling for the one she knew she could carry no matter what. The one she knew she could pick up and actually run with if she had to. And then Mariah took her time packing, letting her mind wander from the task at hand to all those videos she'd watched online about how to pack a carry-on bag for a monthlong trip. Or three months. Or an indefinite amount of time. It had been one more way she'd tried her best to fit in with the effortlessly languid set of people she knew during her marriage. Women who seemed to be able to trot off to Europe for a month with either the contents of their entire house or nothing more than a handbag, a single black dress, and a few scarves.

David had mocked her, of course, though she'd convinced herself it was good-natured teasing at the time. Sure it was.

Maybe you can watch a video on how to make a baby, he had said once, smiling at her across the bedroom as if he'd been whispering sweet nothings in her ear.

The cruelty of it took her breath away now, the same as it had then. This time, however, she didn't have to hide it. She blinked away the moisture in her eyes, then threw the shirt she'd been folding to the side because her hand was shaking.

Had she really tried to tell herself he hadn't meant that? She knew better now. But she'd spent years excusing everything and anything David did.

Because she'd been the one who'd been broken, not him.

David had kept up his end of the bargain. He'd swept Mariah away from that abandoned backwoods town and he'd showered her with everything his life had to offer. He'd paid to give her a makeover. To make her teeth extra shiny. He'd found her a stylist and hired a voice coach so she could transform herself into the sort of swan who belonged on his arm. Or at the very least, so she wouldn't embarrass him.

All she'd ever been expected to do was give him a baby.

Looking back, it was easy to see how David's behavior had worsened with every passing month she didn't get pregnant. Less Prince Charming, more resentful spouse. And increasingly vicious.

When she'd walked in on him and one of the maids, he hadn't even been apologetic.

Why should I bother to give you fidelity when you can't do the one thing you low-class, white trash, trailer park girls are any good at?

She would hate herself forever for not leaving immediately that first time. For staying in that house and sleeping in that bed for months afterward. For telling herself that it was a slip, that was all. That they could work through it.

As if she hadn't seen the hateful way David had looked at her.

She had. Of course she had.

The charming man she'd fallen in love with had never existed. David could pull out the smiles and the manners when he liked. But it only lasted as long as he got his way.

The trouble was, Mariah had turned thirty. And despite years of trying, they hadn't ever had so much as a pregnancy scare. She'd found David with the first maid the week after her birthday. But it had taken her months to leave.

He never bothered to pull out his charm for her again, and she'd spent more agonizing months than she cared to recall imagining she could fix something he didn't care was broken.

In the end, after the second time she'd caught him in their bed with another woman employed in their household, Mariah had been faced with a choice. She could look the other way, as she knew many wives in their social circle chose to do. She could figure out a way to keep what she liked about life as Mrs. David Lanier and ignore the rest. It was a dance she'd seen performed in front of her for years, from David's parents right on down.

But the part of her that had been sleeping for a decade had woken up. That scrappy, tenacious McKenna part of her that she'd locked away. McKennas had *rough and tumble* stamped onto their stubborn, ornery bones. They fought hard, loved foolishly, and didn't take much notice of anyone else's opinions on how they went about it or what kinds of messes they made along the way.

Roll over and play dead long enough, her grandmother used to say, *and pretty soon you won't be playing.*

Mariah had decided she'd played enough. And maybe it had taken months of humiliation, but she'd left.

And she would live through this, too, by God.

"I should watch a video on what Mama would do to a man who treated her like this," Mariah muttered to herself, aware as she spoke that *her* accent didn't slip no matter how angry she got.

The idea of a video made her laugh a little. She already knew what her mother would do in this kind of situation. Country folks weren't society folks, and McKennas were a whole different level still. Back in the day, Rose Ellen had reacted to Mariah's father's infidelities by throwing his drunk, cheating butt out. She'd never let him back in.

That was when it came to her.

It wasn't the family legend of her mother tossing her naked father out of the house at gunpoint, then all his belongings after him, though that was one of Mariah's most tender childhood memories. It had to do with all those videos she'd watched so obsessively over the past ten years. Her own private version of higher education.

And then it clicked. Just the trickle of a memory of one of those late nights she'd sat up, pretending not to wonder where her husband was—or who he might be with, which was better than when she hadn't needed to wonder because he'd made sure she knew. She'd clicked through video after video on her phone, careful to leave all the lights out in the bedroom so she could pretend she was sleeping and David's spies could report back to him accordingly.

She'd found herself watching an unhinged conspiracy theorist ranting about satanic signs he alone had found in a children's television program. Maybe she'd found a little comfort in the fact that there were people out there a whole lot crazier than a lonely Buckhead trophy wife whose husband openly hated her. She might have been the one staying in a marriage gone bad, but at least she wasn't broadcasting her every paranoid notion with a video camera.

But the man had said something interesting at the end

of his garbled insistence that the end was nigh, and in puppet form. He'd mentioned a group of superhero-like men off in the wilderness somewhere. Like the A-Team, Mariah had thought at the time. But not illegal. Or faked for television.

Mariah cracked open her laptop now and got to work. It took a while for her to find her way back to that odd video. And yet another long while to try to figure out whether anything in that video was real.

But eventually she found her way to a stark, minimalist website that had a name emblazoned across the top of the page. *Alaska Force*. And a choice between a telephone number and an email address. Nothing more.

Mariah didn't overthink it. She typed out an email, short and sweet.

> My husband is trying to kill me. He's already come close twice, and if he gets a third try, he'll succeed. I know he will.
> Help me.

Two

As soon as she hit send, Mariah felt silly.

When was she going to learn? There was no use believing in things that might as well be magic. Fairy tales were fairy tales, whether she was telling herself lies about Prince Charming in a backcountry diner or larger-than-life, military-trained superheroes who could save a damsel in distress.

Even if such men existed, why would they save *her*?

"You got yourself into this mess," she told herself sternly, the way she knew her own mother would. With absolutely no sympathy, only that hard certainty that Mariah was going to figure it out herself. Because she had to. "You're going to have to find a way to get yourself out."

Mariah sat there in front of her laptop, clicking around aimlessly until she found herself on a crafting blog, frowning with great concern over something called *mindful making*. One more thing she wasn't doing, apparently. She concentrated on her breathing. On the fact she *could* breathe. She reminded herself that she was alive, and that was what mattered.

It could have been hours or mere minutes. She couldn't tell. But when her email beeped to indicate an incoming message, she jumped like she'd been shot. Her heart clattered, the way it kept doing, as if her natural state these days was panic. When her airway didn't close up tight as a fist—panic wasn't anaphylactic shock—she took a few more deep breaths and made herself click over to her email, certain she would find yet another mailer from some clothing company.

But it wasn't one of the approximately nine thousand online catalogs that were emailed to her daily, urging her to buy more stuff. It was an email from that same address she'd written to earlier. It was direct. To the point.

Almost terse.

> Get to Juneau, Alaska, in time to catch the Friday morning ferry to Grizzly Harbor.
> If you are not on the Friday ferry, consider this offer rescinded. Further communications will be ignored.
> If you can't leave your current situation unassisted, advise us and we will consider options.

Mariah could hear her heart drumming in her temples and the same kick in her throat, her gut, even her feet— but she knew it wasn't panic or shellfish this time. It felt a lot more like relief. Possibly even hope.

No wonder she didn't recognize it. It had been a long, long time since she'd felt anything similar.

I'll be there, she typed in reply, hoping no one could read her giddiness through the screen.

So much giddiness, in fact, that she had to sit there a moment, in case moving too fast made her dizzy.

When she shut her laptop, she felt that same, drumming sense of purpose she'd felt when the McKenna spirit in her had dusted itself off and marched her straight out of that house she'd shared with David and the staff he apparently sampled at will.

Mariah had been out of the hospital for a total of five hours when she left her apartment again.

She tried to convince herself she was on an adventure. Not a life-or-death race toward the unknown thanks to a random email. Not because she was afraid she would die before the week was out, accidentally eating something dressed up with essence of crab, or eating nothing at all out of fear and starving herself to death.

Whatever waited for her on the other side of that email didn't matter, because it wouldn't be David.

Mariah could handle pretty much anything but another dose of David.

She raced downstairs, ignoring how terrible she felt, and got into her car. She checked the back and then tossed her bag on the passenger seat beside her. And then she drove, making her way through the typical Atlanta traffic until she hit I-85. She pointed the car north and east, heading for the coast.

You might feel lethargic, the doctor had told her. It was a whole lot more like being run over by a very heavy truck. Twice. But she could drive her car, so she did.

David had always mocked the thrillers she liked to read, but Mariah put them to good use that day. She deliberately laid a trail. She drove through the Georgia countryside up into South Carolina, then continued straight into Virginia, filling up her car along the way and buying snacks she knew no one could have doctored. She continued out to the coast, and some ten hours after she'd gotten that email, locked herself in a motel room with a lurid green carpet and a view of the Virginia Beach Boardwalk. And the ocean beyond it, which she could hear but not see.

She paid for three days on her credit card but left the next morning, after she'd fallen asleep exhausted and woken up too many times with her heart pounding, certain that someone was in the room with her. Before she climbed back into her car, she took her coffee down to the water's edge and stuck her feet in the ocean. She might not have felt quite like herself just yet, but she was out of Atlanta.

Whatever else happened, she'd made it out in one piece. And for the moment, anyway, with her cell phone firmly switched off, no one on earth knew where she was.

She drove back inland, then turned north, leaving a trail of receipts along the I-95 corridor from Richmond through Baltimore, then on into New Jersey. She crossed the bridge over the Hudson River, sneaking glimpses of New York City standing proud in the spring sunshine, then drove on to Connecticut. She stopped in a town called Fairfield that she'd located on the map the night before, found another hotel, then settled in for the night.

She ordered room service, deliberately. She went online and bought a plane ticket for the following evening, from New York to Athens, Greece, because she'd always wanted to see Greece. The following morning, she bought a one-way Metro-North train ticket back down to New York City.

But she didn't get on the train. Instead, she got in the car again and drove up the coast to Providence, Rhode

Island. She stayed over that night in a motel on the outskirts of the city that took cash and didn't ask for ID. She took out the cash maximum from ATM machines every day—because she was sure David would cut her off at any moment, the way he liked to. And she needed more time to access the accounts he didn't know about, which she hadn't set up with a debit card. Early on Thursday morning, she drove her car to a different hotel in the center of Providence and left it there.

Then she got on a bus to Boston Logan Airport. She bought herself a ticket to Juneau, Alaska, with her cash, and boarded it a little before noon.

Mariah was feeling pretty pleased with herself by the time she landed in Juneau that night.

Spring in Atlanta had already been warm. All the flowers in bloom and temperatures in the seventies. Mariah had only taken clothes appropriate for that same kind of weather, in case whoever would be breaking in to her apartment would take stock of her wardrobe and be able to figure out where she was headed by what she took with her. Luckily, she'd had a layover in Seattle, and she'd outfitted herself there for whatever spring looked like so much farther north.

Friday morning, as she found her way to the only ferry that headed to Grizzly Harbor—a village on an island out in the moody Alaskan sea—it was cold. Crisp and clean and almost unbelievably beautiful, but cold.

Colder than Mariah had ever been in her life, though she tried to wrap the woolly things she'd bought in Seattle around her twice to combat it.

The chill in the air was sharp and sweet, and it slapped her awake.

It felt like hope.

When she finally boarded the ferry, she took a seat near a window and tried to take it all in. She'd spent the better part of the last week on interstate highways or in motels nearby. She'd seen a lot of truck stops. Grimy fast food restaurant bathrooms with that cloying, astringent smell to mask the more unpleasant smells beneath. More construction than should have been possible, all kinds of traffic choking the different eastern cities, and, apart from the glimpses of the Atlantic Ocean she'd had here and there, there had been tarmac, concrete, and steel as far as the eye could see.

Alaska was like an antidote.

There were mountains everywhere, some draped in white with a comforting canopy of dark green pines and imposing rock faces. Some pasted across the horizon, so stark and white she'd assumed they were clouds at first. Everywhere she looked, mountains sloped down into the mysterious blue inlets and sounds, beckoning and beautiful.

It had been downright cold outside at the ferry terminal, despite the sun. In the course of the ride across the water, with stops at tiny Alaskan villages bristling with the masts of boats and the hint of wood smoke, there was rain. Then fog. Then more sun when Mariah least expected it, doing its best to burn the fog away.

When the ferry finally reached Grizzly Harbor, Mariah moved to the outer deck with some of the other passengers, smiling her apologies when a woman with a young boy bumped into her at the railing. She felt the wind on her face, a sharp slap that left salt behind. The water below the ferry boat looked dark in the fog, and she could smell the rich scent of ocean life. It was the same as it had been in Virginia Beach—only deeper. Wilder and unspoiled by high-rises and too many people.

David had taken her to exotic places—or, at least, they had been exotic to a girl from the middle of nowhere, who'd gone nowhere and seen nothing. New York City. Paris. A yacht on the Caribbean.

But she'd never seen anything quite like Grizzly Harbor. The spring sunshine danced in and around the clouds, lighting up the hardy fishing village, which clung to the steep sides of another imposing mountain. All the buildings clustered together there, above the water's edge, were painted in different bright colors, most of them peeling and weathered—though that in no way took away from their appeal. There were boats at the docks, pleasure boats and fishing vessels alike. Mariah had never given Alaska a whole lot of thought, but she discovered it looked exactly the way she'd imagined it would. All it needed was a moose cantering down from the woods or a bear roaring up on one of the narrow streets, and the image would be complete.

She was smiling to herself as she walked off the ferry, swept up with the rest of the passengers getting off here. The whole town had come out to meet the boat and were applying themselves to helping unload supplies or greeting returning locals. Maybe everyone was as charmed as she was, she thought, as a bearded man in made-to-order Alaskan flannel jostled her slightly as they disembarked, as if he were rushing to get out into all that goodness.

Mariah couldn't blame him. It was like walking into a postcard.

A postcard that highlighted the adorable wooden boardwalks that made up some of the streets climbing up the hill—as well as what had to be the most lethal man she'd ever laid eyes on in her life.

She could have sworn he hadn't been there a moment earlier. He stood apart from the rest of the crowd gathered at the dock, his back to a weathered shack Mariah assumed belonged to the ferry company. Or maybe it was for fishermen, given the number of fishing boats she could see in the harbor.

But she was only looking at the shack because *he* was in front of it. And he was . . . too much to take in.

Too much of too many things Mariah didn't know how to feel.

He was tall and dark and the kind of lean that made her think of sharply honed hunting knives, precisely balanced to kill with a single throw. His arms were crossed over his powerful chest, calling attention to the way his biceps threatened the fabric of the henley he wore, while the larger, bearded men all around him wore coats.

But the most noticeable thing about this man was his unflinching gaze. It was much, much colder and harsher than the Alaskan afternoon settling deeper into Mariah's bones with every step she took.

And he didn't pretend he was staring at anything but her.

Mariah felt something in her shake. As if a critical part of her had come loose and was rattling around in there now, threatening to take her down to the cold dock at her feet.

But it didn't. She ignored the bizarre sensation the way she'd learned to ignore just about everything else. She reminded herself she was still recovering from anaphylactic shock, so of course she felt . . . odd. She felt her smile shift from actual, unconscious delight at the pretty town around her to the familiar baring of her teeth she'd used to hack her way through Atlanta society.

She made herself breathe as she walked over to the terrifying man, because holding her breath could end in embarrassing disaster. He didn't strike her as the sort who would exert himself to catch her if she fainted.

And as she moved closer to him, she couldn't help but notice any number of wholly unfair things. He was already too powerful, too lethal. That had been obvious from the ferry. Was it truly necessary that he have the kind of chiseled jaw that belonged in a lovesick poem or two? Or a mouth that another woman—one who still felt anything at all in her heart, and maybe even places lower than her heart—might actually, physically swoon over? Whether she was breathing or not.

His cold gaze was a particularly compelling brown, lit with a deep gold that did nothing at all to warm it, and a few shades lighter than the brown of his skin.

He was the most beautiful man Mariah had ever seen in her life.

And also, clearly, the deadliest.

"Hi," she said, stopping in front of him.

She was free of Atlanta now. So far away from David he almost seemed like a bad dream, here in all this crisp, cold blue and moody splendor that was making her teeth start to chatter. It had to be thirty degrees, not that anyone else seemed to notice. And still, the man in front of her made her uneasy. He looked exactly the way a lethal special ops "problem solver" ought to look, but it wasn't that.

Maybe it's the way he's already looking at you like he hates you, a sharp voice inside her suggested.

That hurt, and it shouldn't have. Mariah was used to

people hating her on sight. And, like her in-laws, long after—no matter how her father-in-law smiled and pretended otherwise.

She could have dropped her high-society persona, but she didn't quite dare, out here in all this wilderness, so far away from everything civilized. Her usual mask firmly in place, she treated the man before her to the sort of smile her mother-in-law had always employed as her go-to weapon of mass destruction. Because for all Mariah knew, this man was more villain than superhero. And she'd yet to meet a single living human that smile couldn't wither down to nothing.

Mariah aimed it right at him and played up her drawl, too. "You look dangerous enough to belong to that very cloak-and-dagger website. I surely hope that you're here to save me."

If possible, his harsh gaze grew chillier. He was like granite encased in a glacier, except much harder and much, much colder. She told herself it was the stiff breeze from the water that was making her shiver.

Most importantly, he didn't wither.

At all.

"I'm no savior," he said, his voice dark and deep, and if she wasn't mistaken, disgusted. "But if you're Mariah McKenna Lanier, that makes you my problem."

Three

Griffin Cisneros disliked Alaska Force's newest client the minute he saw her.

She looked even more expensive than in the photos. Sleek and sophisticated in a way he knew meant nothing but trouble, with a side helping of aloof entitlement, because that was the way that kind of blonde always went.

It was obvious in the way she walked, languid and easy, as if the world had nothing better to do than wait on her. It was clear in the clothes she wore, high maintenance and fussy enough to make it glaringly evident she wasn't much into the outdoors. Which meant she probably wouldn't take to life here in Grizzly Harbor, where matter-of-fact feats of endurance and bone-deep stubbornness were required to make it through the next storm.

Most clients came prepared for a blizzard or three. But not this one. She looked as if she'd showed up for a party. A very elegant party held somewhere a lot less . . . elemental.

Then there was that voice. It was like sugar and honey, thick and sweet, and it poured all over him whether he liked it or not.

He possibly disliked her voice most of all.

It had been Griffin's turn in the rotation to take the hit and conduct a thorough intake on a new client to assess whether or not she had the kind of problem Alaska Force wanted to solve. Griffin's job wasn't to make the final call, only to gather all the information so the rest of his brothers could vote at tonight's briefing. Once they did, Isaac Gentry—the founder of Alaska Force and therefore its commanding officer, though this wasn't the military any longer, only a collection of former special ops soldiers unsuited for civilian life—would either go with the vote or veto it. If he voted *go,* they would start plotting out mission parameters.

Oz, their resident computer genius, who claimed his surname was restricted on a need-to-know basis—and who also claimed his military specialty was *winning information wars*—had confirmed through his usual internet magic that Mariah McKenna Lanier lived in Atlanta, was recently separated from her filthy rich and well-connected husband, and had suffered two cases of anaphylaxis in the past month for an allergy that had been on her charts since childhood with no other flare-ups. The second attack had happened the night before she'd emailed.

"The IP address matches up. She's legit," Oz had told them in their morning briefing, where they discussed the various requests that came in for Alaska Force's specialized services overnight. The other men who made up their particularly elite team lounged in their usual careless—or decidedly not careless—positions around the big reception room of the rambling fishing lodge that had once belonged to Isaac's grandfather. It now doubled as the group's headquarters, there on the other side of the usually impassable mountain that loomed over Grizzly Harbor in a hidden, deliberately hard-to-reach place known as Fool's Cove. "If she shows, she's who she says she is."

But that wouldn't necessarily mean that she was being pursued and persecuted, of course. Griffin shouldn't have been surprised by the things people lied about, but he was. He always was.

"Are we marriage counselors now?" he'd asked gruffly. He'd stood straight and quiet with his back to the far wall. The way he always did. Because they were highly trained operatives, not a bunch of drunken fraternity brothers.

Templeton Cross, six feet and four inches of an ex–Delta Force, ex–Army Ranger hurricane, was kicked back in a chair with only two legs on the wood floor. He let out one of his loud guffaws. "By the time we get them, the counseling is done. It's all bullets, revenge plots, and regret."

The other men laughed. Griffin didn't. Not only because he didn't like the haughty look of the blond woman on Oz's screen but because it took a lot more than Templeton's usual nonsense to make him laugh.

"Sounds like a love song to me," Jonas Crow had said, his version of laughter another man's threat. Griffin still didn't know exactly what he had done in his years in the service—it was too highly classified even now—but he knew Jonas was a ghost when he felt like it. Also absolutely deadly.

The only thing Griffin liked less than snooty rich ladies—who were probably fine, if way too much work—was love songs.

And princesses, he thought now, staring down at the one before him like his glare could make her turn around and get back on the ferry.

The sleek, manicured blonde wasn't wearing a crown. But she was a princess all the same. And she clearly didn't get the message he was sending, because she stayed where she was, a cool smile on her lips like she was the one in charge of this. Of everything.

Even of him.

Not in this life.

Griffin took another moment to confirm what he already knew: Mrs. Lanier was too high maintenance. And high maintenance, in his experience, always went hand in hand with high drama. Her smile kicked at him, like she was trying to get beneath his skin. No one did that. Ever. Her hair was twisted up into a neat, sophisticated knot at the back of her head, suggesting that crown she wasn't actually wearing. Everything about her was a pointed contrast to all the other passengers disembarking onto this remote island in Southeast Alaska on a spring morning laced with fog and the threat of rain. There were the locals in fleece and camo. The tourists in parkas, laden down with overstuffed backpacks and stamping around in hiking boots so new they squeaked.

But this one was wearing the kind of soft designer jeans that were made to fall apart, not stand up to any kind of utility work. A pair of knee-high boots in a visibly buttery leather that would be about as useful in the unforgiving Alaskan weather as a pair of flip-flops.

And she was draped in wool. Literally draped. And not the functional microwool hikers wore as base layers, which could retain heat, dry quickly, and be of use in the relentless bush. This was the sort of fancy wool she could fling around and make into a kind of cape.

A *cape*. In Grizzly Harbor.

He wanted to order her to turn around, get back on the ferry, and sort her messy life out somewhere else.

But that wasn't the mission. Not today.

"Are you Oz?" she asked, and if she was unsettled by the way Griffin stared at her like he was trying to freeze her solid, she gave no sign. "The person who emailed me?"

Since most people were terrified of Griffin—a reasonable response to a man who'd made himself into a machine a long time ago, and therefore a response he heartily encouraged—he found Mariah's polite, unbothered response . . . unsettling.

And Griffin didn't do *unsettling*.

"Do I look like a computer geek?"

That cool smile chilled further. "I'll take that as a no."

Griffin didn't bother telling her that Oz didn't look any more like a stereotypical computer geek than the rest of them. He didn't see how that was her business when hopefully she wouldn't be here long enough to find out on her own. And he could then go back to the kind of missions he preferred. Dangerous extractions. Kidnap resolutions. Missions that mattered, not petty end-of-marriage skirmishes like this one, which struck him as only slightly more interesting than a corporate security detail.

"I'm Griffin Cisneros," he told her stiffly.

More of that smile. And a cool sweep from her entirely too-blue gaze. "Am I expected to salute?"

"Don't salute." That came out gruffer than intended. And a whole lot harsher. "I'm handling your case."

"All by yourself?" Her eyebrows rose, and it was all so haughty it made his teeth ache. He ordered himself to stop clenching his jaw. When had he started *reacting* to things like this? To civilians like her? Or to civilians at all. "That's impressive."

He knew how people like her operated. He could hear it in that silky, feminine voice no matter the drawl. And he could certainly see it all over her smooth, pretty, made-up face. People like Mariah made sure they were never impressed with a thing because they already possessed everything.

But then, Griffin wasn't easily impressed, either. He'd kept his cool in too many war zones, and he'd done it by making himself into a series of locked compartments, shut up tight and polished to gleam. He never opened those compartments. He never entertained the faintest notion to do something so foolish, because he knew too well what was in them. The same way he knew what the real world was like out there—and there were precious few crowns or capes in the places he'd been and the crap he'd seen.

He was impressed by utter stillness. By men who could disappear while you were staring straight at them. By a single, perfect shot that could save his friends, alter history, change the world.

What Griffin was not impressed by was some society princess in a broken-down marriage, wasting his time.

He jerked his head in a silent order for her to follow

him as he turned. He didn't share his thoughts because he figured his nonverbal communication was doing the job for him. And he didn't offer to take her bag, even though he knew it would horrify his own mother, because he believed in packing only what was necessary and what he could carry himself. Lessons a princess should learn. He set off into what passed for the streets of Grizzly Harbor at a brisk pace, down a winding dirt path, then up onto one of the planked boardwalks over the rocks, and didn't look over his shoulder to see if Princess Mariah was following him.

She was—he didn't have to look to know.

And she kept up with surprisingly little effort. He could admit that annoyed him. He'd expected her to huff and puff and complain with every step, especially since Grizzly Harbor was built on a steep hill between the unforgiving ocean and the encroaching forest.

But when he stopped in front of Blue Bear Inn, a building in the central cluster of the village painted a vivid blue that would give any actual bears a headache, she was right there with him. Looking none the worse for wear.

"I'll show you to your room," he said, and he didn't like the way the hike up from the docks—or maybe just the sea air sweeping in from the sound—made her cheeks look rosy. Or that her eyes seemed about as blue as the freaking inn's lunatic paint job. "How long do you think it will take you to get ready?"

"That depends on what I'm getting ready for, sugar."

How did she make that sound so suggestive? He would have stood straighter if it was physically possible. It wasn't.

"Exactly what do you think is going on here?" Griffin asked.

It wasn't a friendly tone. Grown men had been known to recoil when Griffin hit them with all that controlled fury.

But the princess in front of him did nothing of the kind. She peered at him, her gaze sparkling. He noticed a darker navy ring around her disconcerting blue irises. Her lips curved in a new form of that chilly smile he could really only call pitying. And the way she stood there, her bag looped over one languid arm, that cape of hers tossed effortlessly over her shoulders, struck him as impossibly, dangerously regal.

Griffin didn't enjoy being struck by anything.

"I have no idea what's going on here," she said, almost merrily. As if it were all part of an amusing adventure they were on together. Then she made it worse and leaned in. "This might come as a surprise to you, but I haven't spent a whole lot of my time hunting down mysterious superheroes to help me keep my husband from murdering me. If there's a protocol involved, you're going to have to tell me what it is."

"The protocol is simple. Follow orders. Stay alive."

"That sounds a lot more like the army than I was prepared for, I'll admit."

If she had been someone else, Griffin might have made a crack about the paid vacation the army called basic training, as opposed to his own stint in boot camp as a Marine recruit in San Diego. But he only stared at her until the flush high on those cheekbones of hers was less about the sea air and more about him. He told himself the reasons he liked that had nothing to do with any heat kicking around inside him. He was all ice, no fire. Always.

"If you're going to give me orders, you're going to have to use your words. Not that glare." Her voice was so silky it took him a minute to understand what she'd said. "As remarkable as it is."

Griffin felt his jaw tense again and couldn't understand what was happening. He was not the kind of man who let a woman get under his skin. He wasn't the kind of man who let anything get under his skin. He was unflappable all the way through. He had made an entire career out of it.

The fact that some fancy Southern princess could saunter off a ferry and get to him at all was embarrassing. And unacceptable.

"Alaska Force keeps a few rooms on hand for clients," he said, his voice free of inflection, as it should have been from the start. He was going to have to do a serious personal inventory to determine how and why he'd veered off course. "I'll show you to yours. If you need to change, shower, whatever, now is the time to do it. Then we'll discuss your situation in more detail. Any questions?"

"No questions." He didn't like the way her head angled as she said that, because there was too much defiance in it, but he let it go. Even when her smile tipped over into a smirk. "Sir."

He didn't tell her not to call him that. Because it shouldn't matter what she called him. It didn't. *Sugar. Sir.* Whatever.

Griffin didn't have to like his job. All he needed to do was complete it.

He pushed through the heavy front door of the inn,

putting his shoulder behind the movement with maybe more aggression than was necessary. He nodded at Madeleine Yazzie, who was sitting in her usual spot behind the desk with a fat paperback and her dyed red hair up in her signature beehive, and headed straight for the stairs. He didn't look around because he didn't have to. He knew what the lobby looked like, with its mix of country charm, hunting trophies, and self-conscious attempts to look like some kind of cozy mountain lodge. It failed on almost all counts and yet was so entirely itself that it circled back around to pleasant. Griffin had stayed here himself when he'd first found his way to Grizzly Harbor in search of the legend of Alaska Force and the man who ran it. He almost smiled, thinking back on how different he'd been then, fresh out of the Marines and no good at interacting with civilians.

He'd tried. He'd gone home to Arizona to be the son his parents wanted, the brother and the fiancé he'd been when he'd left. He'd tried to pick up his life where he'd left it before his three tours. And he quickly discovered that a man who'd made himself a machine had no business spending time with humans.

Much less a beautiful, blond princess like his ex-fiancée, who'd acted like a stiff wind might break her and cried so prettily it made him feel like a monster before he'd become one. While all along she'd been lying to his face about wanting to marry him—but that was one of those compartments he didn't open.

He heard Mariah laugh behind him, a breathy little sound that did nothing for his mood. Nothing good, anyway.

"Is that a real bear?" she asked as she climbed the stairs behind him. "Standing right next to the fireplace?"

"It was. Once."

"It's not that I haven't seen my share of taxidermy," she said in a conversational tone that told him two things. First, that she had absolutely no sense of the danger she was in here in Alaska, or here with him, or at all. And second, though she looked unruffled and languid, like she spent her days stretched out on a chaise somewhere, she was a whole lot hardier than she looked if she could take the steep stairs while carrying a load and not pant at the exertion less than a week since she'd been in the hospital. "I am from the South, after all. But my Uncle Teddy's collection of raccoons and possums did not prepare me for . . . what was that exactly? A ten-foot beast of a grizzly bear?"

Griffin got to the top of the stairs, then turned to look at her. "Better a stuffed bear in the lobby than a real one outside. This is Alaska. It is not an amusement park. If you see a wild animal, you better believe you're its prey."

"I will keep that in mind should I take it upon myself to go on a nature walk."

It was that gleam in her eyes, Griffin suspected. That was the problem. She looked almost . . . excited. Wound up and lit up with it. Instead of how she should have looked if she really was running for her life, which was scared.

Or even plain old worried.

"You seem pretty upbeat for someone who thinks they have a murderer on their tail, especially one who almost killed them twice."

Mariah aimed that smile at him again, and it actually took a good-sized chip out of him. But Griffin refused to show it. Not to this woman who shouldn't have registered as anything more than a job.

He would have to examine that, too.

"Funny thing about two near-death experiences in a month," she said, her gaze cool but her voice steady. Light and airy, even. Griffin didn't trust it at all. "It takes all the fun out of curling up in the fetal position, whining and weeping. I'm sure I might get back to it. I like a good cry as much as the next girl. But for the time being, I'm going to enjoy being alive while I still am."

He couldn't say he liked the heat that worked its way through him, licking its way down the length of his body the same way that drawl did. He stalked down the hallway instead of answering her, stopping at the farthest door. He pulled out the key he'd picked up from Madeleine earlier, set it to the lock, and opened the door. Then he took more time than strictly necessary checking the room for potential intruders.

"Do you have a cell phone?" he asked.

"Of course I do. But it's switched off."

"Why?"

A faint dent appeared between her brows. "I was under the impression it could be used to track me."

Griffin nodded, and certainly wasn't *disgruntled* that she wasn't an idiot.

"When you're done, come back downstairs," he told her curtly. "And leave the phone off."

She'd followed him in, looking around as if she'd never seen a hotel room before.

"Is this what it's like when you hire . . . whatever you are? Mercenaries?"

His lips thinned. "I am not a mercenary."

"Is that offensive? I'm sorry."

"A mercenary is a soldier for hire. No loyalty. No honor. Always for sale to the highest bidder, no matter who that is."

"And that's not you."

"Alaska Force solves problems. We are not for sale. We turn down more jobs than we take. And we never ransom our honor. Ever."

Maybe he only imagined that she looked paler at that, because he wanted her to. Because people should be careful asking questions like that of a man who'd dedicated his life to honor, courage, and unquestionable commitment.

"Noted," she said softly.

"I'll be in the lobby," he told her, and then he left before he could do something he would really regret.

Griffin was not a man whose impulses controlled him. The fact that he'd spent twenty minutes in this woman's presence and imagined he might have changed was a problem.

But not as big a problem as the heat that settled there in his sex like a clenched fist as he closed the door behind him and stalked back downstairs.

Reminding him how long it had been since he'd allowed himself any kind of release. Especially that kind.

And worse by far, reminding him in no uncertain terms that there was a man beneath the machine, no matter how much he wanted to pretend otherwise.

Four

When the door shut behind the coldest man Mariah had ever met—even colder than her in-laws, who had always struck Mariah as walking blizzards with fancy Georgia accents, even her relatively more friendly father-in-law—she moved to the bathroom, grabbing her toiletry bag as she went so she could deal with how ragged she must appear after her ferry ride and that march up from the docks.

She washed her face, then paused as she patted her skin dry. She blinked at herself in the mirror, slowly lowering the towel to the lip of the sink.

When was the last time she'd seen her own face without makeup for more than the few moments it took to start applying her foundation to conceal her flaws? When was the last time she'd dared to step out of her own bedroom without making sure she *had her face on* the way David liked it—a habit she'd continued even after she'd moved out?

She couldn't remember. It had become second nature to her. Like her accent, it was a way to make absolutely certain she never backslid and found herself in Two Oaks again. She'd worked so hard to make herself worthy of being David's wife—or at least to look and sound and behave like the sort of woman who might not deserve him but wouldn't reflect badly on him, either.

And yet he had always been the first to remind her she was nothing but trash.

She reached up and took the clip out of her hair, letting it tumble down around her shoulders. It was starting to show its natural wave, which normally she would have already ruthlessly tamed with her flat iron, because she lived in horror of parading around looking messy. Especially where David could see her. But today she ran her damp fingers through her hair instead, fully aware that doing so would encourage it to curl more.

If she was all the way out here on the far edge of the world, she might as well see what it was like to be whomever she felt like being instead of who David had made her.

Even if that meant no makeup and less-than-perfect hair.

As revolutions went, it was tiny and silly, but it was hers.

Mariah left the wrap she'd bought in Seattle on the cozy sleigh bed that dominated one wall and dug out the half-zip fleece and down vest she'd also bought. If her surly, icy guide was going to continue racing up and down hills in this charming little village, she figured she ought to be better prepared for the weather.

She dressed quickly, then forced herself to leave the room without checking the mirror, which was another thing she never, ever did. Because she'd learned quickly that it was better to conduct her own inspection than to fail David's.

The consequences of displeasing her ex had always been much, much worse than taking a few minutes to make sure she looked the part.

Mariah felt giddy and reckless as she closed the door behind her, her heart pounding so hard in her chest that she had to stop near the windows in the hall. She stared out at the water in the harbor, the boats moored down at the docks, and the implacable mountains, which loomed in a way that soothed her somehow. She ordered herself to settle down. And as her heart slowed to normal speed, her gaze moved from the raw, brooding water to the village. The seemingly haphazard collection of bright buildings with hand-lettered signs. The wooden board-walks in place of streets. Grizzly Harbor was as hardy as it was picturesque, and the combination made her . . . deeply glad.

She was smiling when something in her peripheral vision caught at her. She turned to look down at the street directly below. There was a post office sign on a yellow building across the way. And what looked like some kind of antique store slightly lower down the hill, flanked by houses in competing shades of green. And she had the sense of movement between the store and one of the houses, as if someone had stepped back into the shadows.

As if someone had been staring up at her.

But this was Alaska, not Atlanta, Mariah reminded herself as her stomach dropped with a sickening lurch—no one was watching her here. No one knew where she was and her phone was off, so no one could track her.

Still, she couldn't help the shudder that speared its way down her back in an icy, uncomfortable prickle. And she moved back from the window, then toward the stairs, more quickly than she might have otherwise.

By the time she made it down to the inn's lobby, she'd convinced herself she was being paranoid. That she'd spent the whole week looking over her shoulder and didn't yet realize that she could stop. *If you jump at every shadow even here, so far away from Georgia,* she told herself, *David wins.*

Then she forgot about David, because Griffin Cisneros was standing with his back to the far wall of the inn's comfortably eclectic sitting area, on one side of the huge stone fireplace. He mirrored the stuffed, rearing grizzly bear on the other side of the stone too closely for her peace of mind.

"Should I be concerned that *you* think I'm prey?" she asked him, laughing. Maybe a bit too nervously.

But he didn't laugh. If anything, those dark eyes sharpened, and she felt something tighten in her.

She told herself it was a healthy dose of fear. Because it should have been.

His full lips formed a straight line. "If I was hunting you, princess, you wouldn't see me."

That thing she wanted to believe was fear and only fear, nothing hotter or more dangerous, tightened all the more.

And Mariah decided to concentrate on the part that wouldn't keep her up at night. "Princess?"

"If the glass slipper fits."

"Oh, sugar. I've already done the Cinderella thing. Been to the ball. Fit my foot into that cute little shoe and made it work. Lived happily ever after for ten whole years, but the happy part never lasts. Before you know it, Prince Charming is sleeping with the maids, poisoning your food, and threatening you in parking lots all over Georgia." Mariah was aware that the sharp smile she aimed at him had far too much Two Oaks in it. Too much McKenna challenge and not enough Lanier reserve. But she chose not to be horrified by her own transformation. "I can't imagine why they leave that out of the fairy tale."

"Fairy tales are for small children and spoiled women."

"I'm not at all surprised you don't believe in them. I used to, of course. But I think after my last emergency room visit, the urge to dive headfirst into a happily-ever-after might finally have been beaten out of me."

Griffin continued to stand with his back to the wall, and his intense stillness clawed at her. Mariah had never seen a man stand like that. As if he could disappear into the wall if he wanted to.

His intense watchfulness pricked at her. It made her say whatever came to mind without worrying she needed to bite her tongue. It made her reckless and giddy all over again.

It made her more like a McKenna and less like a Lanier by the second, but she didn't do anything to stop it.

And when he moved away from the wall, it was no better. He had a kind of rangy, lethal grace that something deep inside her, some feminine awareness she'd never known was there before, identified instantly.

He was the most *male* individual she'd ever seen. Intense and dangerous from his dark hair to his boots. Not soft and carefully pressed the way the men in David's world always were, as if how they wore their khakis and preppy collared T-shirts decided the fate of the world. Griffin was hard and smooth, lethal and compelling, all over.

And the way he made what felt like every last hair on her body stand on end had nothing at all to do with fear.

Mariah accepted that uncomfortable truth as Griffin headed for the door again, pushing his way back out into the moody Alaska afternoon and indicating that she should follow him.

She did, grateful for the slap of the crisp, cool, fresh air and the cloud cover that felt less revealing than the earlier bursts of sunshine. She took a breath so deep it made her lungs ache, then indulged in a moment to enjoy the fact that she could still do such a thing.

With that in mind, she made herself stare down that alley where she'd seen absolutely nothing earlier. *Don't do David's work for him,* she lectured herself.

When she shifted her attention back to Griffin, he was glaring at her again, his arms crossed and an impatient look on his astonishingly beautiful face.

And for some reason, Mariah melted. Everywhere.

Particularly low in her belly and that place between her legs, where she hadn't felt a thing in a long, long time.

But like it or not, she was still married. Technically. And would continue to be unless and until she survived her divorce.

It didn't matter that she found another man unreasonably, almost unbearably hot, she concluded as she stood there, the Alaskan cold nipping at her despite her layers. Griffin was a work of art, that was all. And despite all her years of overlooking any number of outright slights, she wasn't blind.

Still, she was terrified it was written all over her face when his impatience deepened into a frown.

"Hungry or thirsty?"

Mariah decided not to answer that with the reckless-ness that she could feel pumping through her blood, making her feel entirely too young and invulnerable and foolish, the way she'd never let herself feel when she'd actually been all of those things. "That sounds like a trick question."

Griffin didn't move a muscle. She could see he didn't move at all. And still he managed to turn into granite and ice right there in front of her. Or, really, more of both. "If you're hungry, I'll take you to get some food. If you're thirsty, I'll take you to the bar. It's your call."

Mariah had the sudden urge for what her cousins had always called *the McKenna cure*. Any bar, an armful of shots tossed back as quick as possible, and when you got back up off the floor the next morning, you could count on feeling much too bad to worry about whatever you'd been worried about before.

But Mariah had never been one of *those* McKennas. She'd usually been the one scraping her relatives off of bar floors, pouring them into the back of a pickup truck, and carting them back home to sleep it off.

"I could eat," she said, almost primly, as if that could remind her who she was. Or who she'd spent the last ten years trying to be, anyway.

She followed Griffin's long, almost angry stride as he wheeled around and started down the haphazard lane. She looked around as they went, and not just down the alleys so she could jump at more shadows. The buildings in the village were clustered together, which she figured had to do with the long, tough winters. No need to do more than stumble out of one door and then in through the next, a few steps away. She tried to imagine what it would be like to live in a place like this, filled with people who nodded to Griffin as he passed them and eyed Mariah in a manner that told her they knew she didn't belong.

In a way, it reminded her of Two Oaks. Entirely its own universe, close and contained, suspicious of outsiders. But Mariah could smell salt and pine in the air, mixed with wood smoke. Not honeysuckle, deep green woods, and her mama's homemade biscuits and gravy. This was Alaska. It was nothing at all like Georgia.

And that was a good thing, because David was in Georgia. Her cupboards and refrigerator full of potentially tainted food was back in Atlanta. Mariah went ahead and acknowledged a truth that she knew would horrify her entire extended family, assuming they hadn't all written her off for *putting on airs*.

She'd never been so happy to be out of the South in her life.

Griffin led her to a place called the Water's Edge Café, set up from the water on one of the boardwalk lanes. Outside, it was a sturdy two-story house painted a cheerful yellow. Inside, there were merrily mismatched tables and chairs, everything bright and happy, with charming drawings hung on the walls. Mariah was smiling before she sat down in the far corner, where Griffin directed her.

He sat with his back to the wall, so Mariah had to twist to keep looking around as she shrugged out of her vest and hung it on the back of her chair. Two other tables were filled, one with a group of men she decided were fishermen, with their big boots and waterproof pants with suspenders. They all sported impressive beards and weathered hands, and let out deep and hearty laughs as they shoveled down huge plates of potatoes and meat. At the other table was a tourist couple Mariah recognized vaguely from the ferry. They had a map spread out between them and camera equipment stacked next to the sugar dispenser, and they were muttering at each other through fixed smiles.

A style of argument Mariah was all too familiar with.

And even though the tourist couple had clearly been sitting there longer, the sharp-eyed, dark-haired woman with a black half apron tied around the low-slung waist of her jeans ignored them entirely and came over to Mariah and Griffin instead.

She didn't smile. She didn't offer a greeting. She crossed her arms and glared.

"Coffee?" she asked Mariah. She shifted her gaze to Griffin as if it cost her. "Are you eating or working?"

"Coffee for me." Griffin nodded at Mariah. "She's fresh off the ferry. Jet-lagged."

It was the easiest he'd sounded since Mariah had met him, which didn't help at all with that *melting* sensation that was sweeping over her. His voice was even richer when he wasn't issuing orders. More compelling. Mariah tried to shove that unhelpful observation aside. She concentrated on the fact that the woman's unfriendliness wasn't noticeable or notable to him, which likely meant it was normal.

Mariah decided it was charming, like everything else in this place.

"I don't think I'm jet-lagged," she said, almost idly, because neither one of them was paying attention to her. "I got a great night's sleep in Juneau."

"She could use some protein," Griffin was saying. "But no shellfish."

"Did you really just order for me?" Mariah asked when the woman walked away again. She should have been angrier than she was, but she couldn't seem to muster up more fury at his high-handedness. She suspected it had to do with the impossibly sharp line of his jaw. Or maybe his mouthwatering cheekbones. Or possibly her own shallowness. "I didn't even get a chance to look at a menu."

Griffin's expression tightened as he gazed at her. "There aren't any menus. Caradine cooks what she wants. And if she doesn't like the look of you, she won't cook at all." He did something with his shoulder that made her think he'd shrugged when he hadn't. "Welcome to Grizzly Harbor."

"I'm surprised that there are enough people here that she can pick and choose who to serve and still stay in business."

"Nobody comes to Alaska because they want to be like other people. This isn't a place where anyone conforms, and those of us who belong here like that."

There was a rebuke in that if she wanted to look for it. She didn't.

Mariah considered him instead. "How does that non-conformist thing work when you have to do military maneuvers, or whatever you do? Don't you have to follow orders?"

She had no idea if he did *military maneuvers*. All she knew was what she'd heard in that video and in the other limited comments about Alaska Force she'd found in strange corners of the internet. Corners where everyone was a soldier, according to them, and were therefore forever throwing around nonsensical terms like *alpha charlie whatever.*

"I follow the chain of command," Griffin said stiffly.

"Meaning you follow orders."

"Don't you?"

He didn't look angry, and he certainly didn't sound it—beneath all that tight control. And yet the question was another one of those belted-out sentences that Mariah was starting to realize was a weapon. Because every syllable felt like a blow.

Griffin didn't wait for her to reply. "I read your file. Married young to an older, much richer man."

"You make him sound like he had one foot in the grave. David was twenty-nine when we met. Not exactly ancient."

"It was a Cinderella story, right? That was what you called it. Whirlwind romance. Picture-perfect wedding out in the country at his folks' place. I'm betting they paid for it. Did you call the shots after all that? Is that how things worked?"

Mariah had trouble keeping her gaze steady. But that half smile stayed welded to her mouth, because she'd certainly heard worse things about her marriage. Usually delivered directly to her face with a syrupy drawl and a butter-wouldn't-melt expression.

The sad truth was that she'd been head over heels for David when they married. He hadn't forced her into anything. She hadn't been blind, and she'd walked down that aisle with her head high and her eyes wide open. She'd known what her marriage was. Or at least she'd known its dynamics. She hadn't minded. What did a no-account waitress know about anything outside Two Oaks and the rural county spread out around it? It had been so easy to let David take charge.

It had been a relief, if she was being honest.

All you have to do is stay pretty, he had told her.

That had been a far sight better, to her way of thinking, than having to be responsible for her troublesome younger siblings and her wild cousins and, all too often, her mouthy aunts, drunk uncles, and even sometimes the father Rose Ellen had never bothered to marry before she'd tossed him out. Mariah had been tired of being the one the county sheriff always called to come pick up this or that relative. She'd been neck-deep in all the assorted troubles of every generation of McKennas in the area whether she'd liked it or not, and she'd had no idea what was going to become of her.

Was she going to settle down the way everyone seemed to do for lack of any better options? Have a few babies? And maybe even do those two things out of order, so she could take her turn as the source of family gossip for once?

People in her family barely made it through high school. They certainly didn't prance off to collect degrees, even if there had been money lying around for such rich-person foolishness, which there wasn't. They also didn't up and join the army like some folks in town, and if there were other ways out of Two Oaks, Mariah had never heard of them.

Until David.

It pained her to admit it, even to herself, but he'd been like magic.

Five

"I wouldn't say David called the shots," Mariah said now, carefully. Coolly. And too aware of the weight of Griffin's dark gaze. "That's a cynical way to put it."

"If the two of you had a fight, and you couldn't come to an agreement, who won?"

That shouldn't have scraped at her, but it did. Mariah shoved that away, too, because what did it matter if she felt raw? That was nothing new.

"At first we didn't fight at all. There was nothing to fight about. Then, later, we had discussions about various points of contention. I wouldn't call those fights because I always saw David's point of view."

Because he had known so much more than she did, about everything. Because it was his world and she knew—she knew and he knew and his family knew and all of Atlanta knew—that she would never really fit in. Because he was the one with the college degree from fancy Vanderbilt. Because everything she had, he'd given her.

"Everybody takes orders, princess." She didn't know which was harder, Griffin's voice or the way he was looking at her. Like he'd heard every single thought she'd just had. Or maybe she'd shouted out the way she'd scrubbed her own self out of existence right here in this disconcertingly cheerful café. "The difference between you and me is that the man I take orders from is a man of honor. I would lay down my life for him in a second, and he would do the same for me. I take orders from him because I choose to. Because I trust him with my life. Is that what your marriage was like?"

"I believed it was," Mariah said quietly. "Or I wouldn't have married him."

"Wouldn't you?"

There was a slap in that, but Mariah couldn't do more than frown, because the woman he'd called Caradine was back, all sharp edges and a scowl, thunking down big mugs of coffee on the table between them.

"Food will be another minute," she said in a voice that, again, wasn't remotely friendly.

But Mariah wondered if she was simply used to the South. Everybody sounded friendly all the time back home, especially when they harbored nothing but black and abiding hatred in their hearts. For all she knew, this Caradine woman was simply neutral, but Mariah was too Southern to tell the difference.

"The first thing you need to know about my marriage is that I loved my husband," Mariah said after she'd taken a deep, head-clearing chug of her coffee. She was delighted to find that it was good. Really good. And strong. "It took him years to chip away at that. I was under the impression we were in it together, from his political aspirations to our fertility issues. When I caught him sleeping with other women, it wasn't business as usual. Because it wasn't ever a business to me. It was real. I thought it was real." She took another pull from her mug. "And most of the women in my position stay. They stay and they make it work, but I didn't. I couldn't. By the end, the marriage wasn't what I'd imagined it was when we started, but I never would have left him if he hadn't cheated on me. I wanted it to work."

"If you say so."

"I know so."

"You married an older man with money, but sure. It was love. You were head over heels for the guy. Not his bank account, his big house, his expensive toys. You would have loved him the same if he'd had none of those things and wanted to sweep you away to the house down the block."

Griffin didn't actually call her a gold digger. He didn't really have to.

Mariah concentrated, fiercely, on cupping her hands around her mug and lacing her fingers together.

When she raised her gaze again, she'd gotten control of herself and of the pain he didn't deserve to see. "Who ripped your heart out and stomped on it?"

Another man might have flinched. But Griffin's dark gaze only got colder. Just as he got even more dangerously, lethally still.

"Excuse me?"

"You seem to have a lot of opinions about a stranger's marriage. In my experience, that kind of thing usually comes from a person's own ugly stuff bubbling up."

"I don't have stuff."

She smiled. "Okay."

"I don't have stuff, princess. And Marines don't *bubble*."

"That sounds like a whole lot of stuff. And I'm not a princess. If you know my husband swept me off my feet and let me pretend to be Cinderella for a while, you know that Cinderella doesn't start off with a coronation. I was dirt poor. I came from nothing and expected a long life of the same. There's not a royal bone in my body."

Griffin eyed her for a moment that went on much too long. So long Mariah felt herself start to get much too hot. "You look like you got used to having more than nothing."

"My goodness," she murmured, like the Southern belle she wasn't. "I had no idea that I'd be running from murder attempts to character assassinations. That really should have been included in the introductory email."

But if she imagined beautiful, deadly Griffin would be abashed, she was mistaken. He leaned forward, his face set into a stern expression that she tried to see as commanding and very, very scary. When really she wanted nothing more than to reach out and touch him.

Instead, she clenched her fingers tighter around her mug until the heat of the ceramic burned.

"I'm not assassinating your character," he said, his voice cold enough to make her shiver. She tried to hide it, but she knew that he saw it. The same way she knew he saw everything else. Inside her. Inside this café. And out on the streets of Grizzly Harbor, too, she had no doubt. His *awareness* was like a Southern gentleman's chivalry. Knee-jerk and constant. "I'm trying to figure out if you're a liar. Delusional or dramatic or anywhere in between. Or maybe you're a run-of-the-mill rich man's first wife, who didn't like getting tossed aside for a newer model and suffered through a round or two of self-induced shellfish poisoning to point the finger at the ex. Believe me, we've seen it all before."

"If that's supposed to make me feel better about being the potential delusional drama queen in question, it doesn't."

"I'm not here to make you feel better. If we decide to handle your situation, our goal will be to neutralize the threat, not concern ourselves with your emotional state. You should probably get your head around that now."

"I have to say I'm amazed that a super-secret band of heroes hidden off in the hinterland, who roam about solving crimes and saving folks, would choose *this* as their marketing approach. Do y'all actually have any clients?"

Griffin's hard expression didn't change at all. "Do you have something to feel guilty about? Any lies, omissions? Anything you made up?"

"I don't know a single grown person who doesn't feel guilty about something," Mariah replied, keeping her own voice light and her gaze trained on his. She pretended she couldn't feel any heat. Or that hollow yearning that reminded her of the way she'd always wanted to please David. "What about you?"

"Guilt is a luxury." Flat. Certain. "I prefer action."

That felt a lot like a kick in the stomach.

"Exactly what kind of action are we talking about?" Mariah asked after a moment, when her stomach stopped feeling quite so fragile. "Because I don't want . . ." She couldn't finish that sentence. "I want to divorce David, that's all. I want to live long enough to be single."

"Alaska Force is not a contract-killer service. Jesus Christ."

"What are you, then?"

"We specialize in containment. And solutions."

"Is that a fancy way of saying—"

"It's not a fancy way of saying anything. That's what we do. You've had two separate instances of anaphylaxis in the last month, correct?"

That was a dizzying subject change. Or maybe he made her dizzy. "Yes."

"Why didn't you contact the police if you thought your ex-husband was involved?"

"David's family regularly has the police commissioner over for Sunday dinner. I didn't think that reporting him would do anything except make me more of a target. Because the only thing my in-laws like less than a white trash daughter-in-law who can't even get herself knocked up is any kind of public embarrassment."

"But you didn't test that theory."

"It's not a theory. That's the guiding principle of the family. No public humiliations or scandals upon pain of excommunication."

"So again, you didn't report your suspicions to anyone. Not the Atlanta police. Or any of your doctors."

"I thought the first time could have been an accident. To be honest, I wanted it to be an accident." She felt too intense, too visible, and looked away. "Because if it was an accident, I wouldn't have to make myself face the fact that I spent ten years of my life sleeping in the same bed as someone who could turn around and want me dead. And worse, try to make that happen. I'm still holding out hope that I'm paranoid and crazy and you'll tell me it was an accident after all."

She remembered glimpsing movement in the shadows here, where no one knew she'd gone, and wondered if that was what Griffin was here to tell her. That she was plain off her rocker like her aunt Annie May—because in her corner of the poor, rural South, mental illness was often considered part of a family's colorful story.

"What made you decide to seek out Alaska Force?" he asked instead.

Mariah decided not to share any details about conspiracy theorists and her addiction to online how-to videos, because that would give him ammunition she was pretty sure he didn't need. Not when he was already looking at her like she was wasting his time.

"If I stayed in Atlanta, he was going to kill me," she said. Simply. "And I wanted to live."

It was nothing she hadn't thought before, or typed out to an anonymous email address. But it was different to say it out loud. To say it to another person. Not to hedge or try to pretty it up or contradict herself as she said it. Not to tell herself she was being paranoid in the next breath.

And the fact that Griffin didn't so much as flinch, that all he did was gaze back at her steadily, made it possible for her to continue. More than possible—easy.

"He must have had someone break into my apartment. I can't think of how else he could have poisoned me. And if he could do it once, he could do it again. So when I remembered that I'd heard about Alaska Force, I looked you all up. And here I am."

"Here you are."

Griffin sat back then, but he was only making way for the food.

Mariah automatically smiled her thanks, but she

could barely look at the plate Caradine thrust before her. She was too busy trying to parse Griffin's tone when he'd said *here you are*—and then beating herself up for trying to play that game with him the way she always had with David. Forever on edge. Always trying to predict his moods and what he might find *disappointing* next.

It was only when the tantalizing scent of the meal before her got to her that she blinked enough to pay attention. It was a sandwich, but not any old run-of-the-mill sandwich. A BLT, by the looks of it, piled between thick slices of obviously home-baked bread and smelling so good Mariah thought she might cry.

Or maybe she was already on the verge of crying anyway. About anything.

And for a while, she didn't care that the most dangerous man she'd ever met was watching her. She just ate, because her BLT was better than it looked, and it looked like heaven.

Mariah considered licking the plate when she was done, but she restrained herself. Barely.

She pushed the plate away and allowed herself to look at Griffin again.

He hadn't gotten any less cold. Or astonishingly good-looking.

"Did I pass your test?" she asked quietly.

"There's no test."

"Are you sure? I'm getting the distinct impression you're deciding whether or not to help me."

"It's not my decision. We vote."

"Based on your recommendation?"

He sat there, and it occurred to her that he didn't fidget. He didn't rap his fingers on the table, or jiggle his knee. He didn't rub his hands on his face, or adjust his position in his chair, or any of the things people normally did. If she shut her eyes, would she even know he was there?

That made her shiver, too.

"Here's the thing," Griffin said after another long, tense moment in which Mariah was sure she failed a hundred other tests. "You don't strike me as a damsel in distress."

That made her laugh. "What's a damsel in distress supposed to look like?"

Griffin leaned back then, stretching one absurdly well-formed arm over the back of the chair next to him. He shook his head, forcing Mariah to stop contemplating the difference between the bicep of a man who perhaps visited a gym occasionally and . . . this.

"You're not scared. You don't even look frazzled. You had to run from your home, get on a plane, and fly across the country to meet a bunch of strangers you think are going to help you out of what should be a terrifying situation, and you look as cool and easy as if you're out for a quiet stroll."

Her heart picked up its pace, and she wondered if he could tell. If he could see her pulse betraying her.

"I actually went to a lot of trouble to make it look like I was going to Greece. On a plane, not a quiet stroll."

"I'm trying to tell you that you don't look like someone who's being chased."

"Is that a compliment?" She laughed again, because the notion that this man might compliment her struck her as truly hilarious. Or, possibly, she was finally losing it. "Maybe I managed to get them off my trail."

"Or it means that no one's chasing you to begin with."

"Right." She wasn't laughing any longer, and she was overly aware of all the ways she actually did fidget. She made herself drop her hands to her lap and keep them there. "That would make sense in the scenario where I almost kill myself twice because that somehow sticks it to my husband who wants me dead."

"Why does he want you dead? A lot of people say things like that. Everybody wants to kill everybody else in rush hour traffic. Actually killing another person is a different animal. Taking steps to make that happen is crossing a line, and it's not an insignificant line."

"He wants me dead because I'm an embarrassment." Mariah's voice didn't even shake. She supposed that was more evidence for him. Maybe a good damsel in distress would weep. Fall on the ground. Wail and rip at her clothes. "It was one thing to be dirt-poor white trash. I think David got off on that part, honestly. He got to play at making something out of me. But I was supposed to give him children. That's the whole point of marrying a girl like me."

She'd gotten so good at saying it like that. Like it didn't matter that she couldn't get pregnant. Like it was a joke.

But it was gratifying that Griffin didn't laugh.

"Why didn't you give him children if that was what he wanted and you wanted to stay married to him?"

Mariah smiled and was surprised it didn't draw blood. "Well, sugar. I did try."

"Do you call everybody *sugar*?"

He sounded almost as sharp as her smile felt. And that look in his dark brown eyes was worse.

"How many princesses do you know?" she retorted.

She wasn't sure what she expected, but it wasn't Griffin shooting to his feet. It took Mariah a second to realize why it was so strange and alarming, other than the fact that he was suddenly towering over her. It was because he didn't make any noise. He pushed back from the table and rose, but there was no scrape of his chair against the floor. There was no sound at all.

That fact rolled over her like a shiver, but it was all heat.

"I think I have all I need." He looked down at her as he said it, which meant she had to look up.

And up. And up. He had to be six foot two, and it seemed a lot farther up when she was sitting. All that sculpted muscle made it worse.

"Okay. What happens now?"

"Give me your cell phone."

She didn't want to, but she did, sliding it across the table and watching him tuck it into one of his utility pockets like he was taking a piece of her.

"Now what?"

"You stay here. You wait."

She wanted to sound tough and unconcerned, but she was terribly afraid she sounded nothing but scared. Maybe that would please him. "For how long?"

Griffin threw a few bills on the table, never shifting his hard gaze from Mariah. "The next ferry leaves on Monday. You'll know our decision before then."

And then he left her, his coffee mug the only indication he'd ever been there at all.

Six

"Something about her doesn't sit right with me," Griffin said.

Not for the first time. Or the fifth time.

But his Alaska Force brothers weren't heeding his warning. Jonas was standing across the room, running his hand over his fierce black beard while scowling out the window as the Friday sunset settled on Fool's Cove, no doubt going over the mission he'd run the previous week, solving a kidnapping issue without firing a single bullet. Templeton was lounging the way he always did, making Griffin want—also not for the first time—to knock him and the chair over to prove a point. The only reason he didn't was that he knew precisely how lethal the seemingly affable Templeton was, and how swift the other man's response would be, especially when he was still hopped up from the same bulletless kidnap op.

He swept his gaze over the other members of Alaska Force gathered in the lodge, pausing for a moment on Blue

Hendricks, former Navy SEAL and all-around badass, who had just gotten back from putting down a vicious cell of insurgents in a country he wasn't officially permitted to enter. He was sitting on one of the couches with his legs stuck out in front of him, his copy of Mariah's file in his hands, and that same satisfied look on his face he'd been wearing since last fall.

Griffin didn't believe in happily-ever-afters, not for men like them, but against all odds, Blue was doing a good rendition of one. He'd even gotten engaged to Everly, who was famous in these parts for being one of the few boneheaded, suicidal idiots who'd ever made it over the mountain that protected Fool's Cove from the rest of the island. Locals called it Hard-Ass Pass and avoided it, but Everly had driven straight over it on one of the few days it wasn't a death trap, desperately trying to reach Blue. No one had ever expected that after Blue handled the bad situation Everly was in, she would stay. But she had. She'd even made it through an Alaskan winter.

Griffin was confident Blue was the exception that proved the rule. The men gathered in this room were good at solving issues, with prejudice if necessary. They didn't need to be good at the stuff civilian lives were made of. White picket fences and pretty wives, cute kids and the PTA. That was the world Alaska Force protected, not the one they lived in.

They were men without ties. Some without pasts. That usually meant they didn't have much in the way of futures, either. Not the way other, softer, safer people did.

Griffin was more than happy to live out what future he had right here, doing what he did best until his sight failed and he started missing targets. Or until an enemy had a really good day, for a change.

He dutifully visited his family every holiday season, pasting on the smile they expected and pretending he fit in with them when it was obvious he didn't. He put in his annual time in the tony Catalina Foothills neighborhood in Tucson where he'd grown up, grinning his way through his parents' comfortable high-desert life and performing the role of good son and decent brother for a solid week, which was about all he could tolerate. And when he left again after New Year's, he always figured the Cisneros family gratefully sank back into the old pueblo charm of their fancy subdivision with its mountain views and its air conditioning and its high walls that kept out everything but the dark—and had no idea what kind of big, bad wolf they'd allowed near them.

Griffin viewed his relocation to Alaska as a favor to all of them. He assumed they all agreed. But even if they didn't, they knew better than to ask him to move back home. No one had made that mistake in years.

Not since shortly after his ex had betrayed him so publicly, in fact. Back when he'd still allowed himself to react to things. But that required feelings, and Griffin had turned his off years ago.

He cut his gaze to Isaac, the only one among them who'd actually come home rather than leave such petty concerns behind him, since he'd been raised out here, where glaciers vied for purchase on the gruff, cold seas. The leader of their team was dressed the way he always was, in a T-shirt with a happy saying on the front— designed to confuse the unwary into imagining he was approachable—and cargo pants that did nothing at all to disguise his deadly physique. Outside of the lodge—in town where everyone knew him, for example, and out in the wider world where he had spent most of his professional life blending in with purpose—Isaac worked harder to conceal himself. He smiled more. He pretended to be toothless and affable and a friend to all.

But here, where it was only his handpicked group of ex–special ops brothers who'd left their various branches of the service but not their commitment to righting wrongs, everybody knew who he really was.

Here, Isaac Gentry was a lethal reckoning.

"Is it the fact she's sweet and blond that you don't like?" Templeton asked lazily, though there wasn't a single part of the man that was in any way as boneless or relaxed as he pretended he was. "Because that sits just fine with me."

Griffin's jaw ached. Again. He forced himself to stop clenching it. "Blond, yes. Sweet? No. She's a rich man's trophy wife who hit thirty and got replaced. Generally speaking, pampered princesses don't like that much."

"I personally like a Georgia peach," Templeton replied with a wide grin. "Sweet enough to make your teeth hurt and twice as delicious."

"Careful," Blue said with a laugh as Griffin eyed those tipped-back chair legs again. "Doesn't look like Griffin is feeling like sharing his . . . peaches."

Griffin smirked at Blue and made an anatomically impossible suggestion, which, of course, only made Blue—and everyone else—laugh harder. Smug bastard.

"Do we have rules against helping blond princesses, pampered or otherwise?" Isaac asked mildly, cutting through the hilarity without having to raise his voice. He studied Griffin like he could see straight through him. He probably could. "Because that sounds a lot like your thing, not ours."

Griffin wasn't surprised when the vote went against

him, with more talk of peaches and princesses before they moved on to thornier issues involving ongoing cases. There was a possible situation developing in nearby Juneau, but he gave their disgruntled would-be enemy only half of his attention while his temper kicked at him like a lit fuse.

He knew Mariah was nothing more than another client. He didn't have to like her, he only had to save her, and that shouldn't have been difficult. It was one more mission, and missions didn't require that he turn himself inside out with souped-up enthusiasm—they required his skill and dedication.

That was what he was telling himself after the meeting, out on the rambling porch that ran along the front of the lodge and offered views out over the water of the protected cove in the long blue spring twilight. He didn't need to like any part of this. He'd performed the initial intake, he'd handed her cell phone over to Oz so he could make sure no one could trace it without Alaska Force's knowledge, and now that the vote was in, Griffin was running point on Mariah's situation. He didn't have to start cartwheeling around, pretending he was happy about it. Or her. Like most things in his life, it wasn't required that he love every moment. Or any moment. He just had to do it.

Her case was simple enough. Identify and neutralize the threat. Impress upon her husband that divorce was the better choice, assuming he was behind the attempts on her life. And keep her alive while they did it.

The lodge door slapped open, and Griffin knew it was Isaac who stepped out to join him without having to look. He recognized the other man's tread and the patter of his dog's feet, as Horatio—far smarter than most people, with his different-colored eyes and a huge helping of his owner's attitude—had come outside with him.

The fact that Griffin could hear Isaac coming meant he had something to say. *Great.*

None of his other brothers would roll up on him when he was clearly dealing with stuff. There were certain boundaries between snipers and everyone else. It was the nature of the job. He'd accepted it a long time ago.

Hell, he'd embraced it.

Isaac came and stood with Griffin because he didn't care about boundaries, and for a while it was just the two of them, and Horatio at Isaac's feet. They stared out at the seething dark water of the cove as the tide came in, grasping at the rocky shore. They watched the last hint of light in the sky fade, darkness coming almost two hours later than it had at the start of the month. Spring had finally started showing signs of life around here. The clocks had jumped forward after another deep, dark Alaskan winter, and summer was coming.

But Griffin knew Isaac hadn't come out here to stare at the scenery or discuss the changing seasons.

"Are you going to be able to handle this?"

Griffin shot him a look. "Of course."

"She's not Gabrielle."

He should have known that was coming. He should have expected it.

"I'm well aware she's not my ex-fiancée, Isaac." Griffin could hear his own clipped tone, an unwise choice in Isaac's presence, but he didn't stop. "I can actually tell the difference between pretty blond white women."

But if he expected Isaac to back off, he was about to

be disappointed. His leader reached down and smoothed his hand over Horatio's head. And Griffin was pretty sure the dog was giving him the same *yeah, right* look.

Isaac didn't actually say *yeah, right*. He didn't have to. "You sure about that? I've never seen you get bent out of shape about anything. No mission, no matter how screwed up. No person, place, or thing. And especially not a client. Until today."

"I'm not sure why registering some reasonable skepticism equals *bent out of shape*."

"You seem extra skeptical."

Griffin shrugged. "You haven't met her. Maybe when you do, you'll stop treating me like a high school kid who's knotted up over some cheerleader and remember that my instincts and interpretations of situations have saved your butt more times than you can possibly count."

Isaac didn't say anything. And that was worse than if he had, because it allowed Griffin to replay what he'd said again and again, entirely too aware of how much like a high school kid he'd sounded. He could remember being that high school kid himself before he'd enlisted on his eighteenth birthday, complete with Gabrielle as the cheerleader in question, who he'd been *so sure* he was in love with when really he'd been sixteen and an idiot. And even worse than the unscheduled trip down memory lane was his shrug, which was a giant tell that he wasn't as at ease or comfortable as he was trying to pretend he was—because Griffin wasn't a fidgeter. He could spend astonishing amounts of time without moving, awake and alert, his entire being focused on a target.

He'd confirmed everything Isaac was saying.

"I haven't thought about Gabrielle in a long time," Griffin said stiffly, before Isaac could point any of that out. "It's like that whole situation happened to someone else."

Someone significantly dumber.

"I believe you," Isaac said quietly. Too quietly. Griffin kept his eyes on the water surging at the shore below, but he could feel when Isaac's sharp gray gaze slammed into him. "But here's the thing about betrayal. It gets in there and it changes how you think. How you see things. You don't have to think about it directly for it to color everything."

"Gabrielle did what was right for her," Griffin said, hating that it took effort to sound matter of fact. Not stiff or defensive or gruff, because he didn't like talking about ancient history. Not because she had some hold on him after all these years. She didn't. "Much as that sucked for me at the time, I can't blame her. I wasn't the man she sent off to the Marines."

"Okay."

The placid agreement came too quickly to be real. "I see her every year over the holidays. She and Oscar have three kids now. Good cars. Vacations during summer break. A nice house in the same neighborhood where we grew up. As far as I can tell, she's happy."

Gabrielle had told him so herself at a Christmas Eve party he'd been forced to attend with his entire family during his Wolf in Sheep's Clothing week. She'd gripped Oscar's arm and they'd both beamed at him, obviously terrified. They clearly worried a whole lot about Griffin.

More than he ever had about them, if he was entirely honest with himself.

He might have been tempted to share that fact had his

sister, Vanessa, not steered him away from the pair of them. In a hurry.

"And let's be real here," he continued now. "I could never have been happy in that world. Oscar likes being a dentist. He likes taking his kids to Little League and the Girl Scouts and working on his front yard on the weekends when it's not too hot. That's not the life I want. That's not who I am. If it was, I wouldn't have joined the Marines in the first place. I should have cut Gabrielle loose when I enlisted."

"I said okay, brother."

"And even if I wasn't okay with her choices a hundred years later, it wouldn't affect my work now. I'm offended that anyone would think otherwise."

This time, when Isaac turned toward him, Griffin met his stare.

"I'm not commenting on your work, dumbass. I'm pointing out that you're having a reaction to a pretty blond woman who looks a whole lot like the one who cheated on you with your best friend, then turned around and married him instead of you. It's not crazy that you might have some stuff crop up around that."

"Now I'm offended that you think I need to . . . what? Talk about my feelings? What's next? Are you going to give me a unicorn stuffed animal? Are we going to make friendship bracelets?"

Isaac laughed, though Griffin couldn't tell if the laughter made it to his canny eyes. Horatio's head cocked to one side, as if he wasn't fooled. Isaac clapped a hand on Griffin's shoulder.

"I'll come with you into town," he declared, pulling Mariah's cell phone from his pocket and flipping it over to Griffin. "I want to meet this blond woman who doesn't remind you of anyone, is in no way a ghost of your own complicated past, and absolutely, one hundred percent, doesn't get beneath your skin."

Griffin had a lot of things he would have liked to say to that, but decided it was better to maintain a dignified, affronted silence instead. Because if anyone had ever gone head-to-head with Isaac Gentry and won, he sure hadn't heard about it.

He and Isaac took one of the boats this side of the spring breakup of all the winter ice. The frozen rivers inland were starting to flow again. The snow that had been packed down hard all winter had started to melt, leaving mud and puddles everywhere. Even the sea was settling down as the days stretched out longer and longer.

Griffin had been born and raised in the desert—and he'd joined the Marines, not the navy. He was fully competent, but he was also more than comfortable letting Isaac do the navigating through the dark, with the expertise he'd learned growing up here.

This part of Alaska had been settled by prospectors out of places like Seattle, San Francisco, and Russia, drawn to the mountains by rumors of gold. They'd mingled with the natives that were already here when the gold didn't pan out, then carved out hardy settlements where the edge of the world met the elements and often lost, and they dug in. There was no living here without contending with nature in a major way, day in and day out. No one here was indifferent to the seasons. There were four, they were distinct and challenging in their own ways, and everyone tracked them with the obsessiveness of people whose lives depended on knowing what was coming. Because they did.

Tonight Griffin felt the cold slap of the wind on his

face as Isaac took them out into the swells, then along the coast of the island to Grizzly Harbor. But it was already significantly warmer out on the water than it had been a few weeks back. He'd call it downright balmy.

The members of Alaska Force lived in their own cabins in the woods around Fool's Cove, with views out over the same intense sea. Some of those cabins were connected to the lodge. Some were accessible by a short hike. Still others were set back in the woods, off anything resembling a grid. All that undisturbed silence allowed men like Griffin, who spent most of their time assessing every person they saw for potential threats, to actually relax.

The demanding sea in the distance was the only companionship he really needed. It was as much a part of him as his rifle.

Isaac piloted the boat into town with the same offhanded skill he showed in everything he did. They moored down at the docks, then walked the rest of the way into the village. Everyone in town liked to hang lights on the outside of their houses, all huddled together in the narrow strip between the high tide line and the forest. Tonight the lights blazed against the thick spring dark, as if daring the inky, endless black fist of winter to take another swing. It was a moody sort of night, with a hint of fog pooling between the buildings, and Griffin liked that Isaac kept his own counsel as they headed up the hill when he wasn't fielding mission-related calls.

Griffin found himself thinking about Gabrielle, the girl he'd expected to spend the rest of his life with back when he'd expected to have a completely different kind of life. She was supposed to have waited for him to come back so they could pick up the plans they'd made when they were still kids. And she had waited, or so she said, through his first two tours.

It was when he'd re-upped instead of coming home and settling down that she'd had enough. Apparently. She and his best friend from high school had comforted each other—because Griffin's service to his country was equally upsetting to both of them, they'd claimed. The fact that Oscar had wanted Gabrielle for himself since they'd all hit puberty hadn't factored into it at all, Griffin was sure.

He could have forgiven that. Probably. But neither of them had confessed what they'd done when Griffin had finally come home. Gabrielle had moved ahead with their wedding, acting every inch the excited bride-to-be—until right before the invitations were set to go out.

Six weeks before he'd been set to get married, Griffin had instead discovered that he not only didn't have a fiancée, he didn't have a best friend, either.

He hadn't even been as angry about it as maybe he should have been. He'd taken it as a sign.

I don't know who you are, Gabrielle had told him, convincing tears tracking prettily down her cheeks. She'd always been good at crying, and it always used to make Griffin feel like crap, but he'd changed in the Marines. She was right about that. *I don't know what they made you, but it isn't the Griffin I remember.*

Of course he wasn't the Griffin she remembered. That dumb kid had died in boot camp when he was still eighteen. The Marines had made him a man, then he'd taken it a step further and made himself a perfect machine. One who had seen too much, too fast, in far-off countries, and had quickly taught himself how to feel as little as possible. A sniper, cold and calculating, who needed nothing and no one and could therefore take out anyone on command. He'd been so good at what he did that the enemy had given him their own nicknames but never managed to stop him.

His real secret wasn't that he remembered Gabrielle and mourned for what he'd lost. She was his cautionary tale. He shouldn't have imagined that he could be who he was, do the things he did, and slip back into that kind of life. He shouldn't have tried so hard to convince himself he could feel the things others did, because he couldn't. He'd given that up.

He would never make that mistake again.

He'd left for Alaska the morning after Gabrielle and Oscar had delivered the news, leaving them to clean up the mess they'd made. He'd followed up on that legend he'd heard while he was still in the service, about a dangerous man on the edge of the world and the band of skilled soldiers who gathered there to keep fighting.

All these years later, he still didn't regret his choice.

They walked along the village's winding main street, past the Fairweather, which was doing its usual brisk Friday night trade—or what passed for such a thing in Grizzly Harbor when summer was still a long way off. Griffin could hear loud music from the jukebox and voices to match, but he and Isaac kept on, up the hill past the Water's Edge Café, the peeling yellow post office, and the community center, until they reached Blue Bear Inn.

"She's not here," Madeleine said from behind the desk, not bothering to look up after the first glance she'd thrown their way.

Madeleine Yazzie was a Grizzly Harbor native. She liked to wear her hair in that beehive, the better to contrast with her cat-eye glasses, so that people would mistake her for a very old woman. Griffin figured her to be in her early forties. She married, divorced, remarried, and redivorced her husband, Jaco, in tune with the seasons, so no one could say with any certainty if they were on or off at any given time. She had never been known to suffer a fool, she told better fishing tales than old Ernie Tatlelik, and she'd been a fixture behind the desk at the inn for at least as long as Griffin had lived here.

What she wasn't, usually, was an unreliable narrator. But what she'd said didn't make any sense.

Griffin stared at her. "What do you mean she's not here?"

"I'm surprised you didn't hear the racket on your way over. Last I heard, she and Caradine were going shot for shot down at the Fairweather and causing a ruckus."

"Are we talking about the same person?" Griffin asked, tempted to laugh at the absurdity. "Blond, snooty? The least likely person alive to walk into a dive bar like the Fairweather, much less drink anything there?"

"All I know is that Caradine closed early and headed over to get her drink on with an outsider. Pretty sure she's yours. But it wouldn't be the first time I was wrong, and I imagine it won't be the last, either."

"I didn't think you were ever wrong, Madeleine," Isaac said, flashing the smile that made unsuspecting people think he was safe. Charming, even.

"Neither did I," Madeleine replied, grinning over the top of one of the fat paperbacks she got in crates from her sister in Anchorage. "But who knows? This could be the night it happens."

As they pushed back outside and retraced their steps through town, it took every bit of self-control Griffin had not to ask Isaac his opinion on Caradine Scott, the most prickly café owner in Alaska. And therefore in the rest of the world, too. Because everybody knew that Isaac and Caradine didn't get along. They *didn't get along* to such an extent that there were bets among the Alaska Force brothers as to when and how the tension between them would finally snap.

Every woman in the known universe got silly at the sight of Isaac's patented smile.

Except Caradine. Caradine got mad.

Blue had all of his money riding on there being a solution involving a locked room and a bed. But Griffin figured it would be bloodshed. And as dangerous as Isaac was, Griffin's money was on Caradine winning the inevitable fight.

Like everyone else, however, he didn't push Isaac on the subject.

Not only because it was an unhealthy choice, but because he was certain he didn't want Isaac pushing back.

Either way, the moment they stepped inside the Fairweather, Isaac's gaze went directly to the dark-haired woman leaning back against the bar like she owned it. Caradine was egging on one of the burly locals at the pool table, looking slightly more relaxed than usual—yet no less fierce.

Griffin studied the much softer blonde by her side instead.

It was like Mariah had turned into a different person over the past few hours, and he didn't like it. The princess who'd glided off the ferry like she'd been walking into her own coronation was gone. In her place was a pretty woman packed into well-fitting jeans and a snug, expensive-looking T-shirt. She was also leaning back against the bar, propping herself against it on her elbows so that she looked out at the assorted Friday night shenanigans as if she'd never seen such a show before. The position drew Griffin's attention to the way that T-shirt clung to her sculpted, lean curves.

And if he was drawn to that view, he assumed every other man in the bar was, too.

But far worse than that was her laughter.

She wasn't laughing like she was made of ice. On the contrary. Her laugh was loud, warm, and rich, and it affected him the way her drawl did. Poured honey, sweet and golden. It washed over him, and Griffin was seized with a totally unreasonable urge to bundle her up and carry her out, so no one else could hear. It struck him as entirely too intimate for a dive bar in the middle of nowhere filled with rough, hard men who were always, always looking for a warm body on a cold night.

Settle down.

Griffin checked out the room automatically, letting his gaze move from the pool tables to the jukebox. All the dark, intimate booths along the walls and the more accessible seats in the center where Nellie, who prided herself on being a battle-ax, waited tables with her usual brisk impatience. There was no threat. There were only locals blowing off steam on a balmy spring night between storms.

His attention tracked back to Mariah and stayed there.

Isaac was already moving, forcing Griffin to do the same when he would have stayed right where he was in the doorway. He told himself he wanted to take a minute to fully control his temper, but the truth was that he wanted to keep looking at this version of Mariah, with her head tipped back and a wide-open expression—not a care in the world.

"So you're running for your life," Griffin said in a dark undertone as he and Isaac headed toward the bar and the two merry women who hadn't appeared to see them walk in. "You think your husband is trying to kill you and you think he's probably chasing you, too, so you lay down a little misdirection on your way out of town. It takes you the better part of a week, then you jump on a plane and end up in Grizzly Harbor. You meet someone who isn't all that sympathetic, you pour out your story, and then what do you do? Do you lock yourself in your hotel room, waiting to see if anyone's chasing you? Or even if the men you came to hire will take your case? Or do you go out drinking with a random stranger you met in a café?"

"You have a very specific idea of how this woman ought to behave," Isaac said, mildly enough, and the look he shot Griffin was too amused for Griffin's peace of mind. "Maybe she's happy that there's a continent between her and her ex. He sounds like the kind of guy any woman would want to keep away from if she could. Maybe she thinks she earned a party because she didn't die as planned. Twice."

Griffin bit his tongue. With prejudice.

"Oh goody," said Caradine in her usual dry way as he and Isaac approached. "Someone invited Gentry Company to ruin the party."

"You know it's called Alaska Force," Isaac replied, sounding significantly less mild and amused than he had a moment before. A stranger might not have been able to tell the difference. But to Griffin, it was glaring.

And he shouldn't have taken much comfort in that, but he liked knowing that even Isaac had a weakness. Griffin had tried to rid himself of as many weaknesses as possible, but it was comforting to know that someone as seemingly invulnerable as Isaac Gentry had one lurking around.

Griffin couldn't help but enjoy it.

"We're not in your café now," Isaac was saying, and the look he aimed at her wasn't the least bit safe or charming. "You can't make idle threats about banning me from a bar you don't own. What's your next move, Caradine?"

Caradine reached over the bar, picked up a shot glass, and raised it mockingly in Isaac's direction.

"Bottom's up, jackass," she said, and tossed it back.

And then she proved exactly how tough she was, in Griffin's opinion, by failing to react in any visible way to the menacing, knife's edge of a smile that Isaac aimed her way.

Griffin shifted his attention back to Mariah. "I'm surprised you're out celebrating at a time like this."

It was possible he sounded slightly cranky. Maybe that was why she laughed at him.

And laughed. And laughed some more.

He could have handled more of that cool, haughty politeness she'd tried to slap him with earlier. He liked the cold. He could handle it.

But her laugh was something else. It was loud, it was teetering on the edge of rowdy, and she didn't seem to care at all that it made heads turn throughout the bar.

"If you're trying to keep a low profile," Griffin bit out, "going shot for shot with an infamous local and making scenes in the middle of town is probably not the best idea I've ever heard."

"Am I supposed to be keeping a low profile?" Mariah asked. Her blue eyes danced, and Griffin didn't know what he was supposed to do with that. "You didn't leave me with a list of instructions, sugar. You just left."

"I have things to do, most of them with life-or-death consequences. Explain to me why you—left to your own devices, on the run and supposedly afraid for your life—figured this was a good time to make a spectacle of yourself?"

He expected to shame her. Or offend her enough, anyway, to get them to the same place. What he didn't expect was another one of those wicked belly laughs that rolled over him like a gas fire. And made him feel charred all the way through.

He also didn't expect it when she lurched forward, flinging herself from the bar with such force that she would have toppled over and gone straight to the sticky floor if he hadn't snaked out an arm to catch her.

It was a reflex.

It was also a mistake.

Because she felt even better than she looked, silky smooth and warm where her T-shirt sleeve ended and her arm began. Mariah might not be his ex. She might not even be in particular danger, no matter what she said.

But she was here, she was the softest thing he'd ever touched, and Griffin understood in a sudden flash of unwelcome insight exactly why she got beneath his skin.

Because around this woman, he kept remembering he'd once been a man and could be again—if only for a night.

If he played his cards right, which he couldn't. And wouldn't.

But there was no escaping the fact that whatever else happened, Griffin was already in trouble.

Seven

After Griffin left her in the café, disappearing like a puff of smoke, Mariah had shifted around to the other side of the table so that she could take a turn with her back to the wall and a nice view of all the comings and goings.

She ordered another mug of coffee from the surly waitress, who she was surprised to discover was also the cook. And, as she replayed what Griffin had told her, she realized she was clearly the owner, too, which made all that attitude and grumpiness feel like even more delightful local color.

Mariah sat there, nursing her coffee and watching as the group of fishermen left in a friendly knot. And as the tourist couple continued to fight with each other, punctuating their strained conversation with pointed silences as they ate their soup and sandwiches.

After they stormed out, hiking boots hitting the old floorboards with obvious aggression, only Mariah and Caradine were left in the bright, cheerful space that made as much of the iffy sunshine as it could. Unlike Caradine herself, who sat on a stool behind the counter and scowled out at the village as if it offended her. Just by . . . being there.

"Are they always like that?" Mariah had dared to ask.

"Which they?" Caradine had replied after a long pause and a baleful glare.

"Griffin and his friends. I mean, I'm assuming he has friends. That there's really a thing called Alaska Force and not just . . . him. Running around brooding at people and pretending he's a whole battalion."

Caradine's mouth had curved the slightest bit in one corner. "I'm sorry to tell you that Alaska Force is all too real."

Mariah had sighed. "I don't know if that makes me happy or sad. I was warming to the idea of Griffin being a one-man show."

"What I can tell you about all the men in Alaska Force is that each and every one of them is their own epic show. What you need to ask yourself is whether or not you want to be in the audience."

"I'm not the audience. I'm a client."

Caradine hadn't rolled her eyes, exactly. "That's how they get you."

"Not me," Mariah had said with tremendous confidence, as if she hadn't been easily distracted by Griffin's *arm*. "I already followed one worthless man around for a decade. I don't plan to repeat the experience."

"A woman after my own black heart."

Mariah had waited for Caradine to ask questions. Why she was here, for example. What had made her seek out Alaska Force. But if Caradine had the slightest bit of curiosity about Mariah's story—the way Mariah would have if their positions had been reversed—she didn't show it. She'd made Mariah another outstanding coffee and then, when the door opened, she'd waved away the people who tried to come in.

"I'm closed," she'd said, without a shred of apology in her voice.

"Come on, Caradine," the man argued in a low, gruff voice. "Maria and Luz need to eat before we head out into the bush. It's all mud and puddles and overflow for miles."

"Maria and Luz and springtime are not my problem."

"Please?" It was a female voice that time. Mariah saw that there were two women standing there with the man on the doorstep. The speaker was tall and blond. The other was short and brunette. And both were noticeably pregnant. "You know how long the trip is."

"Get provisions from the general store," Caradine suggested, in a tone that didn't invite any further argument.

Sure enough, the man—another fisherman by the looks of him—backed out of the doorway. Caradine followed, flipping the sign in the window to CLOSED and locking the door behind him.

"Are they both . . . ?" Mariah had asked, watching the trio make their way down the street outside.

"What they both are is a mess." Caradine had actually rolled her eyes then. "The short one, Maria, moved here with her boyfriend. But then she took up with Jared, who grew up here with the tall one, his wife, Luz. Who then got together with Maria's boyfriend instead. Now everybody's pregnant, no one knows who the fathers are, and they're all living together off the grid out there. It's a Grizzly Harbor soap opera. With bears and stupidity."

"You don't like them?"

"I don't like anyone."

"Well, that's handy," Mariah had said with a smile. "Neither do I."

She hadn't thought about it in such stark terms before, but she realized as she said it that it was true. She'd had all kinds of friends in Atlanta. Friends from the Junior League. Friends from every charity event she'd ever been involved with. Friends from the country club, the golf club, and David's other clubs. Friends to go to lunch with, or to Pilates with, or to art exhibitions at the High Museum with when the men were busy, and anywhere else she might want to go, too.

And not one of them had known a single real thing about her. Not one of them had been at all trustworthy. She hadn't even questioned the fact that none of them were likely to support her when she divorced David. She'd accepted it as fact, endured any number of thinly veiled insults from these *friends*, and when it came time to leave town and run for her life, she hadn't contacted any of them.

But it hadn't occurred to her until right that second, sitting there in Caradine's café, that she'd never really liked any of them all that much in the first place.

Her friendships during her marriage hadn't had anything to do with whom she liked or whom she didn't. One of her jobs had been to ingratiate herself with as many of the right people as possible, and she'd launched herself into it, because keeping David happy had been the closest thing to a career she had.

"My whole life has been about other people's expectations," she'd told Caradine, because she could tell by the look on the other woman's face that she didn't care. She had no expectations about Mariah at all. And that made her the perfect person to open up to. "And now that I find myself this far away in the middle of nowhere, it turns out I have a powerful hankering to defy every one of those expectations."

"If this involves pumping our fists and singing power ballads together, I'm going to have to decline."

"I'm tone-deaf," Mariah assured her, climbing to her feet. "I was raised by a long line of people who handled every disappointment the same way. With enough alcohol to take down a horse, a whole lot of bad behavior to go with it, and a vicious hangover the next morning, sure, but precious few regrets."

"I don't do friends," Caradine had said, studying her. "If that's what you're after."

"I'm after getting blind drunk and a little bit rowdy, like God intended when he made tequila."

Caradine's smile had been the kind of pure evil that made bad reputations. "That I can get behind."

And that was how Mariah had found herself embracing her long-neglected inner McKenna, smack in the middle of Grizzly Harbor's disreputable dive bar. Which happened to also be its only bar.

The first shot had tasted like cough medicine, only much worse. Mariah had wheezed and hacked her way through it, her eyes tearing up.

"The only way out is through," Caradine had murmured, sliding the second toward her.

That one had been about the same, with less hacking.

The third, happily, went down smooth.

It was around then that Mariah stopped counting. Or

caring that she'd recently suffered an anaphylactic reaction and maybe shouldn't have been drinking at all. She started laughing instead.

She didn't even know what was funny. She laughed and she laughed, because everything was sunshine, inside and out. She felt silly and free, as if she were a toddler who'd finally learned how to get up on her feet and refused to sit back down again. Her thoughts spun around and around in her head, but none of them really gripped her. She leaned back against the bar so she wouldn't fall off the side of the planet, and she let herself laugh.

Then Griffin walked in. And she couldn't find the edge of the world any longer, so she just spun on out into the Milky Way and focused the best she could on him.

Because he was far more potent than any of the alcohol churning around in her system.

He was cut, sculpted, and beautiful. And he made her nothing short of giddy as he walked up to stand in front of her, looking dark and disapproving and unquestionably delicious. The friend he brought with him was more of the same, a man built powerful and dangerous, sporting a beard like the locals and a similar, glittering intensity in his gaze.

But he could have walked in with a parade. Griffin was the only thing that Mariah could seem to look at.

Especially when he poked at her again.

That made her laugh, too, and she moved forward so she could get in his face the way every female relative she'd ever had always did to the men in their lives, but she stopped short when he wrapped one of his huge hands around her upper arm.

His hand was much too strong. Too tough and capable, indicating he used it for more than the odd golf game.

The heat of his palm felt like fire.

She could feel it everywhere. It rolled through her, charging through her blood and her bones and all the soft, needy areas in between, kicking out the cobwebs and reminding her of all the parts of herself she'd locked away.

So many parts of herself. So many feelings and dreams she'd quickly learned to hide. Need and longing and desire. And that gnarled, battered, sharp-sweet thing she was still inclined to believe was hope.

Marriage is about compromise, her mother-in-law had told her, with standard high-class distaste for her only son's regrettable wife. But Mariah had known better. It wasn't David who had compromised in their marriage; it was her. It was always, always her.

David's single compromise had been marrying Mariah in the first place. All subsequent compromises had been hers to make. And she'd made them. Oh, how she'd twisted and turned, contorting herself until she sometimes wondered if she'd even recognize who she'd been when she started.

Tonight, she knew she wouldn't.

Because she'd been married for ten years and she'd never felt anything in all that time like the roar of heat and greed that nearly knocked her off her feet when Griffin Cisneros grabbed her by the upper arm to keep her from tripping.

And then held on.

"You don't approve of me," she said, tipping back her head to look up at him and take in all that severe masculine beauty. "Every time you look at me your jaw goes like this."

She did an impression of him, jaw clenched tight, though it was possible she looked more like a horse. She wasn't much of an actress.

"I don't approve or disapprove of you," Griffin said, the obvious disapproval in his tone contradicting the statement. "You're a client. Nothing more, nothing less."

But everything was sunshine, and she was, too, so she didn't think twice. Mariah reached out and thunked him in the center of his chest with two fingers. And then, when he gazed down at her in exaggerated astonishment, she did it again.

Because he was shaped like one of the marble statues of Greek gods she'd seen at an exhibit at the High, but he was harder and hotter than marble. And far more impressive than any old Adonis.

"You specifically don't approve of me," Mariah countered. "You think I'm a gold digger."

"I don't think you're a gold digger. Because I don't think about you at all, not like that. What interests me about you is your safety."

She would have believed him without question if he'd said that a few hours ago. If he'd sat at that table in the café, stared her down, and laid it out that way. She would have been deeply embarrassed that she'd made it personal when he was only trying to do his job.

But it was dark inside this dive-bar-to-end-all-dive-bars. There was country music wailing on the jukebox, and Mariah was at least four shots in to a blurry, giddy night. And that gave her insight she wouldn't otherwise have had.

Griffin didn't look at her like she was a client. There

was a difference in the way his trained gaze tracked the noise and chaos around them. The way he seemed to keep tabs on everything that was happening, from the pool tables to the bartender to whatever tense, whispered conversation Caradine and Isaac were having a few feet away.

The way he looked at all of those things was more clinical. More distant.

But when he looked back at her, every time he looked at her, something in him burned.

She didn't ask herself how she knew this. She just accepted it.

And her fingers were pressed into that mouthwatering hollow between his pectoral muscles, so she went with it. She spread out her hand, touching as much of his chest as she could.

It still wasn't enough.

She wasn't all that shocked when he snatched her hand and held it in the space between them.

"You're drunk," he told her. Flatly.

In the exact same tone she remembered wielding on any number of her own relatives in the past when they'd taken their own McKenna cures.

She couldn't help but grin. "Am I? Already? I thought for sure that came with crying in the corner. Trying to curl up and take a nap under a bar stool. Or dancing on the pool tables in some or other state of undress."

"That's wasted. That comes after drunk."

"I wouldn't know," she said airily. "I've never been drunk in my life."

"But you figured you'd start tonight. In a bar where you don't know a soul. Anyone in here could do you harm, for all you know. You might as well paint a target on your back."

"I've drunk some wine here and there, but it was always controlled. Never more than two glasses, under pain of death. David got to get drunk if he wanted, of course. But drunk on a woman is no good, don't you know? It's sloppy. Trashy. And we can't have that."

His lips moved like he was biting back his words.

But all he said was, "I'm taking you back to your room."

She laughed at that, too. But she didn't protest. He kept that hard hand of his wrapped tight around her upper arm as he steered her away from the long, scarred wooden bar. Mariah waved to Caradine, who didn't wave back. She dutifully accepted the bundle of fabric that Griffin handed her, but it took her a few confused moments to realize that it was her own fleece and vest.

"This is all much more forward than I'm used to," she told him as he swung open the door and propelled her outside into the shock of the cold night air. "I don't go to bars. Much less leave them with strange men."

"It's cold," Griffin said shortly. "You should dress yourself appropriately before you freeze."

"I like it," Mariah assured him.

She could feel the cold, of course. It was like a sharp, gleaming scythe, cutting straight into her and cleaving her in two, but it was exhilarating all the same.

She tipped her head back, letting herself topple off into the real Milky Way spread out above her. She had never seen so many stars in her life. Not even when she'd been a child, lying in the back of a pickup truck on those long summer nights out in the country.

And it wasn't until she felt his hand tighten around her arm that she realized Griffin was the only reason she wasn't spinning off into the ether. Or tumbling to the uneven ground.

She smiled at him when she found him there, scowling beneath the surly neon sign from the bar that cast him in a kind of pink shadow. But it did nothing to take away from his breathtaking beauty, which caught at her with the same sharpness as the temperature.

"You're beautiful," she told him.

His scowl deepened. He let go of her, but only so he could take her fleece from her hand and put it over her head like she was a child. She stood there, bemused, as he fed one arm through one sleeve, then the other. He tugged the fleece into place, zipped up the neck, and even tugged her hair free. Not done, he wrapped her down vest over her shoulders, made sure her arms were in the proper armholes, and zipped that up, too.

"Replace this vest," he muttered at her as he did it. "Down gets wet and soggy. You'll freeze in the first rain."

A new sensation swelled in her then. Raw. Fragile. And far more dangerous than too much tequila or that fire in his dark gold eyes. All that sunshine had shifted into something sacred, and it didn't matter that he was scowling at her.

His hands were brisk, efficient, even impatient—but kind.

Mariah couldn't remember the last time anyone had treated her with kindness.

"Why are you crying?"

He sounded harsh, but his thumb grazed over one cheekbone, and there was nothing harsh in the touch. It was more of that same shocking kindness and the faint scrape of his skin against hers. Then a gleaming bit of moisture he held out between them as evidence.

"I'm not crying," she assured him with as much dignity as she could muster.

"Let's get you to your room," he said, and they were walking again.

His hand was wrapped around her upper arm, and once more, she relaxed into his grip. She let him guide her, laughing every time her legs couldn't seem to follow directions. And laughing even more when he didn't join in.

She watched in fascination as he punched a code into a keypad at the inn's front door when they arrived, then had to concentrate ferociously to navigate the stairs that led up to her room.

"Where is your key?" Griffin asked her in a low voice when they stopped in front of a door. Mariah blinked, squinted, and only belatedly realized they were standing in front of her hotel room door. "The key, Mariah."

She smiled up at him, tipping her head back. "You used my name. My actual name."

He muttered a word that sounded like a curse, but she didn't care about that because his hands were on her suddenly.

And she couldn't say she minded that, either.

Though it was profoundly disappointing to realize, when he pulled the old-fashioned key from her vest pocket, that he'd been patting her down to find it. And not for any other, far more thrilling reason.

"Stay where you are," he ordered her as he unlocked the door, then moved into the room ahead of her.

Mariah trailed after him, watching as he looked swiftly around the room. He opened up the closet door, checked under the bed and behind the curtains, and then ducked into the bathroom. Presumably to do the same.

She was half sitting, half leaning on the quilt at the end of her sleigh bed when he came out again, and for some reason, the cold stare he aimed at her made her giggle.

A lot.

"I told you to stay where you were. You're drunk, I get it. But if you don't follow directions, this isn't going to work."

"Okay." She smiled at him again, her own giggles fading away. "Did I tell you that you're beautiful?"

"You're not going to remember any of this, are you?" he asked, but it didn't sound like a question.

That gave Mariah another fantastic idea. "Really? Are you sure?"

"You probably shouldn't sound so excited about the possibility of an alcoholic blackout."

She waved a hand, but noticing it was in front of her instead of beside her where she'd expected it added an extra second or two. "Tonight is all about making bad decisions."

He stayed where he was, still scowling, so Mariah shifted. She launched herself off the end of the bed and moved toward him, aware as she did that she was swaying on her own feet. She was dancing on those tables after all.

She unzipped her vest, then tossed it aside, laughing at her own boldness. Because she would never have dared make a mess like that in David's house, where there was a place for everything, including her. Especially her.

She tried to take her fleece off, too, but got tangled in

it. She was laughing even more when she heard Griffin curse again, then felt his hands on her, setting her free.

She went with it, falling against him when he pulled the fleece off and tossed it.

Mariah could feel his perfectly sculpted chest beneath her hands, and if she leaned closer, she could crush her body against his.

That was even better.

"I'm already drunk," she told him, tilting her head up because being this close to that gorgeous mouth made her head spin. More than it already was. "Drinking too much in that bar was step one. Everybody knows that step two is a drunken hookup. What's that saying? The best way to get over a man is to get under another one?"

And she watched, fascinated, as a storm chased itself across Griffin's proud, beautiful face. Thunder, there and gone, until there was nothing but that burning flame that she knew—she just knew—was all for her.

"I'm not a bottle of cheap tequila." His voice was like frigid cold water, slapping her into a different sort of alertness. He'd placed both his hands on her arms, setting her back from him. Decisively. "You can't tie me on, drink yourself under the table, and forget about it in the morning. I'm not a bad mistake you get to make."

And there was danger all around him. It wasn't simply that leashed power she'd sensed in him from the start. This was different. This was more specific, more personal.

This was a darkness she wanted to taste.

"One-night stands are supposed to be fun."

"I don't do one-night stands." Griffin's tone was as dark as he was. "I don't do any of the things that would lead to one."

"I don't know what that means."

"I don't drink. I don't hang around in bars, picking up vulnerable women. And I certainly don't take anyone home with me."

"I've never had a one-night stand," Mariah confessed, like that might help. Like what he needed while he was seething at her was an argument. "I tried once. Everyone told me he wasn't the kind of man who stuck around. And that part was true, but he ended up taking me with him when he left."

"I'm not a substitute for your husband."

"This I know. For one thing, you've already been much nicer to me than David ever was."

She had the confused sense that this admission startled him, though whatever she'd seen on his face was gone in an instant. And everything was so blurred around the edges. She could hear the sound of her own voice, carrying on as if of its own accord, but she didn't have the slightest idea what she was saying.

"Enough."

She certainly heard that. Griffin's voice, cool and in total command. And hotter than anything had a right to be.

Mariah stopped . . . whatever she was doing. She couldn't really focus, but it was easy enough to let him lead her back to the bed and then slide herself onto it when he patted the mattress. She watched as if from a great distance when he bent in front of her to slide her boots off. One and then the next.

"Lie down," he told her brusquely.

She did that, too, letting out a deep sigh when her head hit the pillows. Everything shifted again, sloshing around a bit and then settling hard, as if she'd been much heavier than she'd imagined all this time.

Griffin moved away, and she forgot to watch him. Or her eyelids were too heavy to allow it. But he returned again, surprising her enough to open her eyes when he set down a glass of water next to the bed. He also set down two tablets.

"Take those when you wake up in the middle of the night. And drink the entire glass of water. Then sleep as long as you can."

"Griffin."

He stared down at her, forbidding and imposing at the side of her bed, carved not from marble but her own secret fantasies. "What?"

"Nothing. I just really like your name."

She was sure she actually heard him laugh, but her eyes were already drifting closed, and that was impossible anyway. Griffin Cisneros didn't *laugh*. She didn't think he could. He might break something.

When he sighed again, she suspected she might have said that out loud.

"I'm locking your door behind me. When you want to leave tomorrow, you can get your key from the front desk."

Mariah meant to reply to that. She really did. But she couldn't get her mouth to obey.

She had the vague impression of him standing there for another moment. She felt the quilt when he pulled it up over her from the foot of the bed. She was already half asleep when she heard the door close, and then the deadbolt as he locked it behind him as promised.

And as sleep spun in to claim her, she didn't fight it.

Hours later, she woke up again in a sickening rush.

Mariah panicked, because she had no idea where she was.

She scrambled to sit up, confused when she realized she was still dressed in a T-shirt, jeans, even her socks. Her hair was down, hanging all around her like a wavy curtain, and her stomach lurched threateningly when she moved.

At almost the same instant a terrible pounding in her temples set in.

She looked around wildly until she saw the vague shape of her bag on the chair next to the bed. Then, on the bedside table, a glass of water, two red tablets, and the cell phone Griffin had taken from her in the café.

It all came back at once. This was another hotel room. No different from any of the other hotel rooms she'd found herself in over the last few days. She'd woken up like this—if less ill—every night, never knowing where she was. Or what was happening. Or why she was half-way into a panic attack, like her throat was closing up again.

You're in Grizzly Harbor, she told herself. In a bright blue inn set up in a pretty postcard of a nearly inaccessible Alaskan island town.

Mariah lay her hand against her throat and breathed. Because she could. Because she was alive.

She was in Alaska, not Atlanta, and she was still alive.

Eventually, the flush of panic dimmed. She shoved the weight of her hair away from her face, not sure why she could feel every single strand like straight torture against her scalp. That was new. And unpleasant.

Her mouth felt like a truck had backfired into it repeatedly, then run her over a few times for good measure. As her panic faded away she felt sicker, and half crawled, half pulled herself over to the side of her bed so she could pick up the tablets and wash them down.

She could remember Griffin, standing there beside the bed with a hint of thunder on his face and his surprisingly kind hands, ordering her to drink the glass down. She followed his orders, but the more water she drank, the more she remembered.

And for a ghastly moment she was afraid that she might actually throw up.

It could have been what was left of all the alcohol careening around inside her. Or it could have been the thick heat of shame. She had the impression of her own voice, too bright and too loud, and her brain helpfully supplied images of her relatives' drunken shenanigans all those years ago, in case she was in any doubt as to how she must have appeared.

Sloppy and embarrassing. Trash straight through, as David had always hissed at her at parties.

This was what you wanted, she reminded herself sternly. *You climbed up on that trash can, set it on fire, and settled in for the night.*

There was no use crying over spilled tequila now.

Even if she had made a pass at her freezing cold, completely unamused, brand-new bodyguard. Or whatever the hell he was to her.

Mariah's stomach lurched again at that unfortunate memory, but there was nothing to be done about it now. She squinted at the clock and saw that it was nearly three thirty in the morning. Everything felt worse at three thirty in the morning. It was an hour of shame and regret, and in all likelihood, things would seem a lot rosier in the daylight.

She slipped from the bed, feeling the room spin around her unpleasantly as her feet hit the ground. Her stomach was iffy and her head kept pounding, but she hobbled into the bathroom anyway, thinking that her usual nightly routine might make her feel better.

And maybe it was that, or maybe it was the tablets Griffin had left her. But by the time she crawled into bed again, this time without all her clothes on, it seemed possible she might actually live.

Shame didn't actually kill a person. It only felt like it would. She'd learned that lesson again and again in her years of never being good enough in her marriage. She supposed this was one more golden opportunity to learn that same lesson.

She shut her eyes, congratulated herself on living through another evening, and tried to celebrate with some deep breaths.

And that was when she heard it.

A faint rattling noise. Soft at first, but insistent.

Her eyes flew open and she stared up at the ceiling, holding her breath. Because if she wasn't mistaken—and of course she was mistaken, she had to be mistaken—it sounded like there was someone at her door.

She sat up in a rush, staring across the dark room. She heard the noise again, that faint rattle of metal against metal—a lot like a doorknob sounded when it was turned by an impatient hand.

Mariah slid out of the bed again, wishing she hadn't changed out of her jeans and socks, because she felt chilled straight through as she tiptoed across the floor.

"You're dreaming," she whispered to herself. "You've had this same bad dream all week."

She reached down and pinched her thigh, viciously, until tears blurred her vision. And even in the dark, she could see a bruise begin to form. She stood as still as possible, one hand on the thigh she'd just abused, then held her breath and stared at the door.

For a moment everything was silent. Relief flooded her, because she was clearly dreaming—

But then she heard it. Again. And the tiny creaking sound of old floorboards bowing beneath somebody's feet, right outside her door.

The headache in her temples pounded to match her pulse. She was frozen into place, watching with sick, mute horror as her doorknob began to turn. All the way to the right, then the left. Then again.

There was another faint, almost silent creak of the floorboards, and then the door moved inward.

Only a tiny half inch, until the deadbolt caught it.

Mariah found her hands in front of her, palms out, as if she intended to catch the door when it swung inward. As if she could fight whoever was coming for her.

For a second, there was nothing. No sound. No movement.

He's listening, a voice said with utter certainty from deep inside her.

But she was listening, too.

Was that his breath she heard? That sharp intake, quickly exhaled? Or was that her?

She couldn't have said how long she stood there, unable to move and barely able to breathe, staring at her hotel room door until her eyes crossed. But eventually the door moved again, that same scant half inch. She heard the floorboard in the hall protest, such a soft sound that if she hadn't been standing right there, if she'd been across the room in her bed, she wouldn't have heard it at all.

She waited. Was he still right there? Standing on the other side of the door? Waiting for her to reveal herself?

Mariah counted to a hundred. Her skin was so cold, goose bumps shivered up and down her calves, her thighs, and all along her arms. But she didn't move. No matter how much she wanted to.

She counted to a hundred again.

Only then, still holding her breath, her pulse like a maddening drum and shaking so hard it made her bones hurt, did she ease her way over to the spy hole in her door and look out.

But there was no one there. And she didn't dare open the door to look out into the hallway in case he'd done nothing more than step to the side and wait for her to do something that stupid.

Just as slowly, just as carefully, she backed up. She kept going until she put the bed between her and the door. She pulled the quilt off her sleigh bed and wrapped it around her chilled body. Then sank down on the narrow strip of floor between the bed and her window with her cell phone clenched in her hand so she could call for help if necessary.

When Mariah woke up the following morning, her mouth too dry, her head still much too thick, and still in a heap on the floor, she was safe and warm and in one piece.

And she told herself it had been nothing but a bad dream.

Eight

Griffin started the following day the way he always did when he was home, with a five- or six-mile trail run to blow out all the cobwebs from sleep—and today from Mariah's adventures in tequila, too. Which definitely hadn't disrupted his sleep, because he'd *wanted* to do a blistering set of five hundred push-ups on his knuckles at three in the morning. The steeper and more dangerous the trail, the faster he ran. Then he made his way over to Isaac's torture chamber of a gym in a cabin on the beach for the daily community sweat session at 0700, where all the Alaska Force members not away on active missions engaged in a nasty workout involving wall balls, burpees, and killer sprints along the tide line.

"I hear your Georgia peach enjoyed herself at the Fairweather last night," Templeton drawled, with that uproarious laugh that made all the insinuations his words hadn't.

"Keep it up," Griffin suggested, his tone rivaling the

glaciers out in the bay. "And I'll use your face for target practice."

Templeton tsked. "That hurts my feelings, brother." His grin told a different story. Especially when it widened. "I'm much too pretty to shoot in the face."

Griffin responded the only way he could—with a burst of speed on the last, uphill sprint, leaving all his brothers in the dust.

Though it didn't get them to stop laughing.

All except Isaac, who Griffin figured wasn't abstaining because he was so much holier than the rest, but because he didn't want to give Griffin the opportunity to comment on Isaac's ongoing Caradine situation.

"What's going on with that idiot in Juneau?" Isaac asked Templeton as they all stood around getting their wind back and stretching out their ravaged hamstrings. "Still ramping up the threats?"

Templeton shoved his hair back from his face. "Probably all talk."

"All talk, but all over some pretty questionable sites," Blue countered. "Sites that generally lead to a whole lot of bad decision-making."

Griffin had taken part in the mission Templeton had led last fall that had liberated a handful of women and their children from the control of an unhinged doomsday preacher—though maybe that was redundant—out in the Alaskan bush who claimed the end was nigh. But the only end that had been nigh for him was Alaska Force, who had relieved him of his power and his unwilling followers in one fell swoop. Now the self-styled preacher was back, shooting off his mouth all over Juneau and, worse, in the darker corners of the internet. The kinds of places people gravitated toward when they wanted to see if their ominous mutterings could render a real-life body count.

Not on Alaska Force's watch.

"Keep me apprised," Isaac said with a frown at his watch, which signaled he needed to get back to the lodge. "I want to know five minutes before it stops being talk."

It was a solid vertical mile back from the beach to Griffin's cabin, and he took it fast despite his body's protests. He took a cold shower to test his resolve and settle himself, put in a call to the Blue Bear Inn to make sure Mariah was up and waiting for him, then took a boat into town again. With Jonas and Blue this time, because they were part of Mariah's designated team. Everly came, too, since she wanted to go into town instead of working like she usually did in the cabin she shared with Blue.

When everyone headed off to the Water's Edge Café to start wheedling breakfast out of Caradine, Griffin went to the inn.

And it was there, down in the lobby after Madeleine called up to Mariah's room, that he finally admitted that he'd been in a low-boil fury for hours. Since last night, in fact. He was . . . agitated.

Griffin didn't normally get agitated. He didn't get much of anything these days. The closest he got to feelings happened over that endless Christmas week, when no one asked him to come home more often. Not directly. Instead, his sister, Vanessa, tried to guilt him into it by parading his nephews around in front of him. His mother cooked his favorite meals, as if that would accomplish the same thing. And his father, who was so good at hiding behind his amiable physician's exterior, tried to make idle conversation about sports teams Griffin didn't follow.

None of them knew the horrors he'd seen out there on his first tour, and he'd never known how to tell them. He'd never known how to tell anyone what it looked like up close, war and human suffering and the kinds of choices a Marine had to make to survive. And worse, to thrive. It had been much easier to close himself off and spend time with the only people who understood without his having to put it all into inadequate words. Other veterans and active-duty military were his people. They got it.

Everyone else was a civilian, a heartbeat away from becoming yet another casualty if Griffin didn't do his job.

He usually sat in his parents' living room like the guest he was and chose to remain, his best polite smile on his face, and wondered why they couldn't all see that he was nothing like them any longer. That he hadn't been since he was still technically a teenager. That he might as well be drenched in all the blood he'd spilled, for one thing, right there on his mother's pristine cream and blue sofa. That he was much worse than the monster they likely believed he was—he was an emotionless machine with no regrets, no complications, no human connections.

His father was a hands-on doctor, engaged in his community and always accessible, but while Griffin admired that, it wasn't him. He'd been raised with the same urge to help people, but he'd gone about it in a different way. And now that he knew precisely what his choices entailed, how could he sit around in his mother's pretty house playing board games and acting like he was normal?

Griffin knew how to protect people from afar, a calling he took seriously.

He'd never been very good at playing games.

Christmas in his hometown was slightly agitating, he could admit, though there was also a significant part of him that enjoyed the annual test. It gave him the chance to prove all over again that he didn't belong there. It reminded him exactly who and what he was.

A blond woman who'd made a drunken pass at him shouldn't have registered. Griffin had long ago decided that casual sex wasn't for him, but that didn't keep enterprising women from trying to change his mind. Why was he letting this particular one get to him?

He stood at the bottom of the stairs, his arms folded over his chest, and heard Mariah coming long before he saw her. He heard her door open and slam shut. He heard her footsteps on the second floor hallway, then the way she jogged down the stairs.

Griffin steeled himself for her embarrassment, a bright red face and an inability to look him in the eye, and maybe a few mumbled apologies.

But when she stopped on the step that put her at eye level, all she did was smile.

She didn't look the worse for wear. If anything, Mariah looked as if she'd had a decent night's sleep and woken up this morning refreshed. Her blue eyes were bright and clear, and if she was embarrassed or had been up in the night counting out her regrets, there was no visible evidence.

"How are you feeling?" he asked, pointedly.

Her smile widened. "Good, thanks."

And that was it.

Mariah looked at him, he looked back, and Griffin didn't know how long that went on before it became noticeably awkward. And he had no choice but to lift his chin like he'd planned to have a stare-down all along, then head for the door.

She had been wasted. She might not remember that, but he sure did. She'd even said—but he refused to dwell on that. He wasn't going to think about the sultry invitation he had turned down, and not only because he didn't think she'd meant it.

And so what if it kept him up half the night, wondering *what if*?

It made no sense that the whole thing scraped at him as they walked down the street in the gray morning toward the café at the water's edge. Because he knew she never would have propositioned him if she was sober. Never in a million years.

What had she called him? *A bad decision?*

"What would you do if there was someone stalking you?" Mariah asked as they walked.

He angled a look down at her and didn't like that she was wearing the same fleece-and-vest combination she'd been wearing last night. Not only because he had a clear memory of how he'd taken both items off her, but because it suggested that she really wasn't the princess he'd accused her of being. She'd even swapped out those ridiculous leather boots for perfectly reasonable hiking shoes, annoying him even more.

"I would politely ask the stalker to find another target," he replied, clipped and unamused.

Not that Mariah seemed to notice his tone. "What if he refused?" There was a hint of that laughter that had sucker punched him last night, though she stopped it almost as it began. He hated the loss of it as much as he hated hearing it. And then he hated himself even more.

"Stalkers aren't exactly known for their ability to see reason."

"I would persuade him," Griffin bit out. She glanced at him as they moved, her blue eyes not at all as foggy or bloodshot as they ought to have been. "This might surprise you, but I'm actually very persuasive."

She laughed. And it was laughter, for God's sake. Everybody laughed. He didn't understand why he was acting like he'd never heard a woman laugh before. Why it felt like a bolt of lightning shot straight through him.

"I believe you," Mariah said when her laughter faded.

Griffin couldn't believe he had to remind himself that this was a job. He was working, not hanging around a pretty woman for his own entertainment. Something he really shouldn't have had to keep telling himself.

"The good news is that whoever is following you is now following me," he told her, stepping back into his usual role. Calm, cool, collected. He had always been an exemplary sniper. He knew how to calm himself down. How to steady himself into perfect stillness. Mariah was no more than a new situation he needed to conquer. But he had no doubt he would, because that was what he did. "It's also extremely unlikely that anyone followed you here, and we're tracking your cell phone now, so we'll know if anyone uses it to hunt you down."

He saw a flash of color move over her face then, but he couldn't tell what had made her flush. Especially not when she trained her eyes on the uneven boardwalk before her. The fact that she no longer had what passed for cell phone privacy? Emotion? A stray memory of last night?

Why did he want to know so badly?

"This is certainly the most remote place I've ever

been," she said after a brief pause he chose not to analyze.

"It's remote. It's also a small town. There aren't that many people here, and we all know each other. Too well, you might say."

The way she smiled clawed at him, but by then they were walking up to the café's front door. He stopped her before she could go inside, not knowing how to ask the question. But he wanted to know what she was hiding from him.

He needed to know it, because he liked to have all the information before he did any job. That was all.

Of course that was all.

"Mariah—"

"Please don't tell me we have to *have a conversation*," she said quickly. "Or maybe you want me to apologize? I do. It's all a blessed blur, I'm afraid, but please accept a blanket apology for anything I might have said or done last night."

"You don't remember?"

"It's just so blurry." He didn't believe that bland smile she aimed at him. Not at all. "Bits and pieces. That's all."

"You don't remember telling me that I'm beautiful."

It was a statement, not a question, and he wouldn't have thrown it at her if he hadn't been so aware that she was lying to him. He'd had no intention of discussing what had happened last night. He'd spent the entire boat ride over patting himself on the back for the high road he planned to take.

But here he was. No high road in sight.

"I sure don't." Her smile was impenetrable, which was how he knew she'd practiced it. It was likely how

Princess Mariah kept people at arm's length. "But I'm sure you're aware that you're a very attractive man, Griffin. I assume they give you access to mirrors out there in the woods, or wherever y'all live. I can only apologize for stating the obvious."

"You also told me that you figured a death threat was as good as a divorce decree, and wondered if I'd like to be your rebound."

Though she hadn't used those words. Not exactly.

"Now you're making me blush," she told him, despite clear evidence to the contrary. She wasn't blushing at all at that point. She wore that cool smile, she was holding his gaze, and there wasn't the faintest hint of embarrassment—or anything else—anywhere on that pretty face of hers. "I sure wish I could remember any of the scandalous things I said to you, but I can't. I hope it wasn't too much for you to handle."

And he knew, without a shred of doubt, that despite the sweet honey of that drawl and the wide-eyed innocence of her gaze, she knew perfectly well she was issuing him a challenge.

"I didn't try to handle you, Mariah," he told her, low and dark and perilously close to out of control. Not that he'd allowed himself to get truly out of control since he was approximately eighteen, and boot camp had taken care of that short-lived impulse. "If I did, you can trust that you wouldn't have any trouble remembering it the next day."

Then he reached past her, opening the door and making a show of ushering her in like the fine, proper gentleman his mother had tried to raise before the Marines had made him into . . . something else entirely.

And she went, gliding ahead of him like it had been

her idea in the first place, but he figured she was showing her hand. If Mariah had been half as innocent as she was acting, she should have been more bothered by him. That she wasn't suggested she was taking pains to cover up her actual reactions. He liked that.

Not that he should let this woman—a client—get to him in the first place.

When he got to the table where Jonas and Blue waited, he was all business.

It took them two solid hours. They dug into every aspect of Mariah's life. Her childhood. Her marriage. The kind of political aspirations David Lanier had; the family connections he had no qualm about using; and the names of every friend, connection, or story someone else had ever told in her presence about people who had known David before she met him. All to build a full picture.

"People don't usually start with murder," Blue told Mariah, kicked back in his chair with his tablet in his hands as he put in requests to Oz for different streams of information on David, his family, and all other aspects of Mariah's story. "They usually warm up with something else first."

Jonas sat next to Blue, giving Mariah his usual dark, grave stare. He didn't say much. He stroked his beard—his favorite fake-out because he was not a man who succumbed to nervous energy unless he was trying to draw attention to his own movements, so that someone failed to notice how little he moved otherwise—and kept his gaze trained on Mariah.

He was looking for tells. Calculating lies and diversions. Running potential scenarios in his head, looking for weaknesses, tallying up probabilities.

"Why does he want to go into politics?" he asked at one point. It was the only question he'd asked in the last forty-five minutes.

"No reasonable man would," Blue replied with a laugh.

"Power," Mariah replied quietly.

Griffin had been proud of the way she'd held up under the intensity of this first, exploratory session with men who had been trained in interrogation techniques suitable for use in some of the nastiest places imaginable. And then he'd been pissed at himself for having pride in this woman when she had nothing to do with him.

Just. A. Client, he reminded himself. *You idiot.*

Still, she sat like a queen in the chair beside him, her blond hair wavier than it had been the day before and all of it loose and inviting around her face. It made her look younger. More approachable. He didn't know if that was a good thing or a bad thing—he only knew that he had more trouble than he should have had looking away.

Especially when she didn't wilt beneath the full force of all their considerable attention.

"I'm not surprised you don't understand," she continued, a thread of steel beneath all that honey. "Y'all are obviously powerful in other ways. David can't perform daring physical feats. He would never put his body on the line for his country or anyone else. The power he has comes from his pedigree. His bank account. For someone like that, a political career makes all kinds of sense. It's a path to celebrity for people who recoil at the very idea of actual Hollywood celebrities."

"Is he running for a particular office now?" Griffin asked.

"He plans to start in city government and work his

way up. He has a very high opinion of himself. White House high, if I'm not mistaken."

"Do you think he can win?"

Mariah considered that for a moment, and Griffin was suddenly aware of how she held herself motionless, like everyone else at the table. *She learned how to conceal herself from the enemy, too,* a voice in him insisted, and something in him lurched at the notion. Her hands were folded neatly in her lap, and her legs were crossed at the ankles beneath her chair. And she sat very, very still, as if the slightest hint of a gesture would give her away.

Which told him things about her life as a rich man's trophy wife that he really didn't want to know.

"What I think," she said slowly, weighing each word carefully, "is that he chose me deliberately. Because it makes a good story, doesn't it? A man like him, respectable bloodlines and old money, taking up with a dirt-poor nobody from way out yonder in the back of beyond? A waitress with no prospects he basically found by the side of the road? I think it was all part of the plan."

"He married you ten years ago," Blue pointed out. "Why did he wait so long to start his political career if that's what he wanted all along?"

"I didn't cooperate as expected." Mariah smiled again as they all stared at her, and this time Griffin could see how controlled it was. "I believe the plan was to produce a few towheaded, photogenic babies first. Some adorable tykes for the Christmas card, who he could trot out behind him on stage while he made his acceptance speeches."

"You said it was your job to keep him happy," Blue said. And Griffin couldn't possibly have explained why he wanted to punch his friend at that moment. Only that it was a challenge to repress that urge. "If that's what it took to make him happy, why are you here without the Christmas-card kids in tow?"

Mariah's smile widened, but Griffin felt her get more distant.

"David would tell you that I tricked him. A good old-fashioned bait and switch, he called it once." She laughed, but it was a hollow sound that bore no resemblance to those deep, problematic belly laughs from the night before. "He expected that one of the benefits of marrying a white trash girl who was more or less straight from the trailer park is that I would shoot out babies like a gumball machine. Instead, I never got pregnant. I never even had a late period, if you're wondering."

His brothers maintained stone faces, but Griffin was pretty sure neither one of them had wondered anything of the kind. He certainly hadn't.

And he suspected Mariah knew that, since her tone got lighter as she kept going.

"He never liked me much, now that I look back on it. I was a project. I was good optics. He and that nasty best friend of his—who I'm sure has aspirations of becoming his campaign manager and chief of staff down the line—plotted it all out. Everybody loves a Cinderella story, after all. And I'm sure he'll even use our infertility to keep climbing on up that ladder. It's amazing how many voters find him sympathetic, especially when he pretends he's in pain." Her nose wrinkled slightly, as if she were holding back more of that laughter. Or something else. "I've always heard tell that the camera adds ten pounds, but in David's case, it adds a soul."

There were a few more probing background questions, all to give them as much insight as possible into

Mariah's take on her current dilemma. Then, as things were winding down, Jonas took a call from Templeton.

"Things are ramping up with the preacher," he said curtly when he hung up, his gaze shifting between Blue and Griffin. "I'm on it."

He nodded at Mariah, then took his leave, disappearing out the back door of the café. Blue and Griffin checked their phones and clearly both sent Templeton the same text, offering immediate assistance if necessary, because the same response came back to both of them.

Not there yet.

"Spiritual concerns?" Mariah asked lightly.

"Something like that," Griffin replied.

"Piety can be so thorny," she murmured, and despite everything, he almost laughed.

Blue kept his phone out as he went and stood at the counter where Everly had spent the morning with her laptop, a bottomless cup of coffee, and Caradine.

Griffin stayed where he was next to Mariah, shifting so he could look directly at her. Which shouldn't have felt significant in any way, especially when another situation had shifted from a mere possibility to potentially active.

"So now what?" she asked, still sitting in the same unnaturally rigid position. "Do you all ride off into battle in Atlanta? Or start a blistering media campaign to expose David? I don't actually know how you do what you do."

"The first thing we do is identify and isolate the threat," Griffin said. Maybe in a gruffer tone than necessary, but he felt like he was fighting when all he was doing was sitting next to this woman. And he was maybe too aware of the scent of the soap she'd used in her morning shower when he should have been pressing for details about the deranged preacher on the loose. "Your food was tampered with in Atlanta. But since you left, there have been no attempts on your life. It's possible that means the threat is localized. That your life is only in danger in Atlanta, not outside it. And if it is, our approach will be different than it would be if this was an active-pursuit situation."

"I thought there was somebody at my door last night."

Everything in Griffin sharpened. "When?"

"I woke up sometime after three thirty. I was . . . not well." She made a face that was probably the most honest she'd been about last night so far, not that he could enjoy it. "And I don't know if it was real. I've been having the same nightmare all week long. Every time I'm in a new hotel, I wake up in the middle of the night halfway into a panic attack thinking someone's trying to break into my room."

One elegant hand crept up to her delicate throat and rested there.

"Is the nightmare always the same?" Griffin asked.

"No. One time I dreamed David was standing by my bed. Another time he broke in through the window, leaving glass everywhere. Once he kicked and kicked the door until it caved in. Last night wasn't like that. It was just the doorknob rattling and no David. Floorboards creaking outside in the hall. Someone breathing out there. Listening." She lifted her shoulder, then dropped it. "Maybe."

If the nightmare had been the same as every other night, or a repeat, Griffin would have dismissed it as stress. But he didn't like that it was different from the others. She couldn't wake up in the morning and dismiss it the moment she saw that her door wasn't broken in, her window was intact, and, most of all, she was fine.

"Why didn't you tell me this the minute you came downstairs this morning?"

"I still don't know if I dreamed it. There's no proof I didn't. It's entirely possible I'm just being paranoid."

"You almost died. Twice. In a short period of time and following a very distinct threat on your life from your ex-husband. It would be weird if you weren't paranoid. My issue with you yesterday was that I didn't think you were paranoid *enough*."

"I don't want to overreact."

"Mariah." He had leaned closer than he'd meant to, but when he noticed it, he didn't put any extra distance between them. He kept his gaze on hers. "You've hired one of the most elite bands of ex-military operatives in the world. We don't vote to handle overreactions."

"I can't be sure anything happened. I was still drunk, and it was the middle of the night in a strange place." She pulled in a breath. "Just like when I first went into the room. I looked out across the street and thought I saw . . . something. But it was a few shadows between the buildings, that was all. There was nothing there."

Maybe it was nothing. She could be jumping at shadows, sure. It was also possible that someone had followed her back from the Fairweather last night. Just as it was possible that her troubles from Atlanta had followed her here.

"You don't have to be the judge of whether or not something is happening," Griffin told her, flipping through possibilities in his head. "That's my job."

"But—"

"Is this what you did in the hospital?" She blinked, making him feel like he'd slapped her. But he didn't take it back. Or change course. "Did you lie there with your airway constricted, falling all over yourself trying to find a reason why you ate a stray shrimp for the first time in your life? And then did it again a couple of weeks later?"

Mariah's mouth curved. Her expression was wry. "Yes, as a matter of fact."

"I can't promise you that you're not delusional, if that's what you're worried about."

"I wasn't worried about it, actually. But I think I am now."

"What I can promise you is that I'll take you seriously. I take this seriously. Whatever is or isn't happening, I will get to the bottom of it. I promise you."

He could see he wasn't the only one aware of how things shifted then. There, at the farthest, most tucked-away table in Caradine's restaurant. The table Alaska Force always used for client meetings because it offered the illusion of transparency by being out in the open, but with more privacy.

And here he was making vows.

Mariah didn't let out a laugh, hollow or otherwise. And her mouth shifted to something more solemn. It was reflected in the blue of her eyes.

"Thank you," she said.

That was all.

And Griffin felt as if he'd been running again, straight up and all out, when he stood up. He stared down at Mariah like that could make sense of her, or of him—but it didn't. He couldn't.

No matter how much his chest ached.

And then, worse, when he walked away, his limbs felt jerky and stiff, like they weren't his.

Not like a machine at all.

"All good?" Blue asked, his expression mild and his voice scrubbed free of any inflection—as long as Griffin ignored that speculative gleam in his eyes.

"All good," Griffin replied, trying to sound like his usual, coolly unbothered self. Mostly for the benefit of Caradine and Everly. He eyed Blue when he failed. "Though there are a couple of things I want to check out."

Blue nodded, his gaze sharpening.

"You look very serious," Caradine murmured in the voice she liked to use when she was being her most provocative. She was standing with her arms crossed, her usual friendly way of welcoming in any customers. "I guess last night didn't go the way it looked like it was going when you left the bar."

"I don't know what that means." Griffin went glacial. "I escorted our client back to her hotel after you encouraged her to get drunk. In a strange place where anyone could be her enemy and, for all you know, planned to target her after you made sure she was even more vulnerable."

And possibly did.

"I'm going to take that as a no," Caradine replied in the exact same tone she'd used before, as if Griffin hadn't said a word.

The restaurant's phone rang and she answered it in her usual surly manner, leaving Griffin with nothing to do but pretend that the kick of temper rolling through him as he imagined what could have happened—if he wasn't around, if Mariah hadn't been dreaming—was a purely professional thing.

Because it couldn't be anything else.

"*I* didn't get her drunk," Everly said, and Griffin realized he'd slid his glare to her.

Blue laughed, then slapped Griffin on the back. The way all his Alaska Force brothers did, never seeming to get the hint that Griffin didn't do it in return because he didn't like it.

Or, now that he considered it, maybe they all did get the hint and did it anyway *because* he didn't like it. That was more their style. Jackasses.

"Let me know if you plan to let Caradine get you wasted at the Fairweather," Blue told Everly.

"Why? So you can try telling me what to do?"

But she grinned, wide and happy, as she said it.

"So I can come watch," Blue drawled. He leaned in and dropped an easy kiss on Everly's mouth, the kind of light and simple peck that spoke volumes about their intimacy without having to shout it. "And then make sure I'm the one who takes your drunk ass home."

Everly laughed against his mouth, but Griffin looked away, his gaze settling on Mariah, there across the restaurant where he'd left her.

She still hadn't moved. She hadn't relaxed her ruthlessly straight posture. She hadn't unlaced her fingers or even changed the angle of her head.

And something about how solitary she was, how alone and yet committed to sitting there so gracefully, made his chest ache more. So much he found himself rubbing at the place where it hurt like it was a tight muscle after a tough workout.

He was nothing short of grateful when Blue clapped

him on the shoulder, waved his phone to indicate there were messages waiting, and then headed toward the door. Griffin could follow and concentrate on things like whatever was happening with that lunatic in Juneau, not the phantom pain in his chest.

"Templeton says Oz received reliable intel this idiot stole a boat and has it outfitted with his personal arsenal," Blue said as they hit the street outside and the crisp, head-clearing air. "And if he did, you know he's heading our way."

"Bring it on," Griffin replied, and meant it.

He could use the focus of real work. And when the preacher was handled, again, he could try to figure out if someone really had been at Mariah's door in the middle of the night. It was what she'd hired Alaska Force for, and had nothing to do with how blue her eyes were or that crooked smile she pulled out sometimes when she wasn't pretending.

God help him, but he needed to concentrate on saving her from whoever was after her, so she would go away again. All the way back across the Lower 48, where she could wield that honeyed drawl however she liked and he wouldn't feel it inside him.

Because after his first tour had torn him up and wrecked him from the inside out, Griffin had spent the rest of his adult life making sure he couldn't *feel* much of anything. He had systematically cut himself off from anyone and anything that threatened his ability to do his job. That was how he liked it.

But with every step he took away from her, he had to force himself not to look back.

Nine

"I'm Everly," the redheaded woman said, smiling. "And Caradine says you're in some trouble."

"I would say I *was* in some trouble, but have recently relocated so that someone else can handle it," Mariah replied, not sure why this woman—who'd been sitting over at the counter all this time, messing around with images on her laptop—had come to talk to her. "Someone far better equipped for trouble than me."

"I also heard that you and Caradine went out drinking last night." Everly snuck a look over her shoulder. Caradine was banging pots around in the tiny kitchen where she worked her magic, all scowl and fury. "She won't admit it, but I think she's hung over."

"It's all a blur to me," Mariah said sweetly.

Too sweetly, she realized, when Everly's gaze swung back to hers.

"I hate when that happens," Everly murmured.

And they gazed at each other in a moment of perfect communion.

"Such a shame," Mariah agreed brightly. "I've heard all manner of salacious reports on my behavior, but I can't confirm or deny a thing."

And this time, when they smiled at each other, it was a lot more real.

"I'm obsessed with the hot springs here," Everly told her, her grin bringing out the freckles across her nose. Mariah couldn't remember the last time she'd seen freckles on a woman her own age. Everyone she knew went to obscene lengths to remove them or hide them, as if they were evidence of a crime. "I was going to head over there, if you want to come. I don't know if you're supposed to be doing things with the guys."

" 'The guys' . . . ?"

"Alaska Force. But every time I say that I feel like I should be in a comic book."

"I think 'the guys' have left me to my own devices," Mariah said. Carefully, in case this was some kind of trap. "They're 'identifying and isolating the threat,' if I remember right."

"My suggestion is you let them do that. They're good at it. You can spend the afternoon soaking with me. And Caradine, too, assuming she's not pretending she hates hot water this week."

There was another crashing sound from the kitchen.

"You know I can hear you, right?" came Caradine's voice a moment later, floating out from behind the wall.

"We're thinking about an afternoon in the hot springs," Everly sang out. "Want to come?"

There was a snort from the kitchen. "I would obviously rather die."

Everly rolled her eyes. "You say that about everything. It's really losing all its dramatic effect."

Caradine came out of the kitchen wiping her hands on the black half apron she wore tied around her waist. "I don't think a bath should be a social occasion. Call me crazy."

Mariah considered that. "It's a communal bath?"

"They're natural hot springs, and they're glorious," Everly retorted. "And yes, they're open to the public, though there are also women-only hours."

"It's a bunch of people getting naked, together, and then sitting in their own filth while pretending it's a privilege," Caradine said flatly. "Also together."

Everly shook her head at Mariah this time. "She acts like she's never been in the hot springs when I can tell you that's a lie."

"I go when no one else is there, in a bathing suit like a normal person, and leave the moment anyone else shows up." Caradine shook her head. "And I don't like either of you. Certainly not enough to run around and do group activities."

She wheeled around as if to prove it, barking out a greeting to the old man who shuffled in the door. Meaning she ordered him to sit down. Then she stomped back into her kitchen and started banging pots around again.

"I can't say for sure," Everly said over the noise, "but I'm pretty sure that's her love language."

Mariah lifted her hands from her lap, only then realizing she'd been clenching them there for what seemed like forever.

"I'm not sure I'm a communal bath sort of person," she said. The shadow she'd seen out her window could have been anything. Or nothing, more likely. The doorknob twisting had been terrifying because it hadn't been dramatic or explosive like the rest of her nightmares. And if she hadn't found that bruise on her thigh this morning, she might have dismissed it as a new take on the same anxiety dream. But she'd pinched herself. So hard it ached when she moved. And it was all well and good to think that Griffin and his friends could help her. Protect her. But what happened when they couldn't? When, like last night, she was on her own? "Unless there's some kind of self-defense class along with the bathing. I think I would be up for that."

"A martial arts bath? Like water aerobics, only with actual front kicks?"

"Maybe just the martial arts part." Mariah smiled. "It wouldn't be the worst idea in the world to start protecting myself. Trouble being what it is."

Everly brightened. "Funny you should mention that. Blue's been teaching me some things, but I've been thinking that he should teach them to more people. More women, I mean. This is Alaska. It can get dangerous out here in the last frontier."

"Sign me up," Caradine said brusquely as she stalked back out and slapped down two big mugs of coffee on the table between them. It was the very thing Mariah had wanted but hadn't asked for, since she'd been sitting like she was in rigor mortis for the past few hours. She took hers gratefully.

Everly squinted at Caradine. "Why am I not surprised that you don't want to sit in a nice, spring-fed hot pool, but if there's a possibility that you could learn how to maim someone, you're all in?"

"I don't need to soak," Caradine replied. With great

dignity. "I have a private shower upstairs, thank you, because I live in the twenty-first century. But I wouldn't mind learning how to kill people with my hands."

Everly shook her head as Caradine stomped away again, then slid into the chair across from Mariah to claim her own mug.

And now that the caffeine was doing its work and Mariah had unclenched from that fierce position she'd learned to hold for hours while David performed one of his devastating *critiques* or while she was surrounded by the sheep-like wolves at Atlanta's high-society dinner parties, she could focus more squarely on this overly friendly woman.

Mariah was from the South. The Deep, kudzu-choked South. The sweeter and more friendly the smile, the less she trusted it.

"Why are you doing this? Is this a Grizzly Harbor thing? An Alaska Force thing?"

Everly froze with her mug halfway to her mouth. "Which thing?"

Mariah knew the smile she gave in return down to its last contour. Polite. Nonthreatening. She'd practiced it in the mirror for years. "Is this part of the intake process? They question me officially, then you invite me to get social so you can dig deeper when I'm not expecting it to see if there are discrepancies?"

"Uh. No. None of that. I have nothing to do with what Alaska Force does. I'm with Blue, that's all."

"Then I don't understand."

Everly started to reach her hand out on the table and then stopped, as if she'd considered touching Mariah but had decided against it. And her gaze was almost uncomfortably bright.

"When I found my way to Grizzly Harbor last summer, I thought—I knew—that I was going to die. Maybe not that day. Maybe not that week. But almost certainly before the end of the summer. I remember what that feels like. I guess I just wanted to let you know that you're not alone."

"That's really nice of you. Are you this nice to all of Alaska Force's clients?"

Everly grinned. "Only the ones who go shot for shot with Caradine and walk away. Allegedly."

Mariah felt her own smile thaw. "That's fair."

And after that she allowed herself to get swept along in this odd day that felt stolen. She should have died twice now, by her count. The fact that she was alive and kicking and tucked away in pretty Grizzly Harbor was a gift.

Mariah had spent so many years trying so hard to be more, better, different. It felt like some kind of liberation to simply . . . let herself be there. No more and no less. Nowhere to go and nothing to do.

Everly and Caradine bickered good-naturedly for a while longer, giving Mariah the impression that they did it all the time. Then Everly had set out into the village, so Mariah went with her, soaking it all in as Everly consulted with Blue via text, then decided to rouse up local interest in the self-defense class she wanted to put together. She made flyers, then posted them in the bathhouse and the general store, chatting with people she ran into along the way.

But Mariah didn't have to charm anyone. She didn't have to pretend that charming them was possible when she knew full well it wasn't, the way she always had in Atlanta. Nothing was expected of her on these twisting streets, some muddy in the spring afternoon and others made of wood that creaked satisfyingly beneath her feet. All she had to do was act like Everly's shadow, maybe throwing in an affirmative comment or two when pressed.

This is what a safe, comfortable life feels like, she told herself. And if she was a touch too wistful, no one had to know. *This is what happy looks like.*

And while Everly lived out a random happy day, Mariah could simply tag along as if she were on a holiday in the other woman's life. She didn't have to make decisions. She didn't have to worry, either. There was no one to impress, no one to disappoint.

And besides, every time she looked up, she saw one of Griffin's friends. Alaska Force in action, she assumed. Impressive muscles everywhere and a matching stern, uncompromising expression.

"That's Rory, and he wants you to see him," Everly told her when she caught Mariah staring up at the watchful, sculpted man on the next street, higher up the hill. He'd been tailing them all over the village without ever venturing close enough for Mariah to tell if he was actually as attractive as he appeared. A requirement to join Alaska Force, apparently. "He's brand-new, but even if he wasn't, if any of them were really tracking us, you'd never know it."

When Everly ducked into the post office, open for the first time since Mariah had arrived, Mariah stayed out on the street. She wanted to stare at the harbor and the sea beyond. She wanted to gather it all inside her and hold it there. The sturdy green of the forest clinging to the hills, the mountains capped with snow above and wreathed in fog lower down. The rocky shore and the houses and shops that clung to it, stretching from the docks in a semicircle studded with bright colors against the gray. The moody afternoon that seemed about to clear at any moment but never did.

The only constant was the ocean in the distance, a symphony of blues with whitecapped waves, and the mountains keeping watch all around.

This. She leaned into the unfamiliar feeling that washed over her like another gust of salt-edged wind. *This is what it's like to feel content.*

When her cell phone buzzed in her pocket, she almost didn't recognize the sound. It seemed out of place here, as if she hadn't only run across the country but had gone back in time, too.

She fished her phone out and frowned down at the screen.

David.

Mariah stared at the cell phone in her hand like it was suddenly a snake. A spider. Something repulsive that could bite—and would if she moved a single muscle.

She didn't decline the call. She didn't toss the phone aside. Or even shove it back into her pocket. She was as frozen in place as she'd been in her hotel room last night.

It kept buzzing.

This time she didn't pinch herself.

And she felt out of time and place here, standing outside on a breezy, chilly afternoon, with mountains looming everywhere and the constant murmur of the sea in the background. Alaska didn't feel real. She was so far away from everything she had ever known. She wouldn't say she felt truly happy or content so much as adjacent to both, but she was reasonably sure that she was about as safe as it was possible to get, and that felt like a blessing. It felt new.

Seeing David's name on her phone made her feel like Alaska was the dream and this phone call was waking her up, whether she wanted it or not.

Maybe you're hung over, a caustic voice inside her suggested.

It was possible it was all of the above.

But she picked up the call.

"Hello, David," she said, as calm and composed as always.

He'd taught her well.

"Where the hell are you?"

"I can't imagine how that's any of your business," Mariah said. Pleasantly. Because the nastier David got, the more perfectly ladylike she became in response.

Mostly because it drove him crazy, she could admit.

"You haven't been back to that stupid apartment in days," David snarled at her. "Chandler Stanhope said you'd been to the emergency room. I've been looking for you, expecting to hear you'd been found dead in a ditch."

No such luck, Mariah thought.

"Chandler Stanhope is a powerful attorney, as he likes to be the first to remind you, and he should know better than to talk to you about someone else's medical issues when he's supposed to be representing the hospital. There are laws."

"It's time to stop playing games, Mariah. This has gone on long enough and it's starting to get embarrassing."

"Then I can't possibly be doing it right. Or surely the embarrassment would have set in some time ago."

"Let me guess. Did you run back home?"

David's voice took on that nasty tone that always, always boded ill. It was the tone he used when he made her sit, posture perfect, an impenetrable smile on her face, in a rigid-backed chair in his formal dining room. For hours.

It was the tone he used as he'd whispered those nasty things to her, breaking down all the ways she'd shamed him and all the ways she would never, ever be worth the time and effort he'd put into dragging her out of the backwoods.

It was the tone he used to cut her down to size, chop her into pieces, and remind her of her place.

And she wasn't immune. Even here, a continent away from him, she froze. She stood straighter, automatically, and her free hand went to smooth down the waves in her hair, because the sight of her so unruly would send him into apoplexy.

It was a pleasure to remind herself that he couldn't see her.

"I should have known," David was saying in that ugly way of his, his drawl getting clipped right on cue. "You can pick up white trash and polish it, but it's always going to be white trash, isn't it?"

And Mariah's body might have had an automatic, built-in response to him, but that didn't mean she had to surrender to it. Or him.

Not anymore.

Alaska was real.

"Sometimes white trash comes in a big old mansion smack in the middle of Buckhead, David," Mariah replied. Sweetly. "You never can tell."

"You can't hide from me forever." And she could *see*

the look she knew he had on his face then. Eyes bulging, teeth bared. "I'm going to find you. And when I do, you're going to regret all of this, big time. People are talking. And you know how I feel about being the center of gossip around here."

"I left you, David," Mariah reminded him. "I understand that you're used to getting your way. But not this time. You can threaten me in parking lots all you want—"

"That was no threat. That was a promise. *You* don't get to run the show, Mariah. I picked you. I *made* you. If it weren't for me, you'd be living in filth in that same crappy town, broke and desperate like every other member of your pathetic family."

"David." She said his name almost sorrowfully. "Don't you understand? I'm not afraid of you anymore."

She wasn't sure that was true. Or it wouldn't be true, anyway, if he'd been standing in front of her. But he wasn't. He was thousands of miles away, and no matter what he said to her, he couldn't touch her.

Mariah had felt similarly when she'd moved out of the house in Buckhead. She'd packed her two suitcases, that was all. That was the sum of her ten years under David's thumb. Two modest suitcases. But she could carry them herself, and she had. She'd walked out, gotten in her car, and driven herself away.

Such a simple thing. The only difference from any other time she'd driven out of that driveway was that she'd known she wasn't coming back.

And once she'd made the decision, she couldn't believe that it had taken her so long.

She'd spent the first night in her apartment lying spread-eagled in a bed she didn't have to share with a man who had never treated her gently, or kindly, or with any respect—a state of affairs she'd taken to heart and believed she'd deserved. She'd hardly slept, because she'd been sure the cheerful apartment, the bedroom all to herself, was a dream. She kept expecting David to break down the door and drag her back to Buckhead, by her hair if necessary.

He'd convinced her that she couldn't live without him. Not because she didn't want to or because she wasn't capable, but because he would do something to prevent it.

But that first night had passed. Then the following day and the one after that.

A week. A month.

And Mariah had discovered that if she didn't give David the power, it turned out he couldn't do a blessed thing.

She stayed where she was now, staring out at the brooding Alaskan sea and the clouds while David grew more and more abusive in her ear.

Maybe she was perverse. But the nastier he got, the uglier the things he called her, the more at peace she felt.

And when a shadow fell over her, she looked up and was unsurprised to find Griffin standing there before her, a hard look on his objectively beautiful face. Very much as if he knew exactly who she was talking to and wanted to kill David himself.

It made her feel even more . . . settled. Peaceful. *Safe,* maybe.

She wished, with her whole heart, that she could excise the sound of her own drunken, besotted voice from her memories, but she couldn't. And she was certain *he* hadn't forgotten a single moment of what had gone on last night.

But really, it was the least of the things she had to find a way to live with.

Wordlessly, she took her cell phone away from her ear, hit the speaker button, and held it there between them. At that moment she realized that she trusted this man. She'd told him every last detail of her life with David, and if he judged her for it, he hadn't shown it. He'd treated her with a grumpy sort of kindness when she'd been hopped up on tequila. More, she'd been sloppy drunk and he hadn't taken advantage of her. He hadn't used anything she'd said—or any propositions she pretended not to remember—as a weapon against her today. Griffin had seen her when she was anything but at her best, he'd listened to her story anyway, and he'd taken her concerns seriously. Even though she was fairly sure he didn't like her that much.

Maybe that was a low bar.

But to Mariah, it was a whole new world.

David kept right on going. He was spiteful. Creative and mean. Ugly straight through, the way he always was when he hit his stride.

But what Mariah felt then had nothing to do with the names David called her. If she felt flushed, or uneven, it was because of the man who stood in front of her, listening to this same old, familiar song.

It was one thing to listen to David spew his usual insults at her. She was used to it. But it was raw and horrifying to watch Griffin listen to this same tired routine. To know that he was paying attention not only to what David was saying but to how used to it Mariah really was.

She might trust him, but she still felt ashamed. Deeply

ashamed, as if she'd been marked all this time by the things David called her and she hadn't realized that everyone else could see it. All over her.

"I want to sit down and talk to you," David panted, because he'd worked himself up into such a state. The way he always did. "You can't run from me forever. You owe me a conversation, at the very least."

"Do I?" Mariah asked, and the funny thing was that he'd taught her how to sound bored and unmoved. But he'd never taught her what to do when she used the tools he'd given her while being watched so closely by a man whose eyes gleamed brown and gold and made her want things she didn't know how to name. "You just spent a good chunk of time and what sounds like all your energy calling me every name in the book. Why would I want to sit down with you somewhere and hear more of it?"

"I understand that you think you have some power here," David barked at her. "You seem to have forgotten how things work. You have two hours to get your butt back to the house. Two hours, Mariah."

"Or what?"

"Or I'll cut you off," David snapped. "We'll see how mouthy and independent you are when you're not running around spending my money."

And the line went dead. If she knew David—and she did—he'd likely hurled his phone across whatever room he was in.

Mariah clicked her screen off, then tucked her phone into her pocket again, aware of the great Alaskan silence all around her. The immensity of it.

And when she looked back, Griffin only stared down at her, his lips set in a firm line.

"You don't seem particularly worried."

"He always threatens to cut me off," Mariah said coolly. "It's one of his favorite party tricks, as a matter of fact. One time he didn't like the color of my shoes. Another time I didn't hear him calling my name from across the house. And, of course, he didn't always need a reason."

"Is this your version of being upset?"

Mariah waved a hand. "The women David knows would faint if their weekly allowance was taken away from them. But I know how to make a dollar last, believe me. I've had to choose between a tank of gas to get to work and food to eat, more than once. And after the first time David cut me off, then made me jump through hoops to get back the allowance I hadn't spent in the first place, I decided to treat it the way my great-grandmother did when she ushered her entire extended family through the Great Depression. I set it aside."

"You set it aside," Griffin repeated, as if he didn't understand when she was certain he did. Because very little escaped this man's understanding.

"One of my chores was to create an itemized list of everything I spent my weekly allowance on so David could tell me how useless and wrong I was, which, as you've now heard in grand and glorious detail, is one of his favorite topics. After church on Sundays he liked to sit me down and spend a few hours discussing the error of my ways."

She could tell from the way Griffin's face froze that he didn't much like the sound of that. And it was clear to her why she'd never told anyone else the real, hard truth about her marriage.

"I made lists of spa treatments," she told him, carrying on in the same, almost offhanded tone, because that made it almost easy. Almost funny, surely. "Hair appointments. Lots and lots of shopping. Sometimes I even did those things, but mostly, I took the amount from the account he set up for me and hid it away in mine. The one he doesn't know about." She smiled. "In case you were worried about how I plan to pay for your services."

"I wasn't." He studied her face. "You looked spooked when you first saw his name. Then you got less and less scared as the call went on. Why?"

"I don't know," she said, startled. How had he known what she looked like when she'd taken the call? Then she remembered what Everly had told her earlier, and laughed to cover the odd thrill of heat that worked through her at the idea that Griffin had been out there watching her. "I mean, I think David is under the impression I'm in Atlanta."

Griffin nodded slowly. "That's what it sounded like to me."

"So I really must have been imagining that there was someone at my door last night." Mariah shook her head, still seeing that doorknob turn in her head. Still feeling the ache in her thigh from the pinch she'd delivered to wake herself up. "That will teach me to drink so much tequila. By which I mean any."

"How good of an actor is your husband?" Griffin asked.

"An actor? He's not an actor. Of course he can put on a good show when he goes out in public. But I wouldn't call that *acting*, really . . ." Her voice trailed off. "Why?"

"Because the lock on your door was tampered with," Griffin told her matter of factly. Something pitiless in his dark gaze. "The deadbolt kept them out, but the lock is scratched. A lot like someone spent some time attempting to jimmy it."

"Oh. Well." Mariah had no idea what to say next.

And the look on Griffin's face was stern and maybe a bit ruthless, which should have made it worse. But instead, it made her feel safer than she had a moment before.

"So here's the question I have to ask you," Griffin said, as the wind picked up and a cloud rolled over the sun. Mariah told herself that was why she shivered. The sudden gloom, not the implacable intelligence in Griffin's gaze. And certainly not the shuddery way her body reacted to him. "If your ex doesn't know where you are, and he's not putting on an act, we have to ask ourselves: Who else hates you enough to want you dead?"

Ten

A week passed.

Griffin joined Templeton and Jonas as they scoured Juneau for their missing doomsday preacher—surreptitiously, of course, to stay off any kind of local radar despite Isaac's well-known talent for charming any and all officials—but found nothing but rumors. Blue took a team to follow the lead on the stolen boat, searching the waterways between Juneau and Grizzly Harbor but turning up no sign of the boat in question. Or the arsenal that supposedly went along with it.

Another week raced by. Griffin flew out to handle a diplomatic extraction in the face of a burgeoning civil war and was back, problem solved with minimal impact, in a smooth seventy-two hours.

There were no further attempts on Mariah when he was methodically making his way through Juneau. Nothing happened to her when he was out of the country, receiving updates while he was navigating crumbling infrastructure to usher their client to safety. And when he was back in Grizzly Harbor again, taking his turn on the watch rotation that had functioned smoothly in his absence, everything remained peaceful.

Nothing pinged on her phone. If anyone was tracking her, they were doing a piss-poor job of it.

Griffin had been forced to reassess his take on the situation even before Isaac, after turning down three separate celebrity muscle jobs at the evening briefing, had asked for alternate theories on Mariah's situation.

"You know how wasted Ben McCreedie gets when he's on dry land," Isaac pointed out.

"You think he'd show up at a stranger's hotel room and try to break in?" Griffin was skeptical. They all knew Ben McCreedie, an older fisherman who lived in town and kept to himself when he wasn't in the Fairweather.

"Irene Scola claims she ran him off with a shotgun a few years back when they were living together, but the judge gave him the restraining order when they broke up." Isaac's expression had gone contemplative. "I can tell you that whatever happened between them, Ben wouldn't hurt a fly when he's sober. But there's a demon in him when he drinks."

There were any number of men Griffin could say the same about. It was one of the many reasons he didn't drink. He had enough on his hands with the personality he could remember and control every day. He couldn't imagine why people found it entertaining to turn into someone else for an evening.

But he couldn't deny the fact that no one else had come after Mariah. Had it been a drunk local at her door that night?

Alaska Force kept eyes on her all the time, whether Griffin was in town or not. Sometimes subtly, sometimes not, to confuse anyone who might be watching. Meanwhile, Mariah had made herself a part of life in the town. She never repeated her Fairweather performance with Caradine. Once she'd adjusted to the time zone change, she woke early. She liked to take walks down to the water in the blustery mornings, then up along the ridge that led out past the hot springs.

He wouldn't call her a hiker, necessarily, but she liked to follow the first part of the trail high above the water. She usually spent a lot of time gazing out from the trees over the waves until she reached the point that marked the edge of the protected harbor, then turned back. After her walk, she picked up her laptop from the inn and either settled in the breakfast room there or went over to Caradine's. Most days, Everly joined her, hitching a ride on whatever skiff was headed into town from Fool's Cove. Everly worked remotely for an ad agency back in Chicago and was always in the middle of a campaign, but could handle her work anywhere. Griffin figured that Everly would get tired of actually working when all Mariah was doing was surfing around on the internet. But like everything else with Mariah, there was more to it.

"Have you gotten bored yet?" he asked her the following afternoon, stopping into Caradine's for a cup of coffee. That morning, he'd consulted on operation prep for a mission overseas, then spent some time keeping watch on Mariah himself. He stood over her table and did his best to keep from scowling at her, because it wasn't *her* fault no one was coming for her. "Grizzly Harbor must seem backward after Atlanta."

Mariah smiled up at him in that way other people probably believed was polite. Warm, even. Maybe he was the only one who could see the challenge in it. "I'm perfectly capable of entertaining myself, Griffin. Under any circumstances."

"I don't understand spending all day on the internet." Griffin shook his head in distaste. "Or any time at all. It's all liars and self-aggrandizers pretending to care about something other than themselves. Propaganda and the fools who believe every word of it."

"You're talking about social media." Mariah's smile took on that edge he wasn't going to snap and taste one of these days. He absolutely was not. "I don't do much of that. I prefer the stock market."

At first he thought she was kidding. But she gazed up at him steadily, and it occurred to him that she wasn't kidding at all.

"You play the stock market?"

"I told you that David likes to cut me off. And I told you that I knew how to make a handful of change last longer than you'd imagine possible. If you think about it, the stock market is nothing but a natural extension of that."

"You play the stock market," Griffin said again, wondering how Oz hadn't found this out already. What kind of computer whiz missed a hidden investment portfolio?

"It's all a big secret, of course," Mariah said, as if she were the one who'd been trained to read him instead of the other way around. "I add to it when I can and move things around, mostly for fun. I've never taken anything out. I couldn't let David know that I wasn't afraid of his favorite threat. That might have inspired him to come up with a different one."

"So what you're telling me is that you have money. Your own money, having nothing to do with David Lanier or his family."

"I'm doing just fine. I plan to hand David all the money he ever gave me, with interest, in the divorce—a message I feel he'll understand as it's intended. And when I do, I'll still be more than fine." She tipped her head to one side, her blue eyes too bright for Griffin's peace of mind. Making him question if he'd really needed a cup of coffee . . . or if he'd wanted this. Her. He gritted his teeth against the surge of his own temper. "Do you think that's relevant?"

Griffin wanted it to be relevant. He wanted it to matter. He wanted something—anything—to shake free so he could figure out what was happening here, fight it into submission, and send her on her way.

Griffin fired off an email to Oz as he stood there, mulling over the new piece of information. Mariah didn't simply save her money. If he wasn't mistaken, she made her own. He imagined that was the kind of thing a man like David might find offensive.

David, who had gone through with his threat two weeks ago and closed down Mariah's access to his bank accounts and credit cards because he must have thought that would harm her. He clearly didn't know about her stock market adventures. And he hadn't left Atlanta.

They'd kept eyes on him since they'd agreed to take Mariah's case. They also monitored his phone, yet could find no evidence that he was in contact with anyone outside Georgia, and certainly not someone who might have followed Mariah all the way to Alaska.

Still, there was the lock on her door and the fact that someone had clearly gone at it. And there was that uneasy tickle that Griffin kept feeling in his gut, telling him there was more here than met the eye—and it probably wasn't her finances.

"I'll let you know what's relevant," he told her.

"It's a hobby," she said lightly. Her head tipped to one side. "You must have some of those."

"I have missions."

"That's your job."

He stopped fighting his scowl. "No, Mariah. That's who I am."

She was wholly unaffected by his expression. He knew this when she rolled her eyes. At him.

"Everybody has hobbies, though I'm guessing you call yours something else so they seem more important."

"I keep myself in peak physical condition. I train constantly, with and without my weapon. These aren't hobbies, they're necessities."

"What will you do when they're no longer necessities?" she asked.

But Griffin didn't like to think about that inevitable day. He didn't want to imagine what life looked like when he couldn't shoot. When he couldn't keep up with the team. When he wasn't *him*, more weapon than man.

Instead of answering her, he threw back his coffee so fast he burned his tongue, which he figured he deserved for allowing a client to get to him. Again. It gave him something to focus on as he made his way back to Fool's Cove to go over Mariah's finances with Oz now that they had new information.

"How did you miss this?" he demanded, standing in Oz's oversized cabin that was outfitted like spy central.

"Same way you did," Oz retorted, frowning as he accessed supposedly private records on one of the huge monitors in front of him. "Redneck roots plus a trophy marriage isn't the kind of math that typically adds up to *secret stock market wizard*. It didn't occur to me to look."

Griffin didn't want to think of Mariah as a stock market wizard. Or any other kind of wizard.

He thought of her too much as it was.

About a week after the discovery that Mariah was secretly wealthy all on her own, Griffin made his way into town after a long, frustrating day paging through supplementary documents related to Mariah's situation. David's friends. David's connections. The questionable first steps David had taken toward his political career. He'd also run tactical interference for another Alaska Force team that was out in the field on a security detail for a charity convoy in the middle of a bloody little coup.

The convoy made it to its destination without incident. But Griffin was back to questioning Mariah's entire situation. Maybe this was what he'd thought it was from the start: a nasty divorce, with too many threats and maybe an attempt on her life in the heat of the moment. Maybe that first trip to the hospital was a true accident that had given David big ideas. It was possible he really had snuck into Mariah's apartment and triggered her second attack.

But he hadn't followed her all the way here, or made a half-assed attempt to get into her hotel room. If he had, they would have found him. Alaska Force knew every outsider currently on the island—writers and artists, wildlife photographers and extreme hikers—and none of them were David Lanier.

You really want that to be true, a derisive voice inside

him said when he made his way into the community center that same evening and stopped in the doorway of the room where Blue was teaching a handful of women down-and-dirty self-defense. *You want any excuse to make her go away.*

Because the longer she stayed here, the more it felt as if she'd always been here. Because she wanted to know his *hobbies*. Because he'd spent his whole adult life convincing himself it was his calling and his duty to be nothing more than a weapon, with no inconvenient feelings to mess up his aim or his commitment, and Mariah made him question that.

She kept reminding him he was as flesh and blood as anyone, and Griffin didn't know what the hell to *do* with that.

Instead, Griffin concentrated on the fact that she, Everly, and Caradine did self-defense with Blue in the afternoons when Blue was in town. It was smart. They gathered in the community center that was also Grizzly Harbor's City Hall—containing its mayor's office and set next to the post office that was open only at the postmaster's whim—in the multipurpose room that was mostly used for garrulous town meetings and the occasional flea market when the weather was bad.

This afternoon, while the rain poured down outside and Griffin questioned everything, Mariah was practicing how to be deadly. How to strike, counterattack, and explode into decisive action when grabbed. Blue taught them how to fall, how to roll. How to do their best to keep from ever going to the ground, but also what to do if they found themselves there anyway.

And Griffin had dedicated his life to the practical, elegant application of violence. He trained so that he didn't have to fight, and fought so that nations didn't have to go to war. And he had never been a blunt instrument. He and his rifle were lethal poetry, stillness and a perfect shot, fused together and made one on more battlefields than he could count.

He had seen every variation of fighter possible, from street brawlers to black belts with craft to spare, but he'd never seen anything like Mariah McKenna, with that frown of deep concentration on her face, her elegant hands high and in front of her, moving in to attack.

It did something to him.

She was a pretty blond princess with a killer palm strike, and she made him feel jumbled up inside. She made him want things he knew full well he couldn't have. Things he didn't even want anymore.

That had all shifted straight on into temper by the time Blue's class was over.

"You should join in next time," Mariah said, walking over to him as the class broke up. Like they were friends. Like they had any kind of personal relationship.

Griffin preferred the way Caradine simply walked out, forestalling any attempts to engage her in idle chit-chat. Everly and Blue were more sociable, but they were having an animated discussion about palm strikes with two local women.

Which meant if Griffin wanted to scowl at Mariah, there was no one around to comment on it, for once.

"I already know how to fight," he said. Short and curt. "I don't need a class."

"You mistake my meaning entirely." And she smiled at him, all challenge. "I want to hit you. Hard."

It wasn't the first time she'd said something like that to him. But today, it didn't land the way it had before.

Today it seemed to sizzle, searing into him as if she really had put her hands on his body.

He couldn't seem to keep himself from remembering her husky, intoxicated voice after her tequila night in the Fairweather. The way she'd propositioned him, leaning in close, making him feel like a cursed saint on a pyre of his own morality when he'd refused her.

"It's cute that you think you could hit me," he said, though his voice was too low. Too intense. Too revealing. "Or that you think I'd stand here and let you."

"I have it on excellent authority that my palm strike is fierce."

She was taunting him. He recognized it, and still, the only thing he could really focus on was the awareness in her blue eyes that reminded him of the blazing summer skies of his Arizona childhood, before he'd decided he didn't get to have anything that bright. The same awareness that was like a fire in him, storming through him, changing him. Making him regret every promise he had ever made to himself.

Which in turn made him furious. At her.

"What do you think I do for a living?" He sounded more vicious than necessary. "This isn't a game. The fact that you think it is makes me question why we're trying to help you in the first place."

If he expected her to wilt, he was disappointed. But then, he should have known better. This was the same woman who'd listened to torrents of abuse from her jackhole ex-husband and hadn't so much as blinked.

She regarded him steadily, too. "Let's be honest. You're looking for an excuse. Any excuse. You didn't want to take me on in the first place."

"Correct."

"I imagine it must be upsetting for you that I'm still here. No one's taken me down with a quick dose of lobster, clearing up your problem. That must be hard."

"There's no lobster in Alaska. Crab, sure. Or shrimp."

"I'll make a note."

She was hopped up on a false sense of her own power after another hour spent hitting and kicking things, learning about pressure points, and getting herself out of a series of choke holds. Griffin understood all about the things adrenaline could do.

"And I don't want you dead, Mariah. I want your problem solved. So you can get back to your life."

And leave me to mine. But he didn't say that out loud.

"What life do you think I'm in a rush to get back to? I didn't particularly care for the life I was leading before I met David. Much as I love my family, living anywhere near them means surrendering to them entirely." She laughed, but it was more a sound of surprise than amusement. "And I don't think I realized until this very minute that I had the perfect childhood to prepare me for life with David. Where surrender was also required, daily."

"Now you get to make a new life. No surrender necessary."

"Maybe you haven't noticed, Griffin, but that's what I'm doing. Every day."

"Not here," he gritted out.

But when she smiled, almost as if she felt sorry for him, that made it worse.

He ushered her across the street to the inn and wasn't surprised when Mariah headed straight upstairs, stalking up the steps before him. She stood aside when he opened her door, then waited as he checked her room.

"Thank you," she said when he was done. Icily.

"My pleasure," he replied in the same tone.

He headed back downstairs and took up his preferred position in the lobby, where he could see anyone who came or went. He settled in with his back to the wall, his rifle out of sight, prepared for another long shift. He knew Mariah liked to stay up in her room in the evenings. She read books—mostly the kind of thrillers and historical fiction he read himself, though he had no plans to admit that to her. In case she wanted to talk more about *hobbies*. She watched movies on ancient videotapes and slightly newer DVDs from the general store. She had a hot plate in her room so she could cook modest dinners, because Caradine very rarely felt like cooking dinner, and the other restaurants—such as they were—were either seasonal, indifferent, or the grill at the Fairweather.

She lived like any other Grizzly Harbor resident. Griffin had to remind himself that she didn't belong here, she wasn't a local, and he blurred those lines in his head to his own detriment.

He settled in, tuning out Madeleine's nightly phone squabble with Jaco and the text updates from various active Alaska Force missions in turn. He concentrated on his breath. In, out. He made himself still. Alert and watchful, but wholly capable of staying exactly as he was for hours. Days, if necessary.

And he was surprised, hours later, after Madeleine had closed down the front desk for the night and left to fight with Jaco in person, to hear footsteps in the hall above.

He shifted into a higher level of alertness instantly, and was on his feet before the footsteps hit the top of the stairs.

Long before they reached the bottom, he also knew that it was Mariah.

No one else was staying in the inn this week, but he also recognized the sound of her tread. Light and careful, like the rest of her, even when she barreled into the lobby and then stopped. To stare at him.

She had showered since he'd last seen her. Her hair hung all around her and gleamed in the firelight, smelling strongly of the coconut shampoo she used. She wore those jeans that looked about as soft as her skin and clung to her in ways even he couldn't keep from admiring. She was wrapped up in that wool cape thing again, and yet despite that, her feet were bare and her toes painted a glossy red.

The contrast might kill him.

"Is something wrong?" he asked gruffly, because this was a freaking job, not a date, and he needed to stop obsessing about what she was wearing. "Did something happen?"

She studied him for a moment, as if she were coming to some decision. Then she tipped up her chin, squared her shoulders, and pulled the wrap tighter around her torso.

"Why don't you want me here?" she asked.

Great. They were having this conversation. "It's nothing personal."

"Like hell."

That was all drawl, fire and defiance, and it hit Griffin like a grenade.

"Excuse me?"

"Of course it's personal." Mariah stood even taller. "It's so personal that you can barely see straight when I'm in the same room. Why don't you just admit it?"

"I don't have to like a mission to complete it, if that's your concern."

"That's not my concern. You *really* don't like me, and I want to know why."

She moved farther into the room in that regal manner that drove him crazy. She looked like a queen, and he wanted nothing more than to get his hands on her and prove that she was as flesh and blood as he was.

He told himself it was temper, nothing more, but he knew better. Of course he knew better.

"Let me assure you, Mariah, that I have no personal feelings about you one way or the other."

He couldn't read the glittering expression in her eyes. But that curve in the corner of her mouth was wired directly into his sex. "I don't believe you."

"You want to be careful about throwing accusations around," he warned her. "What happened upstairs? Did you get bored sitting around in your room, pretending that rural Alaska suits you? I don't blame you. This isn't a soft place. It takes a very specific kind of person to make it here."

"And by 'very specific' do you mean . . . condescending? Patronizing? A man so uptight it must hurt when he sits down?"

"I know you're not describing me. I'm not uptight, princess."

"Meticulous. Disciplined. Guarded. Whatever you want to call it."

"I am in complete control of myself. I take pride in it." Griffin didn't restrain the way he glared at her. He told himself it was a choice. "You should ask yourself why you don't."

"I've forgotten more things about control than you'll

ever know," she had the nerve to throw at him. "How do you think I survived my marriage?"

"You haven't survived it yet," Griffin fired back. "Isn't that why you're here?"

"I can't believe that you treat every client like this. In fact, I know you don't. This is personal, Griffin. I wish you'd just admit it. Every single thing I say or do offends you, clearly."

"You don't offend me. You don't bother me." And he'd hate himself forever for the note of desperation he could hear in his own voice. "You're a job. Not a very interesting one."

"And you," she said with too much quiet intensity, her blue eyes entirely too sharp, "are a liar."

Eleven

Mariah had no idea what she was doing.

She should have been tucked up in her room, happily reading a book as night fell—later and later the longer she stayed here—the way she normally did on these blustery spring evenings.

She should have been worried about that fierce look on Griffin's face, as if he were debating between carting her back to her room himself or maybe knocking her out right here. Anything to shut her up.

But she didn't feel much like shutting up, it turned out. Talking to David again the other day had . . . changed her. Or maybe it was learning how to fight back. How to function inside fear, as Blue often told them in their self-defense class.

Whatever it was, she wasn't sitting rigid and still with a smile on her face anymore, taking other people's crap. Those days were over.

She wasn't straightening her hair like her life depended on it. She wasn't making sure her makeup was flawless at every hour of the day and night. She was going straight to seed, in fact.

McKennas might be weeds instead of flowers down there in the backwoods of Two Oaks, but flowers were fragile things. They bloomed awhile then died, and required all kinds of fiddling to stay alive at all. Weeds, on the other hand, took care of themselves, took over, and were almost impossible to kill off.

Just like the extended McKenna clan.

And just like Mariah.

"I know you didn't call me a liar," Griffin said, almost casually. Conversationally.

The ferocious look on his face probably should have scared her down to her bones, but it didn't. He didn't. *Scared* wasn't at all what she felt around Griffin Cisneros.

And she was getting tired of pretending otherwise.

She was tired of *pretending*.

"Here's the thing," she told him, gripping the soft wrap she liked to use as a kind of bathrobe and starting toward him. The floor beneath her feet was cold, but that helped. It made her more *aware*. "I think about my own death all the time now."

"Congratulations, princess. It's called mortality. And guess what? It's going to get us all sooner or later."

"I don't want to die pretending I don't feel the things I do. Even if what I feel happens to make you furious."

And Mariah knew him better now. She'd made an extended study of this still, watchful man. She'd seen how kind he was beneath his bluster. She knew how carefully he listened. And she could see the gradations in all that ice he wrapped around himself, and knew he wasn't quite as frosty tonight as he wanted her to think he was.

"What you feel or don't feel has nothing to do with me."

She shook her head at him. "Liar."

The muscle that flexed in his jaw was almost imperceptible. Almost.

Mariah was tired of waiting. To be good enough. To be accepted. Hell, to be killed.

She was tired of acting like a flower, waiting to be watered, desperate for sun, unable to take care of herself and her own needs unless a gardener happened by.

"I'm only going to say this once," Griffin told her in his precise, furious way. "I do not lie. I pride myself on being a man of honor, and that includes telling the truth. I don't take honesty lightly, and I certainly wouldn't throw it away at the spur of a moment—"

"In the name of all that is holy, Griffin. Just shut up."

He looked faintly startled, which for Griffin was the equivalent of flinching, leaping into the air, and maybe even letting out a scream.

Mariah knew it wouldn't last, so she took advantage. She closed the distance between them, aware of the floor beneath her feet, the uneven wood giving way to the thick rug laid out before the fireplace. She was aware of the crackling warmth of the dancing flames, the wind off the harbor buffeting the windows, and the creaky sounds of the old inn all around them.

She was aware of everything, but all she truly saw was Griffin.

Beautiful Griffin, straight and tall. That impossibly sculpted face, his dark brown eyes shot through with gold and heat. That full mouth, pressed into its usual hard line.

All the lean, hard-packed muscle he carried with such neat, athletic grace.

She walked toward him, and didn't stop until she was right there in front of him, so close that if she breathed too heavily the front of her body would press against his. For a dizzy moment, that was all she could think about.

"I don't know what you think you're doing," Griffin said in a warning tone that made her heart thump. "I'm not sitting in this lobby for my health. It's yours we're concerned about."

"I appreciate your concern," she assured him. "Truly."

"Then appreciate it quietly. Up in your room."

He sounded furious. But Mariah was so close to him now, and she could *see* him. And for all his icy fury, he didn't step back. He didn't set her away from him. He didn't do anything but continue to stand there, straight and stiff, his jaw clenched like he was this close to exploding.

Mariah would bet anything that he was.

"You should be careful who you tell to shut up." Griffin's voice had grown even darker. More intense. Which meant only that Mariah could feel it in even more places. "You might not like the response you get."

"I'll take my chances," Mariah drawled.

And she didn't do what she'd been taught, again and again, by her ex. She didn't wait. She didn't sit sweetly, a pleasant expression on her face, until such time as he felt she was ladylike enough to deserve an advance.

Somewhere inside, she could hear her mama hooting at the very idea of the *ladylike behavior* David had insisted on.

Mariah didn't hoot along, but it was now or never.

She held Griffin's gaze. Then she reached out, entirely too aware of her own breath, and slid her hands over his chest.

It was like sliding her palms over one of the wood-burning stoves that heated the inn. He was as hard as iron and as hot. She could feel the simmering heat and the power of him through the henley he wore, and it made her shudder because it proved what she already believed.

He wasn't cold at all. He burned the same way she did.

She waited for him to order her to step back. But he didn't.

His face still seemed carved from stone. But if he imagined that was a barrier, he was mistaken. She liked the stone, particularly when she could feel that all those sculpted marble ridges in his abdomen were hot to the touch.

He made her want to curl up against him and purr.

Instead, Mariah did the next best thing. She surged up onto her tiptoes, tilted her face to his, and then pressed her lips against Griffin's.

And for a moment, it truly was like kissing some kind of statue.

He didn't move. She would have thought he didn't breathe, either, but her hands were on his chest. She could feel the faint movement. And better still, the wild pounding of his heart.

So she kissed him again. She kept her mouth on his, like she was teasing him awake. Like something out of a fairy tale.

Once. Again.

And then he broke.

One second he was motionless and still, the most beautiful sculpture of a man she had ever beheld.

And the next he was . . . liquid heat.

He angled his head to one side, opening his mouth over hers, and she felt the sound he made—half fury, half need—light her up inside. His hands were on her face, moving her head where he wanted it, and taking control with a swiftness and a certainty that made her toes curl.

And it was better than an explosion. It was deeper. Wilder.

It was greedy. Need and longing, fury and something darker still.

Mariah had never felt anything like this in her life.

She wrapped her arms around the hard column of his neck and arched against him, thrilling to the scrape of her breasts against that iron wall of his chest at last.

The world stopped. Then it spun. And either way, the only thing that mattered to her was Griffin.

He kissed her like a starving man, but she was just as hungry.

She couldn't get close enough. She couldn't taste him enough. She couldn't get *enough*.

And when he pulled his mouth from hers, his hands wrapping around her shoulders and holding her away from him, his gaze was the darkest she'd ever seen it.

Furious all over again, but this time without a shred of that deep chill she was used to seeing in him.

"Griffin . . ." she began, through lips that no longer felt entirely like hers.

"You think this is a game." His face was so close that it was almost like another kind of kiss. "You think— what? If you shatter every boundary I have it will end well? Because it won't. You have no idea who I am. You have no idea what I'm capable of. The control that I keep over myself isn't for me, Mariah. It's for you. It's for the world in general. You don't need to see what happens when I'm out of control."

"Do you even know?" she demanded, spurred on by something she couldn't have named if she tried. It was that ache she felt within her. The taste of him in her mouth. The feel of him tattooed into her palms. The particular scent that was only his, salt and man, that she knew might haunt her forever. "Do you have the slightest idea who you are when you let yourself go?"

"I could tell you what it's like to be a Marine sniper, but you wouldn't understand. I could toss out my number of confirmed kills. But those aren't things I talk about with civilians."

"I don't think the things you've done make you any kind of monster."

"Neither do I. But you know what would? Acting like I have anything in common with all the happy civilians who walk around with no idea what price is paid to keep them free. I know the price. I chose to pay it. And I make sure to keep the weapon they made me under total control at all times, so people like you never have to know what it costs."

She could see how deeply he meant that. How it let him stand taller and wrap another chilly barrier around himself.

But she wanted his heat.

"You don't drink. You don't have one-night stands, and you're certainly not in a relationship. You work out every single day and act as if missing a session might kill you. There's self-control, and that's a good thing. But then there's being a control freak."

There was something like anguish on his face as his hands tightened on her shoulders.

"You don't have the slightest idea what you're talking about."

"I know exactly what I'm talking about." She hardly recognized her own voice. "You're talking to the only person around who wears more masks than you do. Do you really think I don't know what that costs? You think I don't know how hard it is to stay cool and collected no matter what?"

"I must have missed the part of your file that talked about the time you spent having drill sergeants and commanding officers in your face."

"I had David," she threw right back at him. "Ten years of a controlling husband monitoring every twitch of eyelid and every chip in my nail polish. And I'm betting that the consequences I put up with were more unpleasant than an extra set of push-ups."

Griffin let go of her and stepped back, but that only proved she was getting to him. His hands ended up on his lean hips, and he looked male and pissed, yet still so beautiful it took her breath away. And it was worse now, because she'd tasted him.

There was no way she was going to get past that anytime soon.

"The situation is my fault, not yours," he said, sounding cold and detached again. But she didn't believe that distance anymore. "I'm the professional. I should have known better."

"That's what happens when you block stuff up. All that pressure has to come out somehow."

"I'm sure you know you're a beautiful woman," Griffin said with deliberate, pointed courtesy. And a faint note of pity besides. It stung, even though she knew that he was deliberately putting distance between them. "You'd have to know, wouldn't you?"

"Men like my ex-husband don't typically waste their time pulling ugly ducklings out of roadside diners," Mariah replied, letting her drawl get good and thick. "They tend to go right for the swans. If I keep my mouth shut, wear my hair right, and stay pretty, who knows? People might forget that I'm nothing but some no-account country girl, not quite a hillbilly, married to someone way above my station."

"I always assumed trophy wives knew better than anyone else what made them a trophy."

Her lips still felt swollen from his, and he was talking about trophy wives.

So Mariah smiled, letting her voice get sweet and syrupy. "We surely do. Why? Are you looking for one?"

"Mariah."

Her name was a command. One she ignored.

"It's not only about being pretty," she said, feeling dangerous herself as she glared at him. "You have to stay pretty in the very specific manner that appeals to who-ever considered you a trophy in the first place. All the time. No days off. No yoga pants on the sofa, binge-watching television programs. No fluctuations in weight or fitness levels. To be determined by him, not you. Not a scale, not a trainer. He's the final authority on how much you eat, when you eat it, whether it's stuck to your thighs, and what you should do to get it off. Because the thing you really sign up for when you become a rich man's trophy wife is availability."

"Jesus Christ."

But she wasn't done. She leaned in closer to drive the point home.

"Twenty-four seven, three hundred and sixty-five days of the year, you need to be available. In every possible way. There are no shifts, no vacations, and certainly no sick days. Whatever he wants, whenever he wants it. Total, grateful surrender, night and day, forever." She could feel the brittle smile on her face, but it was nothing next to how she felt. Particularly when Griffin only stared back at her, motionless, that dark look on his face. "So yes, Griffin. I know that men think I'm beautiful. Lucky me."

And for what seemed like an eternity, there was no sound in the inn's lobby but the snap of the fire.

"It's time for you to get back upstairs," Griffin gritted out, one or two lifetimes later. "Let's go."

He tilted his head in that way he did, as good as an abrupt order. And Mariah didn't have it in her to fight it, not when she'd flipped over such a terrible stone, exposing all the ugliness beneath it.

She could feel it all squirming around inside her now, raw and unmanageable. Yes indeed, she knew all about being a trophy wife. The shinier she'd gotten, the more obedient, the more David had taken.

Taken and taken, until she had been little more than a flower with its head popped off.

She reminded herself that she was tough as she walked up the stairs, Griffin a silent wall of disapproval at her back. She hadn't been kidding when she'd pointed out that they were the same beneath all their masks. She'd been forged in a nasty fire, too, and she'd never had the opportunity to consider what she'd done honorable.

When she got to her door, she stepped aside as Griffin went in to perform his usual check.

She stayed where she was when he came back, nodding at her to let her know he hadn't found anything suspicious. Because there was nothing suspicious here. This was Alaska, and Mariah was more certain by the day that she'd left her troubles back in Georgia.

"If it helps," she said softly, because he was close again and she had that ache in her that always seemed to grow when she was near enough to touch him, "you're not the only one who's disgusted with me."

He stopped on the other side of the doorway, facing her where she stood in the hall. "I'm not disgusted with you."

"You do a really good impression of it. Must be all that talk about whether or not I know that I'm pretty enough to be a trophy for a man like David." She felt the way her mouth twisted, and it was no mask. It was too real, and she didn't know how to stop it. Much less the words that came next. "But certainly never good enough for a hero like you. You made that perfectly clear."

This time, it wasn't the muscle in his jaw that gave him away. Because maybe he was already too edgy. Or less contained than she'd imagined. Because his eyes flashed, a bright, hard heat.

"I'm no hero," he threw at her, and even his voice was different. Not cold. Raw straight through, like he ached the same way she did. "It's not a question of pretty enough or good enough. You're a beautiful woman, Mariah. I'm not immune to that. To you. But that doesn't mean I'm going to act on it."

A kind of sob rolled through her then, too huge for her to control.

"Why not?" Her voice was as raw as his, too hurt and

too honest. She would feel the shame of it forever. "What do you have to lose?"

"Me," he hurled back at her. "You make me lose control. You make me lose *me*."

She had never heard him sound like that. Wild, uneven. Not icy or controlled at all.

"Griffin," she began, putting out her hand to touch him again, finding that hard line of his mouth and smoothing her fingers over it. "You don't have to—"

He muttered something that she knew was a curse, and she could feel the heat in the words, but she didn't recognize the language.

And then it didn't matter.

Griffin hauled her into his arms, kicking the door shut behind them to lock them up tight in her hotel room, and took her mouth with his.

Twelve

She tasted like things Griffin didn't believe in.

Magic. Heat and desire.

And he knew he would regret this. Maybe he already regretted this.

But he couldn't let go of her.

This time, when Mariah wrapped her arms around his neck, he indulged himself. He ran his hands down her back, vaguely recalling that she'd lost her wrap downstairs, and then not caring at all because the only other thing she was wearing was an absurdly soft T-shirt. He tested the curves that he'd been much too aware of for far too long. The delicate line of her spine, the mouth-watering flare of her hips.

He lifted her against him, letting out a groan when she wrapped her legs around his waist and crossed her ankles, holding on tight.

God help him, the ways he wanted this woman.

But he'd waited much too long to rush things now.

He carried her over to the bed, tipping them both down onto the mattress, and for a long while, there was nothing but heat. Need.

And greed for her like a fist that gripped him, hard.

He kissed her until they were both out of breath, and then he helped himself to that line of her neck, the ridge of her collarbone where she often rested her hand and drove him crazy.

She rolled on top of him, settling herself in just the right way against him so that they both caught their breath.

He liked it when she sat up. It was easier to pull that T-shirt off, then get rid of her bra, so he could finally get a look at the perfect curves of her breasts and, better yet, fill his hands with them. Her hair was everywhere, curling between them, sliding this way and that, and as he tugged her down to take her mouth again, he buried his hands in all that blond silk.

Then he flipped her over, because she wasn't the only one who liked being on top, and found himself grinning against her mouth as she fought him to get his henley off. He reared back, tugging his shirt the rest of the way off and tossing it aside.

"All of it," she ordered him. "I want it all off."

"Stop," he told her when her hands moved to her jeans. She stared up at him, her hair tousled and her lips swollen from his, the tips of her breasts pink and inviting while passion turned her blue eyes navy. "I want to undress you myself."

She actually obeyed him for once, and he took care of his clothes, coming back to her like a man possessed. He kissed her until she was squirming against him, into him, and then he started all over again.

Griffin found his way down the column of her neck, back to her beautiful breasts. When she was arching against him, her head thrown back and pretty keening noises coming out of the back of her throat, he moved lower. He tested the shallowness of her navel and the sweet slope of her belly. His hands found her hips and caged her, enjoying the way she bucked against him.

He took his time finding the button to her jeans and tugged them down, but not all the way off, trapping her. He settled where he was, holding her down, and then pressed his mouth to that pretty bit of lace between her legs.

She tasted like sugar and smoke, and he was only getting started. Her hands were on his head, and she rocked against him. Harder and more insistent, until he took pity on her.

Griffin angled himself up and tugged her jeans off of one leg. He went down again, pulling her leg over his shoulder to hold her open and wide before him.

And this time, when he bent to taste her, he let his fingers slip beneath the lace. She was scalding hot, entirely too beautiful, and he couldn't keep himself from toying with her. When she started to moan, he bent close again, held the lace to one side, and licked his way into all her sweetness.

She shattered almost instantly.

Griffin rode it out, then moved, shifting back off of her. He freed her other leg from her jeans and pulled her panties down. Then he tossed them aside so she was as naked as he was.

Mariah was still shaking while he dealt with the condom, and her eyes were dreamy and hot when she opened them again.

She took his breath away.

But she was talking, her drawl even more honeyed than usual, and now he knew that she tasted the way she sounded. "To clarify, the man who had no intention of ever having sex carries condoms around?"

"I like to be prepared for any eventuality."

"Oh sure. You're just like a Boy Scout."

Griffin gathered her against him, pulling her knees up on either side and settling between her thighs. He notched himself against her heat, watching her eyes grow dark and wild all over again.

"On my honor, I do swear," she began chanting, taunting him even now.

But that only made it hotter.

Especially when he thrust in, deep.

They both made a noise at that.

"Yes," she whispered. "Finally."

And then, because he could, he went slow.

Hauntingly, deliberately slow.

Griffin didn't speed up when she started to shake. Or when she started to sweat, her face red and her hair damp.

He didn't pick up the pace when she begged. Or when she stopped begging and tried to do it herself, rolling her hips against him and trying her best to speed them both toward that edge.

He went slow. So deep it almost hurt, then out again, over and over. Until he wasn't sure which one of them he was driving insane.

Mariah shattered again. She wrapped her arms around him, tried to climb him and control him, but all she did was toss herself over that edge again.

"Please," she whispered. "Please, you're killing me."

But Griffin kept it slow.

Because he could. Because he had made an art out of waiting.

Because this was a lesson, for both of them.

And because he shouldn't have allowed this to happen in the first place, and he had no idea if he would ever allow himself to do it again.

He drank up her responses like the whiskey he no longer indulged in.

Each time she broke into pieces and shattered in his arms, he took it in and gloried in it. And only when she was mindless beneath him—only when he was crazy with the scent of her skin, the clutch of her body, and his name on her lips—did he allow himself to break.

Griffin dropped his head down, clasped her hands in his, and let himself go.

At last, something in him roared, as he hurtled over that cliff.

And lost himself completely.

It could have been days before Mariah came back to herself. Years, maybe. She was surprised to find Griffin stretched out there on the bed beside her, more astonishingly perfect than she'd imagined.

All the lights were still on, so she indulged herself, turning on her side and letting her gaze trace over him. His beautiful brown skin was like satin to the touch, and he had what she instantly determined to be the perfect amount of hair dusting his chest, then starting again below his navel. He lay with one arm beneath his head, and she didn't know how she knew when he shifted to alertness, because he didn't move.

One moment his eyes were closed, the next they were open. And on her.

She could have felt shy, maybe even awash in regrets, but she didn't. Maybe that would come later, when she had time to process this.

But she doubted it.

She reached over and traced a tight ridge sculpted into his abdomen, and took it as a triumph when he didn't tense.

"How long has it been since you last let yourself lose control?" she asked.

She felt his gaze on her like a new heat. "There are a lot of ways of losing control. Are you talking about my temper? Do you want to know the last time I let myself get mad?"

"If that's what comes to mind as you lie here naked, in bed with a woman. Sure. Let's talk about your temper."

"The last time I lost my temper was when my fiancée and my best friend informed me that, really, they would rather be married to each other than have anything to do with me."

He propped himself up on one hand and faced her. And his gaze was no less intense than it had ever been, but this was different.

It took Mariah a moment to realize that there was no trace of iciness in there. At all.

"Ouch," she said, noting that he didn't seem particularly messed up about it. She suspected that meant it had happened a long time ago. "Is that the last time you had sex?"

His mouth curved. "I spent a good while making my own bad decisions."

"I'd say you were entitled to some bad decisions."

He reached over, a look of intense concentration on his face, and traced his own trail between her breasts, then lower. He grinned with pure male satisfaction when she shivered in reaction.

"I've never found that entitlement gets anyone very far. What starts with entitlement ends in excuses. I decided I didn't want either."

"No entitlements, no excuses." She studied his face. "But you're okay with me being the enemy?"

"I don't think you're the enemy. Not my enemy, anyway."

"Are you sure?"

Griffin sighed. He reached over and took hold of her, rolling until she was sprawled across his chest, and then held her there until she settled. She was unnerved by his casual strength, and if she was honest, fascinated by it. She piled her hands beneath her chin and gazed at him, trying not to think too much about how intimate this was. How . . . unmasked and vulnerable she felt.

"Control isn't something I do," he told her, his gaze intense and his voice serious. "It's who I am."

"Does it have to be all or nothing?"

He smoothed her hair back, focusing on the task as if it were the most important thing in the world.

"I've never known how to do anything halfway," he said after a moment, and it sounded like a confession.

Mariah was enjoying all of this too much—Griffin stretched out beneath her, hard and warm. His gaze took in everything and still focused on her like she was the only thing in the world.

And the fact that she didn't have to figure out a way to hide while he was looking straight at her. She could tell he liked the mess of it. The realness. The salt on her skin, the way her hair tumbled everywhere, the drag of her body against his.

He liked it—but she did, too. She more than liked it. It felt different from sex. It felt like some kind of sacrament.

His confession fit right in.

"I don't think you're all that different," he was saying in his typical gruff manner. "You walked off that ferry like a queen. Now you're running around with your hair wild and your feet bare, kind of like you're trying to go full Grizzly Harbor. I might like to control myself, and everything else while I'm at it, but you like to disappear into whatever role you're playing. And if you think about it, it's really all the same thing."

"I'm not disappearing," Mariah told him, an odd certainty washing through her. "Maybe for the first time in my whole life, I'm not trying to disappear at all."

"Good." His gaze searched hers, and she wanted . . . too many things she didn't know how to name, much less ask for. Especially when he stopped arranging her hair and ran his hand over her cheek instead. "You've got nothing to hide, Mariah."

"Griffin," she whispered. "Neither do you."

She couldn't have said if she leaned forward, or he did. But either way, they were kissing again.

And the heat grew quicker this time. From sweet to wild in an instantaneous blaze.

Mariah felt him stir beneath her and couldn't seem to keep herself from rocking against that hard ridge. He let out a low noise, then rolled to the side to deal with the condom.

When he was done, he pulled her back on top of him. Griffin wrapped his hands around her hips, lifted her up, and then settled her back down against him so she could take all of him deep inside her.

"I should punish you," she whispered, bracing her palms against his chest and letting her hair fall down to trap them. "I should slow it down and drive you crazy."

Griffin's grin edged toward cocky. "Go right ahead. If you think you can."

She couldn't.

Mariah moved over him, losing herself far too quickly in the exquisite sensation, the friction and the delicious fullness, and most of all the golden heat in that dark gaze he never moved from her.

And this time, when she broke apart, he flipped them over again, bracing himself against the bed so he could drive into her, swift and sure, until she was meeting him, crashing against him, and shattering all over again.

Only then did he go with her, his head next to hers and her name on his lips.

When she stirred again, the room was dark but Griffin was still there.

He pulled her against him, her back to his front, and took her that way, both of them coming hard and fast, a part of the inky darkness.

The next time she woke, she was alone.

There was light outside the windows. And Mariah felt different.

Reborn.

She swung her feet over the side of the bed, cataloging all the delightful aches and tugs that reminded her what kind of night she'd had. She saw the wrap she'd worn downstairs folded neatly on the chair and smiled. She couldn't remember wearing it when they'd been standing in the doorway up here. She'd likely dropped it downstairs.

Meaning that after Griffin had left her, he'd snuck back in and neatly folded it while she slept.

It was absurd how warm that made her feel. It was a folded length of merino wool, not some kind of valentine.

But she couldn't seem to wipe the smile from her face.

Mariah made her way into the shower, aware of her body in a way she wasn't sure she had ever been before. Every square inch of her skin felt alive and brand-new, so that even the water running down her arm made her shiver.

By the time she came out of the hot water she was warm and pink, and still couldn't stop smiling.

She left her hair to dry as it liked, made herself a cup of the inferior coffee she could produce in her tiny microwave—because she needed some caffeine before she let anyone see her in public, even someone as uninterested in her nonsense as Caradine—and settled back in her bed with her laptop.

She felt dreamy. Sated all the way through.

Happy, a voice in her supplied, and goose bumps rose up and down her arms in a kind of alarm.

Because that was a magical word. And one she hadn't ever used before about her own life.

She went through her email, deleting all the usual junk, then took a quick glance at the news before catching up with the New York Stock Exchange. It was while she was scanning the *Atlanta Journal-Constitution* online that her email pinged. She clicked over automatically.

Then stopped, frowning.

It was a weird email address she would have deleted as junk, but the subject line caught at her.

Blood always tells, it read.

Her pulse was hammering and she hadn't even opened the thing.

Mariah couldn't help herself. She clicked on the message, frowning even harder when it opened to show her an embedded video clip.

She knew better than to play random videos that were sent to her as spam. But there was something about this one. The still screen was blurry, so she couldn't make out the image. She could only see the faintest hint of a deep, reddish brown, and the play button.

Of course she shouldn't click on anything sent to her by someone she didn't know. She ran it through her anti-virus software and it came up clean. She told herself that didn't matter, that she should delete it and move on with her life, but there was something about that blurry image—

She clicked on it.

The video opened with a view of a dirt road with lush green trees all around, and even as she identified the fact that the blurry red-brown she'd seen was a road, Mariah also knew where it was.

She knew every inch of that dirt road. She'd walked it. In bare feet, some summers, for the sheer pleasure of the cool patches of mud between her toes. She'd driven it in later years, each and every turn stamped deep into her, like her own breath.

Here, sitting on her bed in an inn in Alaska, Mariah could do nothing but watch, a terrible dread making her feel weighted down and heavy all the way through.

She clicked another button, trying to turn the sound up, but there wasn't any.

That made it worse.

Soon enough, the camera went around the final curve. Mariah found herself with her hands over her mouth once she saw the farmhouse.

Home.

It looked exactly the same. Peeling paint, weeds, and too many cars in the yard—very few of them in decent condition. She saw that old tractor her brother Justin had claimed he'd build back up but clearly never had. She was holding her breath, creeped out and panicked and scared straight through, afraid to draw the conclusions that were sitting there, right out of reach.

There was some kind of cut in the video, and then they were right outside the farmhouse, moving around the side to peek in the kitchen windows.

The kitchen was also the same as she remembered it, with clutter on the counters and pots and pans piled high in the sink. Mariah knew every nook and cranny. She'd cooked there, eaten there, yelled at her siblings and ordered her cousins around on that same old cracked linoleum. She and Rose Ellen had fought there, cried there, and sorted themselves out again as best they could at the ancient kitchen table.

It wasn't until water splashed down on her hands, clenched in place over her keyboard again, that she realized she was crying.

The video cut again. It was darker now, and the filming was more confused. It took Mariah a moment to realize that they were back in the front yard, out in the kind of Georgia twilight that she knew would be loud with the usual backwoods symphony. There were lights on in the house, and then, worst of all, a figure at the screen door.

Then the screen opened and Mariah's mother walked out.

Mariah sat frozen, tears making her cheeks slick, not sure if she was capable of breathing.

She watched Rose Ellen walk toward the camera, a quizzical look on her face, even a hint of her rare company smile that she usually only pulled out in town— never in her own yard.

Mariah hadn't seen her mother in nearly five years, and she hadn't talked to her for months now. And she accepted that she had no one to blame for that but herself.

She had no one to blame for any of this but herself.

She stared at the screen. She watched her mother come closer. The almost-smile turned more confused, then tipped over into a frown.

"Mama . . ." Mariah whispered.

On screen, her mother recoiled.

Then everything went blank.

And for a moment, Mariah felt just as blank.

But when her heart kicked at her again, she leaped into action.

She shot off the bed, clutching her laptop to her chest, and hurtled toward her door. She flung it open, and almost slammed into the chest of the man standing there.

"Griffin—" she began.

But it wasn't Griffin.

It was a stranger. A man with a black beard, a dark green flannel shirt, and merciless eyes.

Mariah had a flash, suddenly, of walking off the ferry and getting jostled.

By a man who looked exactly like this.

"Can I help you?" she managed to get out, but the man didn't answer her.

His hand shot out, catching her just below her jugular and shoving her.

Hard.

Mariah staggered back, somehow keeping her feet beneath her and her laptop from flying out of her grip.

And then watched in horror as the man stepped inside her room and closed the door behind him.

Thirteen

Griffin's phone chimed once with the alert he knew meant trouble, now, and he was already moving before the sound of it faded away in Mariah's quiet hotel room.

He was swift, dressed in seconds and heading for the door, and if there was a part of him that was relieved that there was some action—if he was *grateful* that he was being called in the middle of the night so he couldn't betray himself further with a woman he'd never meant to touch—well.

That was between him and those parts of him that should have stayed in their own damn compartments.

"Preacher's coming in hot," Isaac clipped at him when he shoved his comm unit into his ear, maybe forty-five seconds after his alert had sounded. "Blue picked him up three miles out and gaining. We need you in position."

Griffin swore, stepping into his boots in the hall outside Mariah's room. Then he took the stairs two at a time, as silently as if he'd walked down them in his bare feet. "Where do you want me?"

He was already in the inn's lobby, retrieving his rifle from its place behind the stuffed grizzly, where it would have been in arm's reach if he'd been keeping watch the way he should have been. He gritted his teeth at his own weakness, swung his rifle over his shoulder, and pushed his way outside.

Isaac was belting out orders in his ear, and Griffin grunted his assent to each one.

He waited for his eyes to adjust to the night air, scanning the quiet little town as he did. He was looking for potential plants. If a so-called holy man bent on revenge could hide in the sounds and inlets that made up so much of Southeast Alaska, it stood to reason he could also have friends stashed in strategic places in Grizzly Harbor, waiting for his signal. Like a boat loaded high with potential explosives. But he didn't see anything that looked out of place.

He could pick up the faint sound of footsteps and braced himself, but in the next instant, the new guy melted out from between two buildings.

Griffin nodded his greeting. Rory Lockwood, former Green Beret, nodded back.

"Reporting for watch," he said, and Griffin was impressed, despite himself, that the other man didn't look or sound the least bit pissed that he was being relegated to what was basically a tame stakeout when there was real action going down. He wasn't sure he'd manage it if the positions were reversed.

But then he was moving again, sharpening as he went. Focusing.

Forgetting.

Following Isaac's commands, he ran along the street and then, instead of following it down the hill, jumped onto the slanted roof of the Fairweather, which was nearly scraping higher ground on its back side. He scaled it easily, and quietly, concentrating on nothing but achieving his vantage point.

He got to the highest part of the old roof and set up there, assembling his rifle in moments.

"Ready," he said into the comm unit.

"Hold position," Isaac replied.

And Griffin sank into the quiet, the cold. His steady grip.

He was Plan B. Plan A was Templeton out there on the water with Blue, moving the chase boat into position.

"It's an army of one," Templeton confirmed when they had eyes on the preacher. "We're going in."

When the wind changed, Griffin could hear the faint sounds of engines in the distance, out on the open water, but the bay directly in front of him stayed smooth. Empty.

The very second that changed, he would fire. That was the backup plan.

He was ready.

He was always ready. The whole point of his life was this, here.

He trained to be ready. To be still.

And he needed his life—and his head—to be clean and neat and empty of everything but his skill. His aim. His willingness to take the necessary shot.

His willingness to do what needed to be done so that others might live.

If he wore a mask, if he hid himself, that was for other—normal—people's protection.

He'd worked himself up into a righteous fury when there was an explosion in his ear and a flare of light on the horizon.

Then nothing but silence on the comm.

"Report," Isaac snapped out.

And Griffin waited. Tense, and bright with shame that while his brothers were out there doing their jobs—and possibly paying for it—he was up on this roof thinking about a woman.

He hardly recognized himself.

"He blew up his own boat," came Blue's disbelieving voice after the longest sixty seconds in Griffin's memory. "Jumped in the water and blew it up on the way down."

Templeton's laughter was too loud, the way it always was. "He's an idiot but not a martyr, in case you thought he believed his own crap. We have him."

"Call the police in Juneau," Isaac ordered a moment later, no sign in his voice that he'd been worried about that explosion—unless you knew him. "I think they're going to want to talk to him."

And that was one more situation handled while the oblivious residents of Grizzly Harbor slept.

Griffin disassembled his weapon, then climbed off the Fairweather's roof. He jogged back to Blue Bear Inn, nodding at Rory, who was standing watch outside the front door.

"I left my jacket here," Griffin said.

That was true enough. But was that why he was here?

The other man only nodded. "I have this covered."

Griffin let himself in to the quiet inn and found his jacket where he'd left it. But he also found that ridiculous cape of Mariah's, crumpled in a heap on the floor of the lobby.

And he didn't think while he moved from the lobby to her room, but there he was. Letting himself in with the key he should have given back to Madeleine weeks ago. Folding up the cape and putting it where she could find it.

Then standing beside her bed.

And he didn't want to think about how long he stood there, watching her sleep.

But he knew when he finally tore himself away and pushed his way out of the inn into the cold remains of the night that this had to stop.

Mariah had to go. This had to end.

His unhealthy fascination with this woman *had to stop*.

Griffin had trained himself to knife's-edge precision because he was a weapon, not a person, no matter what she said. And weapons did not *cuddle*—because if they did, they would find themselves on a rooftop day-dreaming when they should have been focused and ready to strike.

He stood out there on the frigid street in front of the inn while his heart kicked at him, betraying him all over again.

Griffin did not panic. Ever. That was not what this was.

Even if it sure felt a whole lot like it.

"I'm headed back to Fool's Cove," he told Rory shortly. "Someone will relieve you tomorrow."

"I'm on it," Rory replied, as if keeping watch over a woman no one appeared to be chasing was his idea of a rocking good time.

Grizzly Harbor wasn't entirely quiet this close to dawn. Fishermen were making their way down to the docks and heading out to sea. Or maybe toward the flames in the distance. On the comm unit, Isaac was outlining the cover story he wanted Blue and Templeton to tell the authorities when they arrived, because admitting they were running any kind of op here could turn into a logistical nightmare.

Out fishing, officers, might not convince anyone, but it wasn't like they could prove otherwise.

Griffin took his own boat back, navigating along the rocky shore where the moody northern sea swelled and surged as he found his way to the entrance to Fool's Cove. And when he moored the boat at the dock below the lodge, then climbed out, he had every intention of hiking the mile to his cabin. At a punishing pace, because he needed to get back in control of himself. Now.

He was cold. He was furious—if only at himself. And he needed solutions, not more problems.

Maybe that was why he decided to add *suicidal* to the mix.

A man took his life in his hands sneaking up on any member of Alaska Force at any time, for any reason, but particularly one like Isaac, who spent so much of his time and energy hiding right there in plain sight.

Griffin might have lost it tonight, because apparently he was nothing but some hound dog incapable of resisting a woman—but he wasn't an idiot.

Not entirely.

Isaac's cabin was set down near the water, accessible from the lodge along a makeshift hanging boardwalk Griffin and Isaac had spent a whole summer painstakingly replacing so it was walkable.

Though the fact it was walkable didn't mean anyone was dumb enough to actually walk on it without an invitation. Griffin made as much noise as he could, broadcasting his footsteps so that Isaac—who would have heard him coming even if he'd been attempting stealth—understood it was a friendly, nonemergency approach.

When Griffin got to Isaac's door, he didn't have to knock.

Isaac was already standing there, fully dressed in his usual cargo pants and a T-shirt, in front of his door. Horatio at his side.

"Aren't you supposed to be back on watch duty in town?"

"The new guy's got it. And I think it's time to pull the watch."

Griffin threw that out there. Then he squared his shoulders as he stood in the cold, the light over the door in his face, and waited for Isaac's response.

Isaac was his boss. But he was also Griffin's chosen leader and friend, and Griffin hated the fact that he was standing straighter, like a guilty recruit. He hoped like hell Isaac couldn't read what he'd been up to tonight all over his face.

"Why?" Isaac asked, with no particular inflection.

"She's been here for weeks and there's been no credible threat in all this time. It's time to dial back our response here and focus on strategies going forward. The ex and the anaphylaxis appear to be contained in Atlanta."

"Why now?" Isaac asked in the same mild tone, which Griffin didn't mistake for anything soft. "Why right now, this early in the morning after a round of excitement on the high seas, when you're supposed to be propping up a wall in Blue Bear Inn's lobby? Why couldn't this wait for the morning briefing?"

"I'm making a tactical call."

"I'm glad to hear that, brother," Isaac said, an affable smile on his face, but it only made Griffin brace himself. Like the beard Isaac wore to disguise the true, hard lines of his jaw, that smile was nothing but misdirection. "Tactical calls I appreciate. What's funny, though, is that this has all the markings of a personal decision."

"I don't make personal decisions."

"You didn't used to, no."

It was a relief to focus all his fury on Isaac rather than on himself. Griffin jumped into it with both feet. "Are you accusing me of something?"

Isaac leaned back against his front door like he was settling in for a cozy chat, leveling his gray gaze at Griffin. "What would you do if I told you a story about a woman who turned up one day bearing more than a passing resemblance to a fiancée I lost way back because my best friend took her?"

"I told you my past isn't a factor. And the only thing Gabrielle and Mariah have in common is blond hair."

"I know what you told me. Now I'm telling you a story. Let's say this woman turns up, suddenly my ghosts are everywhere, and I start acting unlike myself. I start dragging this woman out of bars, let's say. Acting like a boyfriend, not a bodyguard."

"Is this supposed to be a story about me?" Griffin asked, his voice like a blade. "Because this sounds a lot like the Isaac and Caradine story."

Isaac didn't move. He even held onto that grin, but only a fool would look at him and see anything but the potential for his own imminent death, out here where no one would ever find his body. Or dare to look for it.

"And now you show up in a panic in the middle of the night—"

"I'm not in a panic." Though he counted himself lucky to be breathing after that crack about Caradine.

"—demanding that we pull back from this woman, right now, because you had a flash of inspiration in the middle of the night. And you just know, somehow, that we should be looking elsewhere." Isaac shook his head. "You know what that makes me think? You don't want us looking at you."

Griffin was surprised he didn't break in two, he was standing so stiff and furious. "Are you questioning my integrity? My honor?"

"As your commanding officer? Never." Isaac studied him for a moment. "As your friend? Yeah, buddy. You're acting crazy."

But Griffin refused to accept that. Crazy had been that room at the inn. The way Mariah and he had . . . fit.

"I told you," he gritted out. "None of this is personal."

"Griffin. You've spent so many years acting like nothing's personal that I don't think you know how to identify when it is, in fact, incredibly personal."

"I told you what I think needs to happen, but the final vote is yours, as usual." Griffin glared at this man who had given him a purpose and a home, who had allowed him to spend these years on the other side of the Marines continuing to do what he loved. The man who had created this space where Griffin could be who he was meant to be, instead of the shadow of himself he'd pretended to be for those strained, unhappy months he'd played a well-adjusted civilian in Arizona. That was who Isaac was, and Griffin knew it—but tonight Griffin didn't have it in him to access his usual respect. What he wanted to do was punch Isaac in the face. "Or we can keep standing around, gossiping like teenage girls."

This time when Isaac grinned, it was like another man's sucker punch.

"You know I've been thinking we need to reconsider our approach," Isaac said after a moment. "Why don't you take the rest of this ridiculously early morning to get your head on straight."

Griffin started to protest, but stopped when Isaac's gaze hit his.

"Clean your gun a few times," Isaac suggested. Except it was less a suggestion and more an order. "Run up that mountain and sweat out some of this crap you're not feeling. Then come to the briefing with a few suggestions and we'll figure out the next step."

Griffin wanted to fight. He wanted to throw down and get in Isaac's face. And the very fact that he wanted such things was a warning sign. Hell, it was a whole five-alarm fire and then some. Griffin wasn't a fighter—because he didn't have to be. His fight was always and ever with himself. He was the one who had to stay in position, still and ready, until the right time. He fought a thousand wars against his own impatience, his own demons, and his own distressingly human body long before he took a shot.

He didn't need Mariah making his blood too hot. He didn't need her kicking through him, making him over into some kind of hothead, and making him question . . . everything.

But thank God he had the presence of mind to nod, turn, and take himself off into the dark before he did something seriously stupid, like try to take Isaac down.

Instead, he took Isaac's advice. He ran.

He ran as he was, in combat boots with his rifle slung over his back, hauling ass up the side of that steep, unforgiving mountain. He ran past his own cabin and kept right on going, farther into the dense bush like he was trying to make it over Hard-Ass Pass—and only stopped when he hit the snow line.

The downhill was worse, punishing and dangerous at any speed, but he only made himself go faster.

What little sun there was finally got around to appearing by the time he got back down to his cabin, with only a few grazes and bruises for his trouble. He showered, keeping the water icy cold to test the resolve he seemed to have left behind in Mariah's bed.

But no matter what he did, he couldn't seem to get images of Mariah out of his head. Much less the sensations. It was like she'd burrowed under his skin, making herself a part of him whether he liked it or not. Like he'd been starved for touch and was hoarding it now, no matter how he tried to sweat or freeze it out.

He made himself his usual breakfast—the optimal combination of protein, carbs, and good fats—ate it too quickly to enjoy the taste, and then calmed himself down even further by assembling and disassembling his favorite three rifles in rapid succession.

Again and again, eyes closed, then open, then closed again, the way he'd learned to do when he'd been a too-intense teenager who'd wanted more than a life in the Tucson suburbs—not least because he knew he didn't have it in him to follow in his father's footsteps all the way through medical school.

This was who he was. The deceptively delicate barrel, the perfect scope. A rifle so high-tech it always returned to zero no matter what.

A beautiful, lethal machine, good for only one thing.

Griffin was significantly more calm when he went to

the morning torture session down on the beach. The day's workout had a name, which assured it would be brutal. It was.

You're talking to the only person around who wears more masks than you do. Do you really think I don't know what that costs? Mariah had asked.

And maybe that was the problem, Griffin thought grimly as he fought his way through the grueling movements toward the blessed end of the workout. Today the only thing he could seem to feel at all was the weight of his own mask smothering him, even when he was done killing himself in Isaac's box of pain.

But he shoved all that aside, too, and concentrated on his second shower of the day. This one colder than before. And when everyone was assembled in the lodge for the briefing, he took pride in delivering his assessment of Mariah's situation without a single trace of emotion in his voice.

Like he was still glacial straight through. The way he should have been.

"We've got no hits on her phone or on the trail she laid out toward Greece," he pointed out while everyone else looked at their tablets and files. "The only interest we've seen on her apartment in Atlanta has been the ex-husband performing drive-bys at night, consistent with relationship drama, not attempted murder."

He congratulated himself on extricating himself and Alaska Force from this mess. The mess he hadn't wanted to take on in the first place.

"Assuming we're cutting her loose, the question I have is what happens when she gets back to Atlanta," Blue said.

"We can sweep the apartment. Make sure it's clean

and also increase security," Griffin said. Sounding far more unassailable and sure than he felt. "There were already two attempts made on her life. A third shellfish contamination in this short period of time is going to bring in more interest from authorities, and I'm guessing that's not what the husband wants."

"That doesn't prevent other attempts," Jonas pointed out in his usual gruff, irritated way. "More overt attempts."

"Talk to the client," Isaac suggested, and Griffin noted *he* seemed to have no trouble sounding exactly as he should. "She's the one who has to agree to walk back into the situation she left behind, and she might not want to do that. Find out if she's willing to put herself up as bait before we start planning around it."

Griffin nodded an affirmative, and deeply disliked the part of him that clenched tight at the very idea of Mariah being bait for any kind of trap.

Or Mariah at risk. Or Mariah scared in any way.

But he refused to feel this. He refused to *feel*.

And it was going on two in the afternoon when he caught another boat into town to pull Rory and tell her exactly that. What happened last night was a mistake. Every minute that passed made that more clear to him, especially when he was alarming himself with his incapacity to stop. Freaking. Thinking. About. It.

This had to end. She had to go.

The sun had peeked out in the morning, then thought better of it. The day was overcast and chilly, too much like winter, as if spring had been nothing more than a fairy tale they'd all been telling themselves lately.

Rory wasn't outside when Griffin got to the inn, so he went inside, assuming when he didn't see the Green

Beret in the lobby that he'd secreted himself somewhere nearby, the way he liked. If Rory followed procedure, he'd either show himself or call in, and either way, he'd get the same message: Their surveillance of Mariah was terminated.

Griffin nodded at Madeleine. "Is she here?"

Madeleine took her sweet time looking up from her paperback, then shrugged enough to make her beehive shudder. "I haven't seen her all day."

That was weird.

Griffin felt a prickle deep in his gut, the one that too often operated as its own kind of alarm system, cluing him in when something wasn't right.

He jogged up the stairs, rapping on Mariah's door when he reached it. There was no answer. He figured that meant it was unlikely she was curled up in a ball in there, brooding about last night.

But he was sure there was an explanation. Just because Madeleine usually saw Mariah at some point during the course of the morning, that didn't mean her failure to do so today meant anything. And it didn't mean he could justify using his key. Not yet.

Not when she could be choosing to ignore him.

He tried to call Rory, on the phone and on his comm unit, but there was no reply. That was weirder still—but they could be eating. Talking. Hanging out the way people did with Mariah because no one had ever been chasing her.

Griffin walked down the road to Caradine's café, but Mariah wasn't there, sitting at the table he now considered hers with her laptop and a bottomless mug of Caradine's high-octane coffee. Rory wasn't there, either. And Caradine said she hadn't seen either one of them all day.

"But no one actually clears their schedules with me," Caradine said, all attitude behind her counter.

"A simple yes or no is really all I'm looking for."

Caradine smirked. "Did I give you the impression that I've ever cared all that much what you're looking for?"

Griffin walked out without responding to her. He did a circuit around Grizzly Harbor, up and down the streets, poking his head into all the shops—many just opening up now that winter was over and summer seemed almost possible again. He even ran along her favorite trail, taking it all the way out to the point, where the dirt track started to double back on itself and climb.

But Mariah was nowhere to be found. Neither was Rory.

And it was when he got back from the trail, dug out his key no matter what Madeleine might think about it, and found himself standing in the middle of Mariah's room that he accepted the fact that there was a problem.

All her things were there. Her suitcase was right where she kept it. That stupid, ridiculous cape was where he'd put it on her chair in the dark. Her boots and hiking shoes were lined up neatly in the closet. Her laptop was open at the foot of her bed, its screen dark.

He called in and reported, and while he waited for his brothers to show, he went downstairs and asked Madeleine what her morning had looked like.

"What does my morning ever look like?" She scoffed at him. "Not a song and dance, I can tell you. Today was like every other day that ends in *y*. I checked in a couple from the Lower 48 after the ferry got in. They went out again about fifteen minutes later. That's it. That was the big excitement."

"Where's the couple now?"

"I forgot to put a GPS tracker on them," Madeleine said, unhelpfully. "Sorry."

The married couple from California walked in not long after Blue and Jonas turned up. Which meant the tourists got to nervously tell all three of them that they hadn't, in fact, left their room fifteen minutes after checking into it.

"We were tired," the man said defensively. "We have some big hikes planned, so we decided to take the rest of the morning to relax. We went out around noon to explore."

Griffin's first thought was the ferry. He went down to what passed for a ferry terminal at the docks to see if he could look through the security camera footage, while Jonas went upstairs to take a closer look at Mariah's room. Blue took to the phone, calling their contacts in Juneau to see if they could get a handle on a woman of Mariah's description possibly boarding a plane.

But there was no sign of her getting on the ferry no matter how many times Griffin watched the footage. And Blue reported that there was no sign of her at the airport in Juneau, either.

"I found something weird," Jonas said when Griffin went back to the inn.

He showed them a video he had found when he opened up her laptop. It was a series of disjointed silent images around a farmhouse, and a woman at the end who looked a whole lot like Mariah might if she'd lived a whole lot harder.

Griffin didn't need to consult his files to know it was Mariah's mother.

"I'm not liking this," Blue muttered.

"She can't have disappeared into thin air," Griffin said. "Even if it was possible to disappear off of this island without leaving any trace, Mariah isn't the person who would manage it." He faced the obvious. "Do we think the new guy . . . ?"

"No," Jonas said flatly. "He's one of us. I'd stake my life on it."

That was the highest accolade Jonas could give, and he gave very few, so Griffin accepted it with a nod. But that left even fewer good options. For both Rory and Mariah.

"The couple," Griffin muttered.

"You think she's not alone," Blue said flatly. "You think the couple who left fifteen minutes after those people from California checked in was her. And whoever he is, if he's not Rory."

"He's not Rory," Jonas growled.

"If she was leaving voluntarily, she would have taken her stuff," Griffin continued. "And she would have told someone."

He meant him. No way would Mariah leave this place without telling *him*. Especially not after last night.

It took hours of searching every fishing boat that came in and talking to all the people who worked on the water before they found old Ernie Tatlelik's buddies throwing back a few drinks at the Fairweather, talking about the weird couple the crusty old bush pilot had set out to fly all the way to Anchorage in his seaplane. Because Ernie was just nuts enough to fly up along the coast and risk the notorious bad weather and big waves in the Gulf of Alaska. Ernie was nuts enough to do anything if the price was right.

When they got the old man on his phone, he'd bunked

down for the night with his sister's kid up in Anchorage before attempting the flight back the next day. And he'd been happy to describe his customers. The big, burly man with a beard—like all the mountain men wannabes who flocked to Alaska from Outside each spring—who wouldn't listen to reason and fly to the much more accessible Juneau if he wanted a city. Only Anchorage would do. And the woman, who'd done nothing but sit like she was frozen solid through each refueling stop, never so much as cracking a smile—though Ernie allowed as how that could have been due to the inevitable turbulence on takeoff and landing.

"There it is," Blue said in a low voice when they'd let Ernie go back to his dinner.

Mariah wasn't simply gone. Someone had taken her.

Griffin was forced to sit with that. And while he was trying to get right with it, Templeton found Rory tied up and gagged in a backyard shed a few buildings down from the inn, bleeding from the head. Pissed and woozy.

There it is, all right, Griffin thought grimly.

Because Mariah had been snatched from under their noses and his brother was hurt, and there was no pretending this whole mess wasn't entirely his fault.

Fourteen

At first Mariah was in shock.

There was a man in her room.

Inside her room.

A big, terrifying man who looked at her with a certain focused and yet pitiless expression that made her skin crawl. Right there in front of an unmade bed that seemed to her, suddenly, to pulse with a kind of revolting invitation that made her entire body go cold.

Her body that was currently barely covered by a T-shirt and a pair of underpants.

Nausea made her stomach cramp, but she didn't dare bend over or draw attention to all the parts of her body that were so . . . accessible.

Mariah reminded herself—fiercely—that she'd trained for this over the past few weeks, no matter how *accessible* her body currently was. Blue had prepared her, and she'd practiced it over and over in their makeshift classroom. She slid her laptop onto the end of her bed, took a deep breath, and tried to remember all the various strikes she'd been taught.

"You can try one of those cute moves you've been learning with your friends if you want," the man said, and there was a note in his voice that made Mariah's stomach twist harder. Like he wasn't simply doing this, he was *relishing* it. "But you should know that I don't care if you get hurt. And you will. Badly."

In her head, Mariah was bold and mouthy and effort-lessly brave. But her actual mouth was too dry to work, her knees were threatening to give out beneath her, and her stomach was staging a riot. She didn't feel at all brave. She wanted to cry.

More than once, David had looked at her as if she were something stuck to his shoe that he'd very much like to scrape off. Maybe hundreds of times. And she'd been very aware of how dangerous Griffin was from the first moment she'd clapped eyes on him at the docks.

But she wasn't sure she'd ever stared straight into the face of a man who both didn't care about her at all and really, really wanted to hurt her.

"Here's what's going to happen," he told her in that same creepy, casual voice. And it hit her then why he knew she'd been training with Blue. He'd been watching her. She remembered that shadow she'd seen across the street her first night here. That twisting doorknob. It all led straight to this scary man, with his bushy black beard and that glittering promise of pain in his gaze. She wasn't sure she would ever breathe fully again. "We're going to walk out of here. None of your friends are around, and no one is going to recognize you anyway."

He pulled something awful out of his jacket and threw it at her. And Mariah would have screamed as it flew through the air, hairy and wrong, but her throat was as tight as her mouth was dry. It wasn't until it slithered across the unmade bed toward her that she realized it really was hair. A brown wig.

"You're going to put that on," he told her calmly, and even though he didn't do anything else, Mariah got the distinct impression he was enjoying himself. "Then we walk out of here and down to the water on the far side of this shit stain of a town. You're not going to try a thing. You're not going to signal anyone or make a scene or whatever else you think will save you." And maybe he was smiling, then, behind the beard. "It won't. If you do anything, all I'm going to do is send a text, and my buddies down in Georgia will start carving pieces off your mother."

Mariah began to shake, and couldn't seem to do anything about the way her eyes watered as all kinds of images cascaded through her head, each more upsetting and awful and nauseating than the last.

"How . . ." she managed to get out, though she sounded as if this man had already choked her half to death. "How do I know she's okay?"

He was definitely smiling. "You don't."

As her head spun and her calves cramped with the effort of keeping her from crumpling where she stood, only the horror of making herself even more helpless kept her upright. That and Blue's voice, telling them the same thing over and over in class. *Don't go to the ground. Fight to stay on your feet.*

"Get dressed," he told her, no noticeable change in his voice or in the steady, awful way he watched her. "And bring your ID."

He made no move to offer her privacy while she found

her clothes, and Mariah didn't argue. She was picturing all the parts a body could lose before a person bled to death, in far too much detail, and moved around the bed to pick up her jeans from the floor. The jeans that Griffin had removed last night—but she couldn't let herself think about that. Or him. Or how this man had gotten to her when Griffin should have been downstairs.

Was Griffin—

But her mind shied away from even forming that question.

Her jeans were on the other side of her bed. She pulled them on while hiding herself behind the mattress, concealing not only her private bits but the miracle she discovered when she picked them up.

She'd left her cell phone shoved in one of the front pockets.

Mariah expected the man to notice. To see the outline of the phone as she yanked the jeans on, bending over so her T-shirt covered as much of her as possible. To text his friends before she could do a thing to stop him—

But he only watched her like he was bored. He didn't lunge for her phone. He didn't reach for his.

Mariah said a small prayer of thanks that she'd pulled on her loosest T-shirt this morning. She picked up her slender billfold of a wallet from her nightstand and made a show of sticking it in her other front pocket.

Then she pulled on a sweater that was more of a tunic, the hem brushing the middle of her thighs and further concealing the phone in her pocket. She shoved her feet into her hardy flats. Only then did she go about tucking her still-damp hair up under the awful, scratchy wig that made her shudder. Everywhere.

"Remember," the man told her in that same toneless,

disinterested way. "One text and your mother starts losing digits. And if I don't check in at regular intervals, guess what happens?" He didn't wait for her answer. "More pieces. Or, hell, they'll just kill her and pick up another one. I hear you have a lot of family. It could take awhile to cut through all of them."

It didn't occur to her to fight him. Or test him.

Because this is who you are, a voice inside her whispered, sounding a lot like her ex. It felt like one more assault to add to her collection. *Once a coward, always a coward.*

Mariah blinked hard to keep more pointless tears back, because there was no point crying over something that was true. A brave woman wouldn't have stayed with David as long as she had.

The man marched her out of her room and down the stairs, one hand on her arm in a way that made it obvious he was taking her against her will. And Mariah braced herself as they hit the lobby, because surely Alaska Force would do their thing and handle this—

But there was no one in the lobby. There was only the rearing, ferocious stuffed grizzly bear and Madeleine behind the front desk. Mariah expected Madeleine to notice what was happening, or that the man was a stranger—but the other woman didn't even look up from her book.

It was okay, Mariah told herself as the man took her outside. It was still okay. What mattered was that Griffin's body wasn't on the floor of Blue Bear Inn. He wasn't there, but he wasn't dead—and that meant he could be anywhere. She was pretty sure that was the entire point of a sniper. He watched and waited and would handle everything when the moment was right. She felt herself settle at the thought.

All she had to do was trust that he would take care of this.

She did.

Deep down, she truly did, because that was who he was.

And that belief allowed her to take a deep, steadying breath as the door to the inn slammed shut behind them.

The man's hand on her arm hurt. He was gripping her too hard as he propelled her down the wooden street, away from the town docks, and Mariah was sure that she would bruise. He was actually going to bruise her. He truly didn't care if he hurt her, just in case she'd doubted that earlier.

But she couldn't think about that now.

She focused on walking in time with the man's long strides because she worried that he would drag her along after him if she didn't and, worse, would view that as her *trying something*. Mariah couldn't have that. She hurried along with him, waiting for one of the locals they passed to see that she was being marched off right under their noses, but no one looked at her twice.

It wasn't only the wig, she acknowledged as they walked right past the big window at the Water's Edge Café and . . . nothing happened. It was the wig plus the stranger accompanying her. She'd lived in Grizzly Harbor long enough now to know that no one looked too closely at the tourists wandering around unless they made particular spectacles of themselves.

She had Alaska Force, she reminded herself. She had Griffin.

She expected to hear a shot at any moment. Or something less dramatic, like Griffin appearing from behind a tree and the other men falling in behind him, prepared to take this man out. She was ready for it with every step, every breath.

But instead, her abductor marched her onto a private dock on the other end of town, then into a battered old seaplane headed toward Anchorage, piloted by the old man Mariah saw every day at Caradine's. She waited for him to recognize her, to help her—but his gaze grazed right over her as if he'd never laid eyes on her before in his life.

It was a loud, uncomfortable, very long flight, with refueling stops along the way. There was nothing to do but hold on and hope the moody weather didn't swat them down into a bad landing out there in the middle of absolutely nowhere.

And wonder how Griffin and his friends had allowed this to happen.

The only positive about the experience was when the grizzled old pilot gave her thick, faintly musty blankets to huddle beneath, allowing her to surreptitiously sneak her hand into her pocket and access her phone. She wondered if she could manage a text—but she didn't like the way the man was watching her. She was afraid that too much movement beneath the blanket or peering beneath it would lead him to do the same. When she could manage it without moving much, she switched her phone off. Before it rang and the man made her—and her mother—pay.

Once they got to Anchorage, he took her to the airport and bought flights to Atlanta with cash. They flew from Anchorage into Seattle, where Mariah was sure she'd have a chance to make her move. Make a call, at the very least, with the phone she'd managed to get through security and back into her pocket without him seeing it when she'd *accidentally* gotten into a different line from him. Get away from him in a crowd, maybe. But she quickly thought better of it when they got off the plane, because who knew what his friends would do to her mother while she was running around, trying to convince someone in authority to listen to her?

And despite her crisis of faith on that rickety plane earlier, she still believed that Griffin was coming for her. He had to be. All she needed to do was make sure she was ready.

"I have to use the bathroom," she told her abductor.

The look he gave her chilled her straight through. Especially when they were this close to so many TSA agents. Because it told her—once again—that this man didn't care about consequences. He only cared about hurting her.

"Too bad. You went on the last plane. You can wait and go on the next plane, or piss all over yourself. I don't care."

"But—"

"This isn't a negotiation, bitch. I said no."

She didn't argue further. She didn't dare. Mariah followed him meekly to their gate, sat down in the chair he pointed at, and kept her mouth shut.

And tried her best to *think* this through.

If he didn't want her going in a public restroom, she assumed that was because he was afraid of what she could get up to in there. She would have too much time to convince another woman to help her, for example. Or pass on a message, or any number of other possibilities.

She could even barricade herself in a stall and refuse to come out, forcing him to cause a scene when he tried to come get her.

The fact that he was worried about any of those possibilities—even though he'd warned her what would happen to her mother if she tried anything at all—told her he wasn't just some muscle-bound idiot.

That didn't bode well for her.

Mariah's best option was still Alaska Force. She didn't know why no one had been keeping watch in the lobby of Blue Bear Inn. She didn't know why her abductor had been able to take her out of Grizzly Harbor. On that long, low flight to Anchorage, she'd had a lot of time to think it over while she was rattled around in the noisy little plane. And what she'd kept coming back to was the simple fact that even if, for some reason—and she could think of a pretty big reason that had taken up most of the night—Alaska Force had decided to drop her as a client, they wouldn't do it without telling her.

No one had told her. That meant someone was coming.

She believed it with a wild fervor that bordered on religious zeal, and she was perfectly okay with that.

In the meantime, she had no good choices when it came to rescuing herself. Her mother's life and limbs were hanging in the balance. She still had her phone shoved in her front pocket, and that was the only bit of hope she had to cling to just now. But it was of no use to her if she couldn't access it.

Just wait, she told herself, again and again. *Just wait for the right time.*

When they boarded the red-eye flight to Atlanta, the man took the middle seat and trapped her against the window. Mariah made sure not one part of her body was touching his, pressing herself against the cold, smooth side of the plane as it took off.

She wrapped herself in the flimsy blanket that had been on her seat, happy that it let her secretly touch the phone stuffed in her pocket like it was some kind of talisman. Then she squeezed her eyes shut and let her mind spin from last night, and all its impossible wonder, to the grisly future that waited for her in a few hours.

If Griffin didn't show up and handle this, she was going to die.

Mariah had understood that fact the moment the man had stepped through her hotel room door and stared her down. He was taking her back home, no doubt so David could enjoy the spectacle of her death. That was the point of this. And it probably wouldn't be a quick spectacle, either.

Though her mind shied away from all the ways a violent death could go slow.

All she could hope for was that she could get to her mother. And in the meantime, she would have to be glad that at least when she went to meet her maker it would be with the full carnal knowledge of Griffin Cisneros to sustain her through her premature afterlife.

She would have shouted down heaven itself if she'd died without knowing what it was like to kiss him. Or what it was like to take her time exploring that sculpted warrior's body of his. Or better still, what it was like to feel the sheer joy and exquisite pleasure of him surging inside her, driving them both gloriously mad as he took his sweet time.

She had lived all her life without knowing that it was possible to feel that way about anyone.

And up there at thirty-five thousand feet above the earth, chasing the night across the country, Mariah kept her eyes shut tight and did her best not to cry out loud at the sheer unfairness of it all.

It didn't seem right that she'd suffered a decade with David and only got one night with Griffin. She wanted more. She wanted so much more. She recalled what it had been like waking up in that bed, feeling dreamy and satisfied straight through, wondering what it would be like when she saw him again. The man loved nothing more than pretending he was an icicle, so she'd anticipated there would be more of that—but now she knew what it was like when he melted.

How was she supposed to live without it?

A cross-country plane ride in the dark was a lot of time to think about her life.

She had nearly died twice before she'd discovered what it was like to truly live, and that struck Mariah as a terrible shame. If she'd known how little time she had, she would have done everything so very differently. Of course, the twenty-year-old she'd been would always have taken that ride in David's fancy car the night they'd met. Because that twenty-year-old had wanted to get out of Two Oaks more than she wanted to breathe, and Mariah couldn't begrudge the choices she'd made even in retrospect.

But it hadn't taken her ten years to know better. It hadn't even taken a pair of maids in his bed. That was where her cowardice came in.

She had known within eighteen months that David wasn't any kind of Prince Charming. She'd been fully aware he wasn't much of a man well before the five-year mark. She could have left. She could have figured out her life then, instead of waiting for it to get to this point.

But if you'd been that smart, a voice inside her whispered, more kindly than she felt about herself at the moment, *you never would have met Griffin.*

And he was worth it, she decided, somewhere over Missouri. One night with Griffin was worth ten years of David.

She'd had no idea that her body could do the things it had done spontaneously with Griffin. She'd had no idea that she could *feel* those things, over and over again.

She'd had no idea.

And if she wasn't on a red-eye flight headed straight toward what might very well be her own unpleasant end, she might have been more reserved. She might have lied to herself, built a few walls, tried to play it cool to modify her own expectations.

But the reality was, she'd fallen for that man, and hard.

From the very first moment he'd looked at her as if she'd offended him simply by walking off the ferry, she'd been fascinated by him. That fascination had only grown worse over her weeks in Alaska, and by the time she'd stormed down the hotel stairs to get in his face, well. She'd been done for.

Griffin had listened to her. She trusted him. He was kind beneath his gruffness, when the men she'd known these past ten years had been polite on the surface and vicious underneath. He had seen her drunk and scared, all of her Atlanta polish gone, and that hadn't seemed to faze him. He had even let her goad him, repeatedly, without exploding into anything like a violent tantrum.

All that, and he had touched her anyway.

More than touched her, he'd turned her inside out with sheer joy.

He pretended to be so cold, but up in that bed, Griffin had showed her the truth about him. He'd trusted her, too.

No one else in her life ever had.

Mariah didn't sleep as the plane took her closer and closer to the end of the line, because she didn't want to miss a single second of what might be all that was left of her life.

Griffin will come, she told herself fiercely. *He'll come.*

But if he didn't . . .

She wished she had more time. She wished she'd spent what time she'd had better, too. She wished she hadn't let all that distance grow between her and her family, so confident that sometime, somewhere, there'd be some far-off future when she could fix it.

She wished and she wished, but no matter how hard or how fervently, the plane still landed in Atlanta early the next morning.

No Alaska Force men waited for her as the plane emptied. No reassuring officials surrounded them as they walked through the airport.

It was all too tempting to give in to that knotted, panicked weight in her gut and give up in defeat.

Mariah didn't let that happen. Griffin would find her. She trusted him, even now.

The man shoved her into a car he'd left in a long-term parking lot and drove her out of the Atlanta airport. He headed away from the city instead of into it, driving south. He drove for about forty-five minutes, then took an exit toward one of Georgia's many small towns made of tidy brick buildings and lush greenery. He kept going through what passed for the town center, then pulled off the narrow two-lane country road onto a dirt track.

He stopped when the road was no longer visible. And it was suddenly hard for Mariah to breathe. She longed to put her hand to her throat, to check that she was still alive, pulse kicking, but she didn't dare move.

"You're getting in the trunk," he told her when he turned the car off.

And she was relieved.

Actually *relieved* that he hadn't pulled off the road into this deserted middle-of-nowhere to do something far worse.

It took her long moments to realize he was waiting. Watching her.

He didn't move, but Mariah got the distinct impression that he *wanted* her to fight. He wanted her to argue, or make a grab for the car keys, or do *something*— because then he could really hurt her.

She didn't understand why, if that was what he wanted, he didn't go ahead and do it already.

"You can't be serious," she whispered, every upsetting movie she'd ever seen running through her head. Liam Neeson whispering about particular skills. Blue gravely telling their self-defense class that you always fought—you never let them take you to a second location. That you ended them, the situation, or yourself, then and there.

All of that wound around inside her, choking her as surely as an allergic reaction.

"Get out of the car, bitch," the man said calmly.

So calmly.

It made her shake. But Mariah fumbled for her door

and pushed it open, because if she didn't, he'd hit her. And if he hit her, he might keep hitting her.

And that could only end badly. He might knock her unconscious. He might hurt her a lot worse whether she was unconscious or not. And either way, he'd almost certainly find the phone.

Which would lead to more hurt, for both her and her mother. And would lose her the only potential ace she had up her sleeve.

So she pushed the heavy door open with her foot and climbed out of the car, feeling like she had stepped outside herself. The humid wallop of the Georgia air made her feel unpleasantly flushed at once, and the creepy brown hair of the wig she'd been wearing for much too long now stuck to the back of her neck.

She wanted to throw up. Instead, she obediently walked to the back of the boring-looking sedan and stood there like some kind of nauseated, terrified sheep.

Her captor only stared at her, one brawny arm lifted up to hold the trunk wide open, a violent glitter in his flat gaze.

"You either get in or I knock you out and put you in." He looked bored by the whole situation. "I don't care which."

Everything in Mariah screamed at her to *do* something. Run off into the trees. Head for the water. It was a Saturday. Surely there'd be someone around. Or maybe she could get her hands up so she could move in and palm strike him right in his nose, hopefully incapacitating him.

She needed to do something—anything—to stay out of that trunk.

"You have three seconds," the man told her. "If you

make me chase you, your mother loses a body part. If you try to come at me, she loses two. If you argue with me again or even look at me funny, she loses a piece and you do, too. And let's be real clear, bitch. I'll enjoy it."

Mariah chose the trunk.

She pitched herself forward and caught herself with a jarring thud, but then crawled inside—fast—because the last thing she wanted was to be bent over like some kind of invitation. She broke out in nauseated goose bumps at the image, scrabbling her legs in behind her and rolling so she could see him.

As if seeing him coming would make it better.

Her vision was narrowing and she could taste her own panic, metallic and choking. She curled herself into a kind of protective ball when the man moved.

But all he did was slam the trunk shut, leaving her in the close, hot darkness.

And Mariah freaked out.

There was no prettier way to put it. She couldn't breathe. Her heart was exploding in her chest. She was afraid she might pee her own pants, or worse. Even more terrifying, she wasn't sure she cared. It was stiflingly hot in the trunk, she was as sweaty as her stomach was greasy with terror, and the more she focused on everything that was wrong, the worse it got.

Maybe she blacked out. She couldn't tell. There was noise in her head, and she could hear a kind of whimpering sound. It took her long, scared moments to realize the sound was coming from her. She was making that animal noise.

She had to shove her hands over her mouth to stop it.

The car started up again, and that was worse. She could feel every bump of the old dirt road as her abductor turned the car around, then every pothole and jarring bump when he started down the road again.

She felt like she was in a coffin.

But you aren't, she reminded herself. *Not just yet.*

She tugged the awful, sweltering wig off of her head. That was marginally better. She felt around the trunk, but it was empty. And she saw the dim glow of the emergency release lever Blue had told them about but she'd never had occasion to see with her own eyes before.

Mariah ran through her options quickly, but they all came back to the same place. Her mother. There would be no flinging herself out of the trunk and hoping she didn't break her leg, because she had no doubt at all that the man would keep right on driving so he could hurt her mother himself.

She wanted to live. She wanted out of this trunk.

But she couldn't do either of those things at her mother's expense.

And then she remembered her phone. *Her phone.*

She wrestled it out of her pocket, biting her lips to keep from sobbing out her joy. The car rocked her around as she swiped at the screen to power it on, then waited for the phone to find service.

Mariah wanted to make a call more than she wanted to breathe, but she didn't dare. It would comfort her to hear a friendly voice, or really any voice at all, but it was too risky when she didn't know if the man could hear her.

And besides, she wasn't sure her throat worked at the moment, all thick and tight with fear.

She scrolled to Griffin's number, which he'd given her—reluctantly—in one of their situation meetings at Caradine's restaurant.

And something in Mariah hardened as she remembered that first meeting with Griffin. Or shifted, anyway.

She refused to believe that she would never see Grizzly Harbor again.

Or him.

She refused to accept that this was the end, no matter how maudlin she was tempted to get.

And she refused—she absolutely refused—to believe that Griffin wasn't on his way to save her, even now.

In the trunk of a gray Honda Accord heading south of Atlanta, she texted him, fighting to keep from dropping the phone as the car bumped along. Stopped outside of Brooks, then drove on dirt for a while. Now sounds like a highway.

The car sped up, and that was better for Mariah. Smoother.

He hasn't hurt me yet. They have my mother.

She stopped her frantic typing then, panting in the close confines of the trunk. And she believed he was coming. She believed.

But just in case, she added, If you don't make it in time, I would do it all over again.

Then she hit send.

Fifteen

They left Alaska after delivering Rory to the hospital in Juneau and briefing the rest of the team, and were wheels down in Atlanta by six o'clock the next morning, local time. Meaning it was two in the morning in their bodies. But they were all used to handling time zone changes. There was nothing for Griffin to do but suck up the situation he'd caused.

The situation he wasn't sure he could fix.

Isaac had been in communication with their people in Atlanta throughout the flight, so they were good to go when they hit the ground. Oz reported that Rory was mostly thirsty and pissed, which was a good thing. But it was a grim, tight rollout from the plane to the SUV in Atlanta, because everyone involved was fully aware of what was at stake for Mariah—who hadn't been left behind, shoved carelessly into a shed.

And they still hadn't found her.

Mariah's apartment was empty. There was no sign that

anyone had been there in weeks. The rooms were shut up tight, the air was stale, and, as the Atlanta satellite team had assured them, there had been no security breaches since they'd started monitoring the place weeks ago.

Griffin hadn't expected to find her there. Someone had taken her from Alaska. And there was no reason he could think of that anyone would abduct her only to head to an Atlanta apartment building, with its high concentration of potentially nosy neighbors.

Though he didn't really want to consider what might cause the sorts of noises bad men would want to conceal from the neighbors.

He refused to let himself think about it.

Their next stop was Mariah's ex-husband's monstrosity of a house. It was set back from the winding road and hidden behind pretentious gates that were clearly there for show, not real security. Blue and Jonas melted around the edge of the property to access the back. Griffin and Isaac went in the front.

It was always amazing to Griffin what regular people could sleep through.

Fifteen minutes later they knew more about David Lanier than anyone needed or wanted, thanks to both of the women he had sleeping in his bed with him. And the resentful, mutinous staff in the kitchen, who had no qualms about ripping their boss apart in Spanish while they thought they were alone.

But Mariah certainly wasn't one of those women crashed out in her ex's bed. Nor was she rolling her eyes as she talked smack about him over coffee with the gardener. They couldn't find her anywhere in the house.

And the fact that her ex was snoozing away his Saturday morning with last night's conquests didn't mean he *wasn't* behind Mariah's abduction. But it didn't feel right.

"We could check his friends and favorite haunts," Isaac said tersely when they were back in the SUV. "Maybe he stashed her somewhere, like one of those re-markably shiny golf trophies."

"He belongs to a lot of country clubs," Griffin replied, forcing his jaw to work despite the way he was clenching it. "But however much they might like a full roster of nothing but white-collar criminals, I think they might frown on being used as part of an abduction."

"Will it look like an abduction?" Jonas shrugged when Griffin glared at him. "You heard what Ernie said. He took them for a married couple. She's a chameleon."

Jonas and Isaac exchanged looks. Griffin figured they were bonding over the kind of blending in to enemy ter-ritory they'd both done over the years. The kind of blend-ing Griffin had always done was different. He knew how to be mistaken for rock, not . . . an Atlanta society prin-cess on a seaplane jaunt to Anchorage.

His jaw ached.

"What about her hometown?" Isaac asked when he and Jonas were done silently congratulating themselves on their Delta Force days. Assuming that was what Jonas had done in the service. "I feel like a guy who camps out for weeks in Grizzly Harbor and takes advantage of the one time she had a watch change in the middle of the night might like the symmetry of it. If this is connected to her marrying that dumbass, the hometown might make sense."

It took Griffin a minute to realize they were all star-ing at him, waiting for him to sign off on this. And much as he might want to tell himself it was because he'd done

Mariah's intake and had assumed command of her case, he was pretty sure that wasn't the reason.

But that was one more thing he wasn't talking about.

"Why not?" he gritted out. "Nothing about this makes sense."

It was supposed to be a solid three-hour drive from the ex-husband's house deep in to rural Georgia, where Mariah had grown up. The way Isaac drove, Griffin figured they'd make it in more like two.

It gave him just enough time to deal with himself.

Or try to, anyway.

He kept trying to slow himself down and box himself back up. He'd spent his entire adult life packing himself away into separate internal compartments, and he liked it that way. He liked *him* that way. Over time, he'd developed a foolproof system of padlocks and heavy steel doors to keep things where they belonged.

There was no cross-contamination. There were no feelings that started in one compartment and poisoned the whole.

Machines ran on proper fuel and maintenance, not feelings.

But today he couldn't seem to get a handle on himself no matter what he did. He was all temper and fury, running hot and much too intense, and he might have been worried about what was happening to him if he hadn't been a whole lot more worried about Mariah.

Griffin had failed completely. It wasn't only that he'd let sex get in the way like some punk. It was much worse than that. Mariah had become a distraction to him. He'd let that happen, day after day. And that was a piss-poor excuse for missing the fact that some jackhole had been trailing her the entire time she'd been in Grizzly Harbor.

They'd all missed him. As far as they could tell, he'd come in on the same ferry Mariah had taken and settled in to one of the rental cabins in the woods, claiming he was a writer on a creative retreat. No one had thought twice about him.

But thinking twice was Griffin's responsibility.

Any inventory he took of his behavior since the day Mariah had showed up tallied up the same way. He'd missed everything. He'd been wrong about her, but that wasn't likely to kill her. That was simply more evidence of what a bastard he'd been, pretty consistently, since he'd first laid eyes on her.

That he'd been wrong about the threat against her, on the other hand, might have already killed her.

It had been almost twenty-four solid hours. They'd tracked her to Anchorage and assumed she'd headed to Atlanta, but there were a whole lot of ways to get there, and not all of them direct. She could have been taken anywhere. She could *be* anywhere right now, in any condition.

He wasn't sure he could breathe through it—and until today, he would have said he could breathe through anything.

"This isn't on you," Isaac said, an hour into the drive.

Griffin automatically checked his six, but Jonas and Blue were sacked out in the back and snoring, because soldiers slept wherever they could. Whenever they could.

Griffin didn't look at Isaac when he turned back. He kept his gaze trained on the two-lane highway in front of them. "You told me I was acting crazy. You were right."

"Sure. But everything isn't all one thing or the other. There are gray areas."

All his locks and steel walls were melting, compartments flying open and slamming into each other, and Griffin didn't know how he was sitting upright with all that agony tearing his ribs apart. If this was a gray area, he wanted no part of it.

"Maybe for you. I either make a shot or I don't. It's that stark, brother. Every time."

"You're going to make the shot, Griffin. You always do."

That was supposed to be encouraging, Griffin guessed. He could do without it. It made his skin feel like it was peeling back off his bones, exposing all the muck beneath.

He'd survived a whole lot of terrible things in his lifetime. It was his job. His calling, even. But he didn't know how he would survive this.

"Besides," Isaac was saying, as if nothing out of the ordinary was happening in the passenger seat, "you didn't make the call. I did. I could have ordered you straight back to the inn when you showed up at my front door like a wild man before dawn. And I could have overruled your request for a shift in our approach. I didn't."

"You operated on intelligence I gave you. Faulty intelligence."

Isaac sighed as he sped up to get around a slow pickup truck.

"I hope you're having fun up there on your cross, friend. I hear martyrdom is real entertaining."

Griffin entertained himself the next few miles by imagining all the ways he could kill—or at least stun—Isaac without even breaking a sweat or necessarily crashing the vehicle. And when he'd finally soothed himself enough to break through the murderous red haze that wasn't helping anybody, his phone buzzed in his pocket.

He pulled it out, expecting it to be an update from Oz, then froze.

"She's alive," he told Isaac.

Isaac belted out a command that had both men in the backseat sitting up straight and alert before he was done.

"Alive and unhurt, for now, but in the trunk of a Honda Accord," Griffin told them, staring down at his phone while everything in him roared. *She was alive.* "Headed south into the woods. And they have her mother."

He heard Blue flip open his tablet, and knew without having to ask that he was getting Oz on that Honda Accord. And the GPS coordinates to Mariah's phone, which they hadn't been able to lock in on before now, suggesting she'd had it turned off all this time.

Griffin relayed the rest of the information in the text, except for the last line.

That was his.

Though the heat that moved through him because of it was shame. And guilt.

Because it was ridiculous that she would want to repeat anything that ended with her in the trunk of a car.

He only hoped he had the opportunity to tell her how ridiculous it was.

To her face.

And soon.

Isaac kept driving, even faster than before.

It took Oz minutes to find Mariah's phone. Jonas calculated the change in their direction, directing Isaac off the main roads and into the spiderweb of back roads that laced the rural Georgia countryside.

"We're about twenty miles outside Two Oaks," he said from the backseat. "And headed away from the crossroads that marks the town center."

"It makes sense." Blue levered himself forward. "Whoever's doing this—and I'm thinking it's the husband less and less—they're zeroing in on her family."

"It pains me to admit it," Griffin agreed, "but I don't like the husband for this at all."

And he didn't need anyone to chime in then to remind him what that meant. That they had nothing. That Mariah was in the trunk of a car and they didn't know who was doing it or why.

But at least they knew where.

Griffin was going to have to be happy with that.

Isaac kept a ten-mile cushion between them and the signal from Mariah's phone. And when the signal finally stopped bumping its way deeper into the countryside, he moved in closer, then pulled over to the side of the road so they could rustle up intel. There was no need to go in hot and make everything worse than it already was.

It was the same protocol they would use in any situation, but this was the first time in Griffin's memory that he felt each second that dragged by like fingers digging into his throat.

Deeper and then deeper still.

Oz sent satellite images of the big falling-down red barn out in the middle of the woods where Mariah's signal was holding steady. The perfect place to take someone, Griffin thought, as they all stood outside the car on the quiet dirt lane. He adjusted the strap that held his rifle in place as if that, too, were choking him.

"We need to get eyes inside," Isaac was saying. "We need to get eyes on Mariah. And I don't think we want to wait for dark."

"We're not waiting," Griffin bit out.

And he knew how bad it all was when no one even bothered to throw him any side-eye for leapfrogging the chain of command or throwing his weight around.

He didn't care.

Isaac found a better place to stash the vehicle, and then the four of them set out, making their way through the woods the way they'd trained a thousand times before. It was a good five-mile hike, but it was flat here. Easy.

No snow and, better yet, no bears.

When they reached the clearing where the barn was located, Isaac gave the signal, and they fanned out.

Griffin knew what he was supposed to do. He knew it made sense to follow the established protocol, the way they had at the ex's house. Do some recon, get a sense of what was going down and how many people were involved, ascertain proof of life, and then consult with his brothers before doing anything rash.

He'd never done anything rash in his life, until Mariah.

But once it was clear the two guards ambling around the field in a lazy patrol were the entirety of the security system, he didn't have it in him to wait.

"I need a diversion to the southwest," he said under his breath on their comm channel.

"Negative, dumbass," Blue growled back, from his position to the southwest.

"I need it now," Griffin retorted, already moving.

He heard Blue curse. And he didn't have to hear Isaac or Jonas to know they shared Blue's feelings on this.

Griffin cared about one thing, and she was inside that barn.

He scaled the tree before him, then swung out on one of the wide upper branches. He crouched where he was, waiting.

Because Blue might curse, but he wouldn't leave Griffin hanging.

There was a sudden, loud sound from the southwest quadrant. It sounded like a heavy branch cracking—or someone cracking a heavy branch—and it easily got the attention of the two men patrolling the clearing. They whirled toward the disturbance, guns high, and moved in. Fast.

Behind them, on the far side of the barn, Griffin jumped.

He aimed for the questionable, patchy roof of the barn, spreading himself out as he went to make sure he landed lightly. He rolled almost before he hit, spreading out his body mass and getting the hell away from the point of impact in case anyone was waiting for him.

The roll took him toward the edge of the roof, and he didn't wait for the guards down below to start paying more attention to their surroundings than to a mysterious noise in the woods. He swung himself down and straight through the looming opening high up on the barn's side that he assumed had something to do with hay.

He landed the way he always did, light and easy, the weight of his rifle a comfort against his back, the way it was supposed to be. Then he waited for his eyes to adjust.

When they did, he found himself in a loft that ran the

length of the barn. There was no hay, though he couldn't tell if the dirt everywhere suggested it had once been here. There were rusted old farm implements shoved haphazardly against the walls and unidentifiable mounds covered in tarps.

And in the center, near an open trapdoor that led to the ground floor, was a woman duct-taped to a chair.

It isn't Mariah.

It wasn't Mariah, he told himself sternly a split second after his adrenaline kicked in like an elbow to his sternum.

And he would have known it was Mariah's mother even if he hadn't seen pictures or that video on Mariah's laptop back in Grizzly Harbor. It was the narrow way the woman stared at him, as if she were gathering her wits before handling the armed man who'd just swung in to her hayloft.

Rose Ellen McKenna reminded him of her daughter in other ways, too. Suspicious blue eyes, a mutinous chin, and no apparent fear when she should have been pale with it.

Griffin didn't move. He was listening while he held her gaze, trying to figure out who else was in this barn and, more important, where they were.

"Where is she?" he asked, his voice barely a whisper.

Rose Ellen had duct tape over her mouth, but angled her head toward the floor below them with a certain regal air that Griffin recognized all too well.

He started to make his way across the loft, going carefully because he didn't trust the wood beneath his feet not to creak and give him away. When he got close to Rose Ellen, he squatted down beside her and did a quick check for injuries. He found a few bruises, but nothing serious. And no blood.

She could still be hurt, of course. But he didn't think she required medical attention.

"I'm going to get you out of here," he promised her. "But I need to get Mariah out, too, so I might have to leave you up here and come back while I figure out how to do that. Do you understand?"

Rose Ellen nodded decisively. And something else flashed in her gaze that Griffin recognized all too well. Sheer fury. Like Mariah's mother wanted to tear herself out of this chair and go handle whoever was downstairs herself.

He related.

"There are two men outside," Griffin said quietly, right next to her ear. "I need to know how many more are inside. Nod when I get there."

He lifted up a finger. Then another. Then one more, and she nodded.

Griffin eased himself over to the trapdoor opening and peered down, but he couldn't see anyone. He could only hear them. Male voices, laughing with a sort of low, easy malice.

He turned back to catch Rose Ellen's gaze, and waited until she nodded at him. Then he carefully, slowly moved back over to the far part of the loft so he could look outside and get eyes on the two men who had taken up their patrol again.

He spoke quietly into his comm. "The mother is here and unharmed. There are three douchebags downstairs plus the two outside. I can't see Mariah without exposing myself."

"Five on four isn't a fair fight," Jonas complained from his position to the east. "I can take five by myself. Where's the fun in that?"

"I get the impression there'll be fun to go around," Blue chimed in. "Not much I enjoy more than relieving an idiot of his AR-15."

"All I've seen so far is hired muscle," Griffin said. "Which means that even if we relieve them all, we're still going to have a problem. We don't know who's paying for this party."

Griffin stayed in position but eased his head through the opening. Nothing had changed. A pretty day, a green field and greener trees, and no one in sight except the two goons. Now jumpier than before.

He shook his head as he ducked back into the shadows. "I don't think you cart someone across the country to hang out with hired muscle in a barn."

"Agreed," Blue said.

Jonas made a low sound that Griffin interpreted as his agreement.

"Unless you hear something in there that changes the game, I think we wait," Isaac said finally, once again making the call.

Once again based on Griffin's intelligence.

But this time he had no intention of leaving Mariah out to dry.

Everyone muttered affirmatives, and then they all settled into radio silence.

Griffin spent another long while listening, tracking the sounds until he'd come up with a map of where the men were down below. He couldn't hear Mariah, but he also didn't hear anything that suggested she was being abused in any way.

If he had, he would have kicked a hole in the floor and gone down shooting.

When he moved again, his eyes were fully adjusted to the gloom of the barn's interior. He walked the length of the loft once more, keeping his gaze trained to the significant cracks between the floorboards.

And this time, he saw her.

Mariah was tied to a chair of her own, also with duct tape. Her head was slumped forward slightly, making her hair a kind of wild blond curtain around her face. He couldn't see any evidence of a gag, but that didn't mean they hadn't shoved anything in her mouth.

And when he stopped and stared hard, he could see that she kept testing the duct tape around her wrists and ankles.

If she was hurt, she wasn't too hurt to keep looking for a way out.

And Griffin took the first deep, real breath he'd allowed himself since he'd realized she was missing.

The three douchebags were arranged around her. One was sitting with his feet thrust out before him like he was at a picnic, his back to an old stall. The big, burly one with a beard was muttering into his phone and pacing. And all Griffin could see of the third one was a hint of his boots as he walked back and forth in front of the barn's big doors, suggesting he was the guard.

When he satisfied himself with what he could see through the floorboards, he carefully made his way back to Mariah's mother, crouched down before her again, and eased the duct tape gag from between her lips.

She swallowed and worked her jaw. He knew from experience that she was trying to make her mouth feel like hers again.

Then she leveled those eyes that were entirely too much like her daughter's at him.

It felt like a blow.

"Tell me why I shouldn't scream and let them know you're here, whoever the hell you are."

Her voice was raspier, but it was the same honey-and-cream drawl that made a meal out of every word and then some.

Griffin didn't shift his gaze from hers. "Because you want to live."

"Not sure that's on the menu, sugar."

Sugar. He felt the last of the barriers he'd built inside himself crumble, and he didn't fight it. Not there in a sweaty Georgia hayloft with a woman who looked too much like Mariah but wasn't her.

He wanted to hear Mariah call him *sugar* again, assuming she lived through this.

Griffin intended to make sure she did.

"Did they hurt you?"

"It didn't feel real good to get bashed over the head and tossed in the back of a pickup truck, but that's any old Friday night around these parts." Rose Ellen's mouth curved into a smile that didn't reach her eyes. "But no. They didn't really hurt me."

He nodded gruffly, happier to hear that news than maybe he should have been. And relieved in ways he didn't want to examine.

"Is she okay?" Rose Ellen asked, her voice scratchier than before. "I heard her when they brought her in, but . . ."

"She's okay, as far as I can tell from up here."

Rose Ellen swallowed again. "You're going to have to put that gag back in."

"I know." Griffin shifted his weight to his heels. "But not yet."

Rose Ellen's eyes gleamed as if she were fighting back emotion, but all she did was offer a jerky sort of nod.

And then they both settled in for the wait.

Sixteen

The whole kidnapping thing, horrifying from the start, wasn't getting any more fun as the hours dragged by.

Mariah was exhausted. More than exhausted. She wished she'd actually tried to sleep on the plane, where the man who'd abducted her couldn't actually have hurt her. Not in any serious way, surrounded by so many people. But she hadn't, and she knew that was making all the many ways she ached worse.

It had been bad in the trunk. Dark and bumpy and sweltering, and she kept slamming against the trunk's interior no matter how she tried to brace herself.

But it had been worse when the car stopped.

Her heart had pounded so hard she worried she might be sick, but there was nothing she could do. The engine turned off. She stayed where she was, curled up in a sweaty ball she knew perfectly well wouldn't protect her from anything, and waited for the man to come and open the trunk again.

When he finally did, the sudden shock of sunlight was so bright it made her eyes water.

And he wasn't alone.

They'd hauled her out of the trunk, and Mariah couldn't remember which one was which. It was all flat eyes and cruel faces, awful laughter, and worse, the sure knowledge that not one of them was going to help her. She kept hearing the same whimpering sound again and understood on some level that she was the one making it—but she couldn't do anything about it.

There were men all around her. Men in a Georgia field that she could tell, with old senses she hadn't used in years, was far away from everything. It was the silence. The breeze in the trees that carried no sounds from nearby roads. The way the men's unpleasant laughter seemed to spread out all around them. At first she thought there were crowds of them, big and scary men with that same dead look in their eyes, like a forest all their own.

It took Mariah a long time to downgrade from *crowds* to *maybe five*, but that wasn't much better.

One of them took hold of her with an unpleasant grip that wrenched her arm from her shoulder, and she blurred it out even as it was happening. There were too many of them for her to process anything too closely. It was as if her brain were curling itself into the fetal position when her body couldn't. Her head was pounding, there was a humming noise in her ears, and it was easier to think about death in the abstract. It was easy to sit on a plane and imagine you were accepting the inevitability of your own end . . .

But there was so much light everywhere. There was sunshine and the smell of home, honeysuckle and deep green mixed in with the rich smell of the Georgia dirt. There was the soft press of the humid air against her face, feeling cool and very nearly refreshing after the trunk. There was the salt in her mouth, tracking down from the water in her eyes, and all these things seemed like reasons enough to live.

She wanted to *live*.

They'd hauled her into a big empty barn, and one of them had shoved her, hard. Mariah should have expected it. The force of it knocked her straight off her feet, sending her tumbling for the floor, where she'd hit her face on the way down before she caught herself on her palms.

She'd been so dazed, it had taken her a long time to realize that what she'd hit was a metal folding chair, set out in the middle of the barn floor.

But she had Griffin's cool gaze in her head, watching her from the open door of the community center the way he had on so many afternoons. When she'd practiced situations like this over and over again. She heard Blue's voice in her ears, ordering her to get up. Now.

She wanted to crumple on the floor, bury her head in her arms, and cry for a year or two about the flaring pain across one cheekbone and the panic and fear that felt like more bruises all over her body.

But there were men behind her. Awful men wearing the same nasty, pitiless expression as the first one, and she didn't dare stay where she was.

She swiveled around as she rose, careful not to make it look like she was trying to do anything but get up quickly, because the fact that she'd practiced getting up off the floor—a lot—seemed like a good thing to keep to herself.

But none of them were actually paying any attention to her. Not really.

They have you. You're here. The voice inside her was far more matter of fact than she felt. *Why should they pay attention to you now?*

The men were talking to each other, but her head was filled with too much noisy chaos to hear what they were saying. The man who'd pushed her to the floor shoved her again, this time down into the chair. And he barely looked at her as he tied her to it, using strips of duct tape he ripped off with his yellowing teeth.

Mariah used it as an opportunity to count her blessings.

She was fully dressed and no one had seemed all that interested in changing that. No one had patted her down for any reason, which meant she still had her phone tucked into her pocket. She was still wearing a sweater over a T-shirt and jeans, and they'd tied her to the chair this way, suggesting no one was going to try to take her pants off.

Just now, anyway.

She tested the duct tape on her hands when the man walked away, wiggling it this way and that to see if she could loosen its hold. She couldn't.

The sound of her voice when she asked "Where's my mother?" electrified the cavernous space. It quieted all the men, and Mariah couldn't say she particularly enjoyed the way they all swiveled around to look at her. Each one of them more terrifying than the next.

Maybe it had been better when they hadn't paid her any specific attention. When they'd acted like she was nothing but an inanimate package someone had delivered.

"What did you say?" asked the man who had brought her here, in that oddly mild voice. The same one he'd used when he'd talked to her about the things he'd do if she defied him.

"I'm wondering where my mother is," Mariah said, and she sounded weird. So weird that if she hadn't felt herself speak, she might've doubted it was her at all.

It took her another moment to realize that she was shaking.

And she couldn't lift a hand to soothe herself the way she wanted.

"She's fine," the man said. "Or she's dead. Which do you want it to be?"

That didn't help. Mariah swallowed, hard.

"You should worry more about yourself, girly," one of the new men said, and the way he stared at her made her breath stutter to a stop in her chest.

But when she dropped her head as if she were overcome—mostly because she was—all that attention eventually drifted away from her.

Mariah braced for the next slap. For an actual punch. For some of the dread and threat that seemed to be weighing down her bones where she sat to burst, one way or another.

But nothing happened.

She watched the shadows move across the barn, tracking the way the sun fell through the wide-open door. She thought time was passing, though she couldn't tell for sure. They'd gotten off the plane sometime before eight. The last time she'd looked at the clock on her phone in that stifling trunk, it had been closer to noon.

The longer she waited with nothing awful happening, the easier it was to breathe. It wasn't that she stopped being afraid, but she was slowly able to make herself focus. She listened to the muttered conversation the man who had brought her here had on his phone, but she couldn't quite make out the words.

One of the other men carried the most enormous gun Mariah had ever seen in real life, and she'd grown up out in these woods, surrounded by hunters and gun enthusiasts of all shapes and sizes. The gun was worrying enough, but the tweaked-out way the man holding it was walking back and forth was truly disturbing.

Mariah knew a meth user when she saw one.

The third man in the barn, the one who'd shoved her, tied her up, and called her *girly*, was sitting down. He stared at her. A lot.

And unless she'd panic-hallucinated the whole thing, there were more men outside.

But still they waited.

Mariah kept her head tilted down for a while, then tilted it up for a change of pace.

"What are you looking at?" the staring man asked, a touch of Alabama in his voice and straight evil in his gaze. He followed her line of sight to the ceiling. "If you listen real good, I bet you can hear your mama sniffling up there. She's a feisty one. I'm wondering if it runs in the family."

Mariah had to bite down on her tongue to keep from screaming. For her mother, to her mother, or just to scream.

But whatever expression she wore on her face must have satisfied the man, because he let out a creepy giggle, and then resumed that dead-eyed stare.

Like he was already dead. Or she was.

And this time, when Mariah studied the battered old

ceiling above her, she could have sworn she saw a shadow move, almost as if Rose Ellen was up there wandering around.

If she was, God help these men.

Mama was the one who had taught Mariah how to shoot when she was seven.

More time dragged past. Mariah had to go to the bathroom, but she refused to ask. She didn't want to introduce the idea of pulling down her pants.

And she didn't understand how she could be bored and terrified at the same time, but this was a long day of unpleasant firsts.

She didn't want to call attention to herself—or no more attention than she was already gathering simply by being the guest of honor, tied up in the middle of the room. She sang herself songs inside her head. She recited every prayer she knew, and came up with quite a few new ones.

The shadows lengthened. She could see a difference in the way the sun hit the field outside and the way it moved through the big trees on the far side.

"It's time," growled the man who'd brought her here.

Mariah shifted instantly from a sleepy sort of daze—with nothing to do but contemplate shadows and recite song lyrics in her head—to total alertness. She braced herself again, as if that could help her if they decided it was time to really start hurting her.

The staring man giggled, then rolled himself up into a squat, so close she could smell him. Old fish and motor oil. She didn't know how she kept from wrinkling her nose in disgust.

"Soon, girly," he crooned.

She fought off the shudder she felt deep in her gut,

like everything inside her was on a roller coaster and there was no getting off.

"You can scream your head off," her original abductor told her, flashing her an impatient sort of look that didn't take away from the flatness of his gaze. Nothing did. "No one will hear you. No one will come. And the only thing you'll manage to do is piss us off. So go right ahead."

And then the men walked out, pulling the barn door shut behind them.

Leaving Mariah in the gloom.

She fought to *think*, though she wasn't sure that in her present condition she would be able to tell if she was being the least bit rational or not . . . but she didn't have to be rational to work to free her hands. Twisting and turning her wrists this way and that, she tried her hardest to loosen the grasp of the duct tape. She wanted to call out to her mother in the hopes that she could hear, that she wasn't unconscious or worse, but Mariah didn't know where the men had gone or when they might be coming back.

Was this a test? Were they standing right there on the other side of the door, waiting for her to make a noise so they had an excuse to start . . . doing things to her?

Her breath was a shuddery thing over her lips. She was working up a sweat and no doubt tearing open her wrists as she fought to loosen the duct tape, but she didn't stop. She couldn't stop.

If she could get it to go slack, even the slightest bit, surely she could pull her wrists through—

"Mariah."

She jerked. Then blinked.

She must have died.

Her heart was so painful in her chest that she assumed that was the explanation.

She must have simply . . . up and keeled over, right here in this chair.

That was the only reason she could think of to explain how Griffin Cisneros was standing in front of her, scowling down at her, as if this were any old afternoon in Grizzly Harbor and he'd appeared to walk her from Blue's class to her room at the inn.

"You're hurt."

She had seen him cold. Grim, even. Rough and still and sometimes mean.

But Mariah had never seen anything like the darkness that moved over Griffin's face then. He reached out and brushed his fingers over her cheek, and that felt real. Too real. She'd forgotten that she'd fallen until he touched her there, and it was unfair that she could feel a bruise coming in when she was already dead.

Not to mention the sweetness of his hand on her.

"I'm fine," she said. "My mother . . . ?"

She couldn't bear to finish the question. But he nodded as if she had.

"She's upstairs. And as far as I can tell, she's also fine."

And he crouched down in front of her, his expression fierce and focused entirely on her. It occurred to Mariah that the last time she'd seen him, he had been in her bed.

She could feel the warmth of the backs of his fingers against her cheekbone. That drugging, comforting warmth of his skin. She felt entirely too warm herself, suddenly.

And it dawned on her that she might not have died after all.

"I knew you would come," she whispered. "I knew it."

If he had been another man, she would have called what washed over him then pure anguish. But this was Griffin. And the emotion was gone again so fast she almost thought she'd imagined it.

He looked stern. "We both know how this happened. It was my blunder. But I promise you, I'll make up for it."

"I love you," Mariah said.

She felt delirious, only worse. She'd been sure she was dead two seconds ago. The likelihood was still that she would be dead a few moments from now. There were men with semiautomatic weapons roaming around, and every one of them had looked at her as if they couldn't wait for the opportunity to tear her apart with their own hands. She had been awake and more or less alert—and scared—for at least twenty-four hours.

There was almost no possibility that she was in her right mind. Mariah accepted that.

And still, the minute she said those words, she knew they were true. She loved him.

She said it again, just to be sure.

Griffin dropped his fingers from her face. But he didn't rise from where he was crouched down before her, looking dark and furious and emanating all that leashed brutality. He rested his elbows on his powerful thighs and regarded her sternly.

She might have said he had no expression on his face, but she had made a study of him. She could see that what burned in his eyes when he looked at her wasn't impassive at all.

"That's the abduction talking."

"It's really not."

"I'm still in love with every man who ever delivered

me safely from a war zone," he told her, his voice clipped—but his eyes gleaming. "It goes with the territory."

"Did you have sex with all those men?" When he scowled at her, Mariah smiled. She didn't realize until that moment that she hadn't expected she would ever get the chance to smile again. It made it that much sweeter. Or bittersweet, maybe. "Because I'm betting that sex changes the equation. I'm pretty good at math. You should trust me on this."

"We don't have time for this." His hands moved to test the duct tape at her wrists. Her calves. "As far as I can tell, our friends have headed out there to have a discussion about payment with whoever just drove up in that Mercedes with tinted windows. But sooner or later they're going to come back in. We need to be gone by then."

"Get my mother out first."

Griffin's hands were already working, pulling apart the duct tape that held her to the chair, and then inspecting the damage she'd done to her wrists when she pulled free. But Mariah hardly noticed a few more abrasions.

"You have to get my mother out," she said again, fiercely. "It's my fault she's here in the first place."

"It's not your fault I went out to greet a stranger on my land without a rifle in my hand," a familiar voice said.

So familiar that Mariah's whole body jerked in recognition almost before she'd processed it herself. She twisted in her chair, only dimly aware that Griffin was muttering curses in a language she didn't understand. She felt tugging at her calves as he handled the duct tape there, too, but she was already standing, then stumbling across the barn floor.

Her legs felt useless, thick and sound asleep, as if she'd never learned how to walk. But that didn't stop her from tilting herself toward the woman who stood there at the bottom of the ladder Mariah hadn't seen behind her.

She fell into her mother's arms like she was starved for it. Like she was a child again, with a skinned knee that only her mama could cure.

And just like when Mariah was a child, Rose Ellen held her tight, rocked her, then set her back on her heels.

"No time for that now," Mama said in her matter-of-fact way, though her eyes were suspiciously bright. "I don't intend to spend one more minute in this barn than I have to."

Griffin was standing by the chair, his head angled slightly to one side, a faraway look in his dark eyes. When he focused on them again, Mariah realized that he'd been listening to voices in his ear.

"Let's go," he said, all business now.

It made her love him all the more.

He started toward the back of the barn and a dark corner where a big chunk of the wall was kicked in. Leaving a big old hole in the side.

Escape, an urgent voice whispered in Mariah.

She'd started following Griffin automatically, but something had her twisting around to look behind her.

Where her mother was following her, or trying to, but was moving much too slowly.

Because she was limping. Badly.

Mariah opened her mouth to get Griffin's attention, but he was already brushing past her and heading toward her mother.

"You told me you weren't hurt," he said in a low voice,

with an undercurrent that might have been temper if he'd been a different kind of man. One less capable and lethal.

"Didn't know I was until I tried to walk." Mama shrugged. "The skinny blond one has steel-toed boots. I don't regret kicking him, mind, but it hurt like hell when he kicked me back. Now I know why."

Mariah watched, filled with a mute dread, as Griffin dropped down in front of Rose Ellen, then smoothed his hands down her leg. He tugged the leg of her jeans up to look beneath. Mariah couldn't see past his broad shoulders and back. But she knew when she heard a tiny hiss of indrawn breath that it wasn't good.

"I don't think the bone is shattered," Griffin said after a moment. Gruffly. "But I don't think you can run anywhere on this."

Mama was looking straight at Mariah as he spoke. Mariah watched the way her chin lifted. She saw the familiar light of battle gleaming in her mother's eyes.

"I'll run if I have to," Mama said, like it was a prophecy she had every intention of fulfilling.

Mariah knew she meant it. And that she'd do it, even if she injured herself more in the process. That was what being a McKenna was all about.

But Griffin was talking. And not to them.

He relayed the injury into his earpiece, then waited, his gaze shrewd and intense as he looked from the opening in the wall in the back of the barn, then toward the chair and the front again.

He did that a few times, and then he stiffened, his expression going sharp.

"ETA?" he barked.

And Mariah didn't need him to translate what *ETA*

meant while he scowled at the door all those men had gone through.

They were coming back. With reinforcements from the Mercedes, if Mariah had to guess.

They'd been waiting for hours. Mariah didn't want to stick around to see what was in store for her now that the waiting was done.

She wanted to throw herself out of that hole in the wall and run for it, more than she'd ever wanted anything else in her life. She could *taste* it.

But Mama couldn't run.

Mariah was closest to the opening in the wall, and she could see out of it. The barn sat in the middle of a field that stretched off toward the woods. But the woods weren't right there on the other side of the barn wall. The tree line—and safety—had to be a good two hundred yards away.

And she had always been such a coward. Hadn't she proved it time and again?

This, here, was her chance to be brave.

She was going to take it.

"Mama can't run," Mariah said, a kind of peace coming over her as she spoke. A lot like when she'd told him she loved him. "You're going to have to carry her."

"We need to move," Griffin said, rising to his feet with a smoothness that made her breath hitch. "We just ran out of time."

"You need to carry her," Mariah said more calmly. "And if you're carrying her, I have to think that's going to slow even you down. What's going to happen when they walk in here and I'm not sitting there in that chair?"

"Over my dead body," Griffin seethed at her, like he knew where she was going with this.

"They're going to chase you. Us. It's not like any of your friends are going to start shooting if they might hit us. But these men will. And they'll enjoy it, trust me."

"I said no."

She smiled at him, this beautiful man who was looking at her like he wanted to sling her over his shoulder and end the conversation that way. He probably would have if he hadn't had to carry her mother, too.

"I can occupy them, Griffin. You'll have plenty of time to get Mama out of the line of fire."

She saw his jaw work. She saw his dark eyes burn. And she told herself she would hold on to that, whatever happened next.

"Mariah."

It was a whisper. A surrender from this man who never, ever gave in. And she knew what it cost him.

"I'm a princess," she reminded him, and it was funny how her voice thickened. How it scratched. "I do what I want, remember?"

She didn't want to say good-bye to him. She couldn't. She forced herself to move past him and stopped when her mother reached out to grab her arm. Or maybe they grabbed each other, holding on tight for a moment that couldn't have been more than a few seconds but felt like a lifetime.

They didn't say good-bye, either.

Mariah threw herself toward the chair again, her gaze blurry but her heart clear.

"Mariah." This time it was a command. She stopped moving, though she didn't turn back to face him. She knew that if she did, she wouldn't go through with this. "You're going to have the opportunity to run. When you do, take it. Promise me."

"I will," she whispered. "I promise."

"Run when you can," he said again, his tone like a caress and a demand at once. Beautiful and harsh. Just like him. "As fast as you can."

Mariah nodded once, jerkily, and then she kept going. She made it to the chair and wrapped herself back up in the duct tape he'd loosened, hoping it looked as if she were still secured.

Then she tried to make herself breathe.

She heard voices on the other side of the barn door. She heard a car door slam.

And she didn't think *brave* was supposed to feel like this. Like she might be sick. Or faint. Or sob.

She snuck a look over her shoulder, but Griffin and her mother were already gone.

And then the barn door was scraping open and there were cold-eyed men everywhere again, and she didn't have time to worry about how brave felt.

She just had to do it.

Especially when the man in the center of the ugly scrum stepped forward and smiled, big and wide, because she knew him.

Dear God, she knew him.

And it wasn't David.

Seventeen

Griffin gritted out a request for cover and potential cover fire into his comm and barely heard the terse affirmatives in reply. Then he ducked down and swept Rose Ellen up and into his arms, shifting her over one shoulder into a fireman's carry with the ease of long practice involving much heavier soldiers.

"Hold on," he told her, when her breath left her in a rush.

He didn't look back.

Not because he trusted Mariah to execute her role like she was an acting member of Alaska Force today, but because he couldn't. He'd never felt that *thing* in his chest before, like a balloon with an ache that kept getting bigger and bigger. . . .

Everything Mariah had said made sense. He couldn't abandon her mother. A decoy was a solid plan.

And he wanted to tear this barn down with his hands instead of leaving her in it.

Griffin knew that if he looked back at her, he wouldn't do it. He wouldn't leave her for even one second more.

He moved to the wall instead, then eased his way out between the rotted old planks, taking care not to slam Rose Ellen's head into the jagged wood. He trusted his brothers to handle any enemy eyes, so he didn't waste time looking around. He took off for the tree line, running as fast as he could while carrying the weight of another human.

He was aware of his heart and the way it beat, strong and true. He was aware of his breath, in and out of his lungs as he moved. He was aware of every inch of the body he'd made into a machine, and how every part worked exactly as it should.

There was nothing but his breath. The weight of Rose Ellen.

And the trees ahead of him, beckoning him to safety.

It felt like it took him an hour to sprint some two hundred yards, but it was likely a handful of seconds.

When he penetrated the forest, he kept going until he was sure there was enough cover. Only then did he stop, shifting to let Rose Ellen down. He helped her stand on that bad leg. And then he checked in.

"Mariah's mother is safe," he said into his comm.

"What's the status on Mariah?" came Isaac's cool voice, after much too long a pause.

"She stayed behind. As bait."

There was another long pause.

"Mariah's mother can't walk much or fast," Griffin said tersely. Rose Ellen watched him as he talked, no particular reaction on her face. Because she was tough like her daughter, Griffin thought. Or maybe Mariah was tough like her. Either way, she wasn't breaking down as he gave his precise coordinates. "I need her picked up."

"Are you thinking another diversion?" Blue asked.

"I'm thinking it's high time I did what I do best," Griffin replied.

He didn't wait for his brothers to agree, because he knew they would.

He bent down and pulled one of his backup pieces from his ankle. Then offered it to Rose Ellen. "Do you know how to operate a nine-millimeter?"

"Oh, sugar," Rose Ellen drawled, a fierce glint in her eyes. "With a merry ol' song in my heart."

"Okay. Shoot anyone who doesn't identify himself as a friend."

"Whose friend?" Rose Ellen asked coolly. She took the gun he offered her, checked the chamber, then held it in a casually firm grip as she pointed the muzzle at the ground. "I don't know as I have any friends running around these woods today, and if I did, I'd have half a mind to put a couple bullets in them for leaving me in there."

"My friends," he clarified, and hated himself for finding this woman charming when Mariah was still stuck in that barn. And he'd put her there. "But I suspect you'll know them when you see them. For one thing, they'll call you *ma'am*."

Rose Ellen almost smiled. "Then I might shoot them first."

He left her with her back to a tree, the Glock in her hand like she'd been born with it.

And he ran.

Under normal circumstances, Griffin liked to pore over maps. He liked to study geological factors, the wind, any and all weather conditions. Under normal circumstances, he planned long before he ever maneuvered himself into position.

But there was nothing normal about this.

He ran through the woods, grateful for every nasty vertical mile he'd ever pounded out in Alaska. Because these flat Georgia woods were nothing in comparison. He ran in a wide circle so no one could see him through the trees, and made as little noise as possible as he moved. When he was roughly one hundred and eighty degrees from where he'd started, he headed back toward the field.

And found the tree he'd spied on the way in, with its sturdy trunk and broad, wide limbs. He scaled it easily, flowing from branch to branch until he found the perfect vantage point. He balanced himself, then reached back around for his rifle.

He could assemble it with his eyes closed. In the dark. Behind his back.

It was even easier here, high up in a big old tree. He felt the smoothness of the metal, the lethal barrel, the scope.

In a few economical movements, he assembled one of the most lethal weapons that had ever been crafted.

He settled down with the scope, focusing it on the barn door.

"I'm in position," he said into his comm.

"Wait for some fireworks," Isaac ordered him.

Griffin muttered an affirmative.

I love you, Mariah had said.

More than once.

He told himself to breathe. To settle. To blank out his mind and focus in on the target.

I love you, she had said, and it had never been like this before. He had never had all this weight and ache sitting on him while he did what he'd been born to do. It was a lot worse than a distraction, because he wasn't distracted. He was focused. He just . . . *felt*.

He could fight it, Griffin realized after a moment of trying, or he could give in.

He had his scope at his eye. He had his gun against his shoulder.

And he'd learned a long time ago that there was no fighting the inevitable. There was only leaning into it, settling into whatever parameters were available, and taking it to that still, focused place where he could exist forever.

I love you, Mariah had said, bright and easy.

He breathed out, then in. And slowly, slowly felt his heartbeat begin to chill.

I love you, she'd said, and it was like those words wrapped around the barrel of his gun, flowing from the elegance of the rifle deep into him, changing everything.

I love you.

He held it like he held his rifle, his aim true.

She loved him. And he would save her.

Those were facts, the same as the weight of the rifle, the angle vectors and wind resistance, all of which he calculated by rote. All of which helped make him who he was.

He leaned into them, they became part of him, and Griffin went still.

Finally, he went still.

And waited.

It wasn't the first time in this long ordeal of a day that Mariah thought she was dreaming. Possibly dead.

But no amount of blinking could change the fact that she knew the man standing there in front of her.

It was her father-in-law, Walton Chandler Lanier.

And he looked the way he always did. Dapper. Put together in a Southern man's outfit of linen and pastels, like he'd gotten lost on the way to one of those garden parties with refreshing mint juleps that seemed to be the entire point of slow, hot Southern summers.

He even cracked the same toothy grin she'd last seen at the Thanksgiving dinner table.

"Walton?" she asked, as if she couldn't believe what she was seeing.

Because she couldn't.

"I get it," Walton said, grinning even wider. "I do."

David took after his mother, and Mariah had always secretly regretted that he'd missed out on Walton's truly luxuriant mane of hair. It had been golden blond in his youth and was now a pure, flowing white. Mariah had never understood how all that hair never responded to the humidity the way hers always did. Even now, when her father-in-law was standing in front of her in this barn where she was tied to a chair—or supposedly tied to a chair, and clearly by his orders—she was marveling at that hair.

"I truly do get it," Walton was saying in his thick, affable drawl. "You're a pretty girl, and men lose their minds over pretty things. I can't say I'm not guilty of the same. But you never should have married him, Mariah." He shook his head as if he were sad. "You should have known your place."

Mariah was glad that she was pretending to still be tied up, because no one was likely to notice it when she clenched her hands into fists.

She was buffeted by competing emotions. First, she still didn't feel anything like brave ought to. She was afraid she might throw up at any moment. And second, she was swamped with an overpowering sense of relief that didn't make the slightest bit of sense under the circumstances, when she didn't have a lot to be relieved about.

It took her a moment to understand that she'd really expected it to be David.

She'd steeled herself for it, in fact.

And Mariah wasn't sure what it said about her that even though she knew what kind of man David was, she hadn't wanted to believe that he could really want to kill her.

Much less do it.

Hate her, sure. Shout terrible things in her face, why not. Their marriage had been ugly, so there was no reason to imagine their divorce would be anything but more of the same.

But deep down, she'd wanted to hold on to the memory of that misty fall evening in Two Oaks, when he'd shown up in that cherry red car, smiled at her as if she mattered, and told her he could change her life.

Maybe that was a strange souvenir from a terrible marriage, but she wanted to hold on to it all the same.

"Walton," she said, and her voice was scratchy. "I can't believe you're the one responsible for all this."

"I'll tell you what, Miss Mariah," he said with that broad smile that, she saw now, went nowhere near his hooded eyes. Had that always been true? Was she only now noticing it? "I never did care for the way you took to calling me by my Christian name. I know I offered, but any good girl of decent breeding never would have taken me up on it. It seems to me that's part and parcel of the problem right there." Another sad, sad shake of that lion's head. "I don't know that I blame you. It's in your nature, after all. It's what gold diggers do. You take advantage."

Mariah revised that feeling of relief and focused on who was in the room instead of who wasn't.

"Walton," she said, lingering on his name because this time she could see that telltale coldness in his gaze. His smile was usually too wide and bright for it to show. "Did you put me in the hospital? Twice?"

"I didn't want to hurt you." Walton looked like he was out making Sunday social calls, shaking hands around white linen-draped tables at his clubs. Not standing in an old country barn, talking about . . . this. "But I don't want my only son divorced from some backwoods trash. Bad enough he married you in the first place."

"You were always so much more friendly to me than Mrs. Lanier," Mariah said, astonished to discover that somewhere inside, that smarted. She was actually the faintest bit hurt. "You were always perfectly polite. You always smiled, asked after me."

"A man either has manners or he doesn't," Walton said, as if she'd suggested he do something truly horrendous, like wear white after Labor Day. "I know I failed with David. I know he's not the man I intended him to be. I know all about his dalliances, and if I could apologize for him, I would. I didn't raise him to flaunt bad behavior."

"But . . ." She swallowed, not sure how to ask the question. "If you're apologizing for him, why am I here?"

Here in Georgia, against her will. Here in this barn, with these men all around. Here in this chair, waiting for a verdict they all knew had been passed already.

This was her sentence, not her trial.

"You shouldn't have left him," Walton said, tsking as if he were admonishing her. *Correcting* her. "The only thing you had going for you was your loyalty. All those years standing by his side, taking all that abuse when you couldn't give him the baby he thinks he wants. I've always rewarded loyalty, Mariah. But then you left."

"Rewarded . . . ?"

Mariah hardly understood what he was saying. And not only because she was too aware of the other men behind him. The staring one muttered to the tweaker, and the tweaker slipped out through the barn door. Taking his giant gun with him.

She jerked her attention back to Walton.

"You were obedient. You were loyal. You stayed with him for ten years, almost to the point where folks were getting used to you and thinking on forgetting where he found you. You should have stayed. I'd just about decided that I could tolerate a piece of trash like you being the mother of my grandbabies, because Lord knew, you have more tenacity than my own flesh and blood."

She couldn't help the way her chin rose then. She'd been letting too much of her McKenna out lately, and there was no putting it back inside. Not now. Not ever again.

"No need to worry on that score." And she let her drawl go deep country, just to remind them both who she was. Where she'd come from. "It turns out I can't have children. A surprise, I know. Your son's been pretty worked up about it for years."

"I've had you on birth control since the day my son brought you home," Walton said, that same merry smile on his face and a twinkle in his eyes, as if what he was saying wasn't impossible. And heinous. "You were a tramp straight out of a roadside diner, like a bad country song. I knew that left to your own devices, you'd have a litter of sticky brats to spend my family's money, and I couldn't have that. If you think on it a minute, you'll see clear."

Her heart was doing things that should have hurt more. Though it hurt enough as it was. "I didn't . . . I wasn't . . ."

"One thing I appreciate about you, Mariah, is how consistent you are. You wake up at the same time every morning. You eat the same thing for breakfast right after you get off the treadmill. Easiest thing in the world to slip a crushed-up pill into your morning oats. There's not a maid in that house who doesn't do my bidding."

Mariah couldn't take that in. All those years. All the terrible things David had said to her, and the way she'd privately agreed, hating her own body for betraying her. All the doctor's appointments . . .

Her stomach lurched. Why had it never occurred to her that she was only ever sent to doctors David approved of—doctors who played golf with him and his father? Why had it never crossed her mind that, really, she ought to find her own?

"You let me think I was infertile for a decade," she whispered.

Walton laughed that same booming, uproarious laugh she'd heard him use a thousand times over the years. She'd found it infectious. She still did, only now it struck her as more of an airborne toxic event.

"You should thank me," he told her now. "Just think how losing a mother can break a child's heart. If you'd had David's babies, they'd have to mourn you, too. Are you really that selfish?"

Pull yourself together, baby girl, she told herself, that voice in her head sounding exactly like her own mother's.

Behind Walton, the staring man said something to her original abductor, then left through the barn door, too.

Griffin had told her to run, she reminded herself. That she would know when she should.

She tensed in her seat, told herself she could and would do this, and then focused her attention back on her father-in-law. Who looked the same as he always did.

It made this worse.

"I'm not following," she said, trying to sound submissive and docile. The way he liked women to address him. "David and I were engaged for months. Why didn't you stop the wedding if you were opposed to it?"

Another chuckle. "It never occurred to me he'd go through with it. He sure showed me."

"I was his . . . rebellion?"

"Let's be real clear, now that it's just you and me." Walton moved closer, and then, sickeningly, reached out to fit his palm against her cheek. He leaned in so close, she had no choice but to look at the red of his nose. Capillaries that spoke of the drinks he liked too much and the dissipation he took as his rightful due. "You've always been a mighty fine piece of ass, Miss Mariah. At first I was going to kill you off. Make it look like an accident, nice and simple, no muss and no fuss. But then you had to go and run. It would have been one thing if you planned to stay away for good, but who stays in Alaska? I knew you'd be back."

Mariah was frozen straight through, but the worst part was that she could still feel her heart kicking hard and panicked. Her pulse was an impossible racket inside her. She wasn't sure if her head ached more than her stomach lurched, but despite that, she stayed still. Entirely too focused on his meaty, damp hand against the side of her face.

"You caused me a lot of trouble, is the thing," Walton said, and his hand moved down to stroke its way over the nape of her neck, making her shudder in revulsion. "I think I deserve a taste of that fine ass. It'd be a shame to waste it, don't you think?"

It took three seconds. One of disbelief. One of sheer horror.

Then one more second of *hell no*.

"Well, Walton," she said, and she smiled as she said it, "since you asked, I would really rather die."

And it was worth it for the blank look on his face. The shock that followed. It was worth watching his temper take hold, his mouth tightening, color flooding his face until he was even redder than he was before.

It was even worth it when he lifted that moist hand off her face, then hit her.

A sharp pain and a dull, deep ache exploded in her cheek at once. She tasted copper. Her head rocked back, and she might have tipped straight out of her chair if she hadn't been holding on to it, pretending to be tied down.

When she turned her head back around to face him, there was blood in her mouth and her face felt swollen. She was pretty sure there were tears on her cheeks.

But she smiled anyway.

She'd thought a slap was supposed to sting, but then again, what Walton had done was wind up and clobber her. So maybe it wasn't surprising that she felt less slapped and more as if he'd tried to cave in her cheekbone.

When her swollen cheek started to feel numb, she decided that was another gift.

"This could have been easy," Walton told her, all red nose and nothing even remotely kind in those deep-set eyes. "All you had to do was be nice to me. I wouldn't have hurt you much at all. But now look what you've gone and done."

Mariah went with her gut instinct then, suicidal though it might have been, and laughed at him.

She laughed until he hit her again, harder this time, then she pulled herself woozily back around to stare at him. And laughed some more.

"I want to make sure you live with this one thought, Walton," she said, and her voice sounded fuzzy. Or maybe it was that her tongue kept snagging on her teeth when he hit her, so it was puffy, too. "You might get a piece of this ass. But you'll have to take it. And the only way you dared try this was by hiring your own personal army, kidnapping me from an island in Alaska, and tying me down to a chair. That's the kind of man you are. For the rest of your life, when you look in a mirror, you'll always know that this gold-digging, no-account, backwoods, trailer trash piece of ass was *that much* better than you."

Walton's face was red again, fleshy and dangerous. But she smiled once more—and maybe this was what bravery was. Doing the thing, saying the thing, because it had to be done and it had to be said, and it didn't matter at all that inside, she was curled up tight and hiding. What mattered was that Walton couldn't see it.

What mattered was that she didn't want to show him how scared she was, so she didn't.

This time when he reached over, he put his hand around her throat and squeezed.

"You're going to pay for that," he said without any

particular inflection, the way he used to ask her to pass the salt.

He'd hit her twice on the same side of her face. Her eye felt weird and swollen, as if maybe she had her first black eye. But she forced herself to hold that awful gaze of his, no matter what.

She didn't want this man to touch her. But if he was dead set on taking his piece, at least that meant she would stay alive that much longer.

Because as far as she was concerned, there was no fate worse than death.

Mariah wanted to live.

She still wanted to *live*.

Walton squeezed, and she knew she had to get her hands up. She had to duck her head to get some air, fight him off, and try to save herself in the maybe six seconds—if she was lucky—before she was unconscious.

She'd hidden the fact that she knew a couple of moves from her abductor, who was standing over by the barn door, watching the interplay between Walton and her like it was a deeply boring television program. She did a lightning-fast calculation. Griffin had told her she would need to run, so she needed to stay conscious no matter what.

Even if she showed her hand.

Or better yet, her elbow.

She moved her head, dipping her chin to see if she could create some space by pressing her chin into the top of Walton's fingers where he gripped her. She tugged her hands out of the duct tape first, then brought them up to yank down on the hand at her throat, creating just enough room to get a breath in.

At the same time, she shot to her feet, slamming down on Walton's wrist with one hand to jerk him toward her, so she could use her other arm to elbow him.

Directly in his fleshy, red face.

It hurt.

That was her first thought. In the next second, she understood that the crunching sound she'd heard was probably his nose. She shoved him back from her, paying no attention to the high-pitched, enraged sounds he made as he fell to the ground with a thud and then writhed there.

Like some kind of insane pig.

"You stupid, stupid bitch," her abductor said quietly.

Mariah pushed away from the chair, kicking it back from her, and then took a few steps away from Walton in case he decided to grab for her.

"I told you I was going to hurt you," her abductor said softly. With great relish. "I'm going to break every bone in your arms and legs. Then I'm going to watch him fuck you till you bleed. Then I'll take a turn, and believe me, bitch, you'll beg for him to come back and give you some more when you see how I do it."

She refused to dwell on any of the vile, disgusting things he'd said, because they might actually kill her where she stood.

This was about staying alive. By any means necessary.

Be a weed, not a flower, she ordered herself.

"That sounds great," she drawled. "I don't know where you're from, but this is Georgia. Out here in the country, we take ugly words like that as an invitation. To end you. Is that what you're looking for?"

"Until you bleed," her abductor said again, with a

kind of fervent delight that Mariah suspected might give her nightmares after she survived this.

But nightmares were a small price to pay for survival. She believed that with every part of her. Every currently intact part of her.

He took a step toward her. Mariah took a step back.

We do what we have to so we can go home, Blue had told them.

She remembered Griffin's face when she'd told him she loved him. The way his fingers had traced over the bruise on her cheek. The way he'd kissed her in an empty inn above a lonely harbor, then taken her to bed.

And after all this time, and all those years in Atlanta, she hadn't truly found her home until she'd taken a ferry across the moody Alaskan sea and stepped off into Grizzly Harbor.

Mariah knew that whatever happened here, she would, by God, be going home one day.

And it was as if someone heard her.

Because something outside the barn exploded.

It sent the man before her diving for cover. It blew Mariah back a few feet. She slammed into the stall behind her, but at least she stayed upright. Her head ringing, her body battered and strange, but upright.

And this was it.

Walton was on the floor, and her abductor had thrown himself into one of the old stalls for cover. There was a clear line to the barn door.

She trusted Griffin. And God help her, but she loved him.

And she wanted to stay alive long enough to celebrate both of those things.

Mariah ran.

Eighteen

Griffin was the tree beneath him, the rifle in his hands, the scope at his eye.

He was the slow, steady beat of his heart. He was his own deliberate breath.

He watched. He waited.

Blue and Jonas moved in, sneaking up on the two men outside the barn and taking them down, hard and silent. Then they dragged them around the side of the building, out of sight, while Isaac went for the Mercedes and worked to lay down the charge.

Griffin waited.

Blue headed out for the woods to find Mariah's mother, while Jonas lured out two more men and took each one down with a certain swiftness that Griffin would remember later, as a clue to the kinds of things he'd done in the service.

Isaac gave the signal, setting the charge and then

breaking into a run so he could join Jonas around the side of the barn for cover.

And still, Griffin stayed where he was.

He allowed sensation to wash over him without giving into it. He felt the faint ache in his muscles that reminded him of the jump he'd made to the barn's roof. He felt a vague itchy sensation on one forearm, then his cheek, but he knew that was nothing more than his nerves resisting the settling. The focus. He observed each new sensation, then let it go.

He maintained his position as Isaac counted down over their comm channel.

"Three. Two. One."

The Mercedes went up in flames with a satisfyingly loud boom.

And Griffin still waited.

The world narrowed down to that barn door and the flames dancing in front of it.

Run, he ordered her silently. *Run, Mariah. Now.*

One breath. Another.

And then Mariah was streaking out from the barn door, pumping her arms as if she were trying to make her legs less wobbly. But the more she ran, the steadier she got.

She didn't look back, she simply kept her head down and hauled butt. She shot straight out of the barn like she was headed for the other end of the field. For him.

He hadn't told her where to go, only to run. And he understood how much she trusted him then.

Maybe even loved him the way she'd said she did.

Because right behind her came a big, burly individual, charging like a pissed-off bull. Griffin recognized him instantly as the one they'd seen on the security tapes from the ferry terminal back in Alaska. The one who'd snuck onto the island and stayed there, hidden right under their noses. The one who likely would have taken Mariah a whole lot sooner if she'd ever been alone.

The moment he'd had the opportunity—the moment Griffin had given him that opportunity—this man had taken Mariah from Grizzly Harbor. Put his hands on her and scared her. *Locked her in a trunk.*

Then brought her here for a whole lot worse.

Griffin felt a whole lot more than mere *sensation*, then. He felt like he'd exploded right along with the Mercedes, every part of him going up in flames and burning down to ash—

But he didn't move.

He waited.

Time flattened out. Stretched.

Mariah had a significant head start, but the man behind her was bigger, fitter, and a whole lot taller. It meant his strides were longer. He gained ground quicker.

And there was no discounting the effects of testosterone and rage, both of which were written all over this animal's snarling face.

Still Griffin waited, because he wanted this gorilla to do exactly what he did next. Reach out his hands, think he had her, shout something Griffin didn't have to hear to know he wouldn't appreciate—

The man lunged.

And Griffin took him out.

One perfect shot, crisp and clean.

A split-second later, Mariah stumbled, and he knew she'd heard it.

But she still didn't look behind her.

She kept right on going, righting herself from her near

stumble and running faster—as if she didn't know or care that there was no longer anyone chasing after her.

Or, possibly, as if she planned to follow the last order he'd given her until he gave her a new one.

Griffin waited until Isaac and Jonas moved into the barn, ready and more than capable of handling any remaining threats. Only then did he abandon his post. It took him seconds to disassemble his rifle, pack it away, and sling it back into place over his shoulder.

He swung himself down from the tree, hitting the ground in an easy crouch.

And when he stepped into the field, Mariah was still running. Straight toward him.

She didn't stop when she saw him. She was panting, loud and ragged, and he wasn't sure if she was breathing or crying. Or maybe both.

Then he didn't care, because in the next second she was hurtling herself forward and into his arms.

Griffin didn't know why he felt so ragged, so undone, as if he'd been the untrained person running for his life across a wide field.

All he knew was that when he ducked his head to bury it in her hair, the sweet scent of her made that ache in his chest better and worse at the same time. Better and worse, and then more of each, until it was very nearly unbearable—but he didn't let go of her.

She wrapped her arms tight around him and kept making that same sobbing noise against his chest, and Griffin felt his head spin, as if she were the one holding him up instead of the other way around. He couldn't seem to tell the difference.

"It's over," he told her, and he didn't recognize his own voice.

Or his own hands when he looked down to see them shaking.

When Griffin was a man who never, ever shook.

Across the field, Isaac was escorting a man with blood all over his face out of the barn. Jonas was briefly visible through a hole in the second-floor wall, moving around the loft, sweeping the building for any surprises. Blue came around the side, Mariah's mother hobbling beside him and leaning heavily on his arm. Isaac met him and helped Rose Ellen find a seat where she could elevate her leg. Then the two of them escorted the men they'd rounded up—at gunpoint and with their hands zip-tied behind them—out to where the remains of the Mercedes smoldered.

No one bothered with the man left in the field. That was a law enforcement problem.

And no one appeared to look over to where Griffin stood with Mariah still in his arms, but he knew they'd all seen him. The fact that he'd have to answer for that nipped at him—but he didn't have it in him to care the way he knew he would eventually.

And he still didn't let her go.

"It's over," he told her again.

Mariah tipped her head up then, and he tensed at the sight of her. One whole side of her face was puffed up and bruised. Her eye was almost entirely swollen shut. And he didn't need her to tell him that someone had hit her. More than once. It made him want to start shooting all over again.

"Griffin," she whispered, as if his name was one of those long, pretty prayers his grandmother used to murmur. "I didn't want to die."

"Good." He didn't sound the least bit pretty. He sounded wrecked. Ruined. "You deserve to live a long and happy life. Away from all of this."

She reached up and fit her palm to his jaw. Her blue eyes were wet, darker than they should have been, but glimmering.

"I love you," she said again.

This time it felt even more like a blow. And that ache swelled until it took over his chest like some kind of impossible pneumonia, and he was surprised he didn't keel over where he stood.

It was ridiculous, he told himself. It was the usual transference that happened in situations like this. Completely understandable and not at all true.

And it didn't matter anyway, because he didn't do love.

But when he opened his mouth to tell her that, to let her down gently because she was still hopped up on adrenaline and fear and it was his fault she'd ended up in this field in the first place, he set his mouth to hers instead.

And he didn't like need, but he understood it. He was suspicious of passion, but that didn't mean he couldn't drown in it when he chose. He had.

But he had no place to put this.

It was a sweet, easy kiss, and it broke him in two. The world split into before this kiss and after it, and he was too broken to figure out what it meant.

Griffin pulled away and rested his forehead against hers.

"I love you," Mariah whispered. "I love you, I love you, I love you . . ."

He thought she might keep saying it forever, and he knew he needed to shut this down. Fast. He needed to cut her off, right here and right now—

But he didn't do it.

It was like her words were sunshine and he'd been lost in the dark for far too long, and God help him, but he wanted to bask in her.

Just for a little while longer.

But there was no time—there had never been any time—and, anyway, he wasn't that man. And when Isaac let out a piercing whistle to call them all back in, it was Mariah who pulled away. She wiped her hands over her face, wincing. Then frowned as she turned toward the barn.

"Mama . . ." she whispered.

She went to take a step, then staggered when her knees failed to hold her, her blue eyes fixing to his in surprise.

He caught her before her legs could give way. Without questioning it, he swept her up into his arms, letting her legs dangle, and started across the field.

Because if he was already ruined, he might as well make sure it went all the way down.

"I almost fell on my face," she told him, and then her wondering tone gave way as her teeth started to chatter.

"It's the adrenaline. Your body doesn't know what to do with it. It will pass."

"Why aren't you falling over, then?"

"I'm used to it."

She looped her arm around his neck and rested her head against his shoulder, and he wasn't prepared for the wave of feelings that cascaded through him. He felt protective. He felt needy and wild for her, but he didn't know if it was because he wanted her naked, or he simply wanted to tuck her up in a bed and watch her sleep, safe and sound. He felt on edge and he felt soothed, all at the same time. He *felt*, damn it.

He felt.

He was the one who had made that shot, but it was as if the bullet had slammed into his chest, cracking him wide open.

He had tried to keep Mariah at arm's length. And he had failed at that, spectacularly. Again and again in that bed of hers in Blue Bear Inn.

And then she was gone.

Griffin hadn't known if he'd ever see her again.

And now she was snuggling up against him, surrendering herself into his arms as if she hadn't been assaulted and kidnapped, then treated hideously by a whole bunch of other men. Bruised and battered. Forced to act like bait, take a few hits, then run for her life.

But she leaned into him as if none of that mattered as much as the feel of his shoulder against the less hurt side of her face.

Griffin felt humbled and exalted in turn.

He figured she'd hide her face when they walked past the man who'd kidnapped her, but this was Mariah. She never did a single thing he expected her to do. She lifted her head, stared at the man as he lay sprawled there, facedown in the grass, and didn't avert her gaze at all.

"I should feel worse," she said quietly. "That's a human life."

"That's the man who would've killed you if he got his hands on you."

"Probably. Though he had a lot of plans to hurt me first." She considered. "A lot."

"Then I wish I could take the shot all over again."

She shifted her gaze to his, steady and blue. "I said I *should* feel worse. But I don't."

Griffin kept walking. Then felt the strangest sensation, and looked down to find her covering his heart with one hand. He was surprised he didn't stagger.

"Do you carry the weight of that life?" she asked him.

He was torn open, again. When he didn't think there could be anything left inside him to expose.

There was something howling in him, old ghosts, maybe. And not of pretty girls who told him lies, but the kind of tallies he'd stopped making a long time ago.

All of those compartments, crumbling into dust.

"I carry all of them," he heard himself tell her, though he had never said that out loud in his life. "But that's okay. It's why I stay strong. I never carry more than I can lift."

She didn't move her hand. He felt her trace a pattern, but he couldn't tell what it was. He didn't want to know.

"But who carries you?"

He couldn't answer her. Or he didn't want to, and he wasn't sure that his throat worked any longer anyway.

It was good that they reached the rest of the group then, and he could set Mariah down on her feet. He held onto her arm as she tested her balance, and he hated the way her sudden smile when she didn't sag burst through him like some kind of heat lightning.

Lightning and sunshine, and he was a goner. He knew that now.

He forced himself to let her go, then watched as she walked carefully over to her mother to grab her in another fierce hug.

It was excellent practice, he assured himself, not making any eye contact with his brothers. He'd let her go. He could do it again.

Because he wasn't the kind of man who could keep her.

He never had been. He never would be.

She had been a job, and the job was done.

And if Griffin was the one who had to live with that . . . Well, he was used to carrying all kinds of weight.

He would carry that, too.

Nineteen

When the ambulances finally came roaring down the dirt road, bringing with them the county sheriff's office and the FBI and a whole lot of painful reality, Mariah was pathetically grateful to crawl up on a stretcher, surrender to the EMTs, and close her eyes at last.

The adrenaline had worn off and all she wanted was to be away from that barn. Her mother was in safe hands in the lead ambulance, and she figured they were both happy to give themselves over to the delights of Western medicine and whatever dripped from those bags. And this time, when she felt all the bumps in the road as the ambulance left the field Mariah never wanted to see again, she got to do it lying down and not stuffed in the trunk of a car.

She could really only count it as a win.

At the county hospital, she was checked over by a battalion of doctors and nurses, then admitted for observation.

"Nothing really happened to me," she told her doctor, trying to frown despite her stiff, swollen face. "It's a black eye, that's all."

"It will be a whole lot blacker tomorrow," the doctor said, already distinguishing herself from the emergency room doctors in Atlanta by looking concerned rather than, say, annoyed that Mariah kept exposing herself to shellfish. "You look exhausted, and I mean that clinically. Lie back. Take some fluids on board. If you're fine now, you can be even more fine tomorrow."

The minute the doctor was gone, Mariah crawled out of the bed. She took a minute to find her balance, which was harder to do without Griffin there to hold her upright, and grimaced at the hospital gown they'd given her. But it was better than continuing to wear the same clothes she'd had on for more hours straight than she could count. She took her IV stand as a convenient walker should her legs give out again, and went to find her mother.

It took poking her head into every room along the hallway, but Mariah found her. Mama was lying in her hospital bed looking mutinous and deeply grumpy, her leg bandaged and propped up before her.

"It's a bone bruise," Mama said in disgust, the exact same way Mariah had said *It's a black eye*. "I don't need all the theatrics."

Mariah shuffled over, then perched herself on the edge of the bed, making sure not to tangle her IV lines with her mother's.

Rose Ellen hadn't said a word when she'd recognized Walton back at the barn. He'd looked diminished and small as he lay huddled at Isaac's feet, bloodied and whining, but Rose Ellen hadn't commented on it. She hadn't said anything while the Alaska Force men did their thing once reinforcements arrived, taking charge of the scene and answering official questions as if they were actually the ones in charge.

Just like Mariah hadn't said anything when she'd watched Griffin surrender his weapon to the authorities, then disappear into the back of an official vehicle without so much as a backward glance.

They'd both stood near that horrible barn, waiting their turn while draped in those funny metallic blankets. They'd held on to each other as if they had never let go in the past ten years, staring all around them as if they were shell-shocked.

Maybe they were. Mariah thought it was entirely possible she was. It wasn't every day she ran like that—or at all—so hard and fast that her thighs now ached. She'd felt her abductor's breath on her neck. She was sure she'd felt his fingertips graze her.

You're going to bleed, he'd growled again.

And then he was gone.

It wasn't every day she fielded rape threats along with death threats, or heard that she'd been dosed with birth control pills for a decade. She couldn't decide which horrendous violation was more upsetting. And the fact that she wasn't curled up in a ball somewhere, sobbing her eyes out, told her that yes, she was in shock.

Mariah expected she might stay there awhile.

But now she concentrated on her mother's hand. And how good the weight of it was on her leg.

"How bad did he hurt you?"

"He punched me in the face a couple of times," Mariah said. Her face was stiffer now, which meant it hurt to use it. She made herself smile anyway. "It's like any given Tuesday night at Uncle Teddy's."

Rose Ellen didn't smile back. "I don't mean him. I mean the other one. The one you married."

"David never hit me, Mama," Mariah said softly, holding her mother's gaze. "If you want to know the sad truth, he didn't have to hit me. I did everything he said anyway. I guess I wanted to."

Her mother looked older, and worse—frail. When she had always been the strongest woman Mariah knew. She told herself it was the harshness of the fluorescent lights. Or the fact that this marked maybe the only time in her life she'd ever seen her mother without her eye makeup on, deep and black and ready to make a statement.

Her tough-as-nails mother had very blond eyelashes that disappeared without mascara. She looked soft and fragile, and Mariah's ribs hurt from keeping in all that sobbing.

"I'm sorry." Mariah heard how choked up she sounded. And the damaged side of her face already hurt. Extra salt wasn't going to help anything. But she couldn't seem to stop the tears that tracked down her cheeks. "I'm so sorry for everything. For leaving. For being so bad about keeping in touch. For being the reason all this happened to you."

"You wanted to better yourself," Rose Ellen said, her voice as steady as the firm pat she delivered to Mariah's thigh. "There's not one thing wrong with that. You don't need to apologize for doing what you always said you would and getting out of Two Oaks."

Mariah shook her head, not willing to hand off the blame that easily.

"Two Oaks wasn't the problem. I was the problem. I let them get to me years ago. I let them separate me from you. I don't know if you can better yourself by pretending that the person you were before didn't exist. That's not improving. That's just hiding."

"You're not the one who stopped calling, baby girl. I was."

Mariah blinked a few times, but she couldn't seem to form the questions that crowded her mouth. Her mother sighed, adjusting herself in the bed, and kept talking as if she'd heard those questions all the same.

"You didn't need all that McKenna nonsense every time you turned around, and you know as well as I do that they would have camped out in your front yard if you'd have let them." She pinched the bridge of her nose. "You had a life, and I thought it was the one you wanted. I didn't see any reason why you should beat yourself up about separating yourself from your roots, so I did it for you."

"I abandoned you," Mariah whispered.

"Baby girl, I let you go." Rose Ellen's tough mouth curved upward. "I wanted you to go. You spent your whole childhood cleaning up messes and taking care of your brothers and sisters. You deserved an easier life. I figured that's what he was giving you."

"You did not. You hated him on sight. And you were right."

"I didn't want to be right." Rose Ellen reached out and took Mariah's hand between hers. "There's precious little happiness in this world, Mariah. I've never had more than a nodding acquaintance with it myself. And no two people's happiness looks the same. You've never heard me call you names for going after what you want, and you never will."

"He made me choose," Mariah heard herself say, as if it was torn from the deepest part of her. "And I chose wrong. I'm so sorry."

Her mother let out that laugh Mariah had always loved. A rough, glorious cackle, made up of late nights and cigarettes and pure joy.

"Who do you think you're talking to?" she demanded. "I've spent my whole life making the wrong choice. I won't lie—that's the only choice I know how to make. And if I've learned anything, it's this: You can't spend your time beating yourself up for doing what you thought was right. You can only try to do better the next time. Life isn't about making the right choice, Mariah. It's about what you do after the bad ones blow up in your face, the way they always do. Do you lie down? Or do you get up and try again? I could personally teach stupid to a bunch of rocks, but I learn from my mistakes. Or I hope I do. And either way, I always, always keep going."

And Mama had never been one for extended displays of physical affection. She didn't like to cuddle, and truth be told, she'd never been all that warm. She wasn't that kind of mother. But they were both in the hospital tonight, and not dead the way they could have been.

Whatever the reason, Mariah lay down next to her mother, resting the unhurt side of her face on the pillow. Rose Ellen wrapped her arm around Mariah, keeping her elevated leg out of the way.

And they lay like that for a long, long time.

When Mariah woke up, it was because she was in Griffin's arms again.

She knew it was him before she knew what was happening. It was the scent of him, maybe. Or the particular strength of his arms and the comforting wall of his chest. She cradled the part of her face that didn't hurt in the crook of his neck, let him push her IV along, and only complained when he set her down in her hospital bed again with a gentleness that might have made her cry if she'd had any tears left in her.

"You can't go wandering off," he told her gruffly, standing there at the side of her bed, his dark eyes glittering with things she knew he'd never say. She felt them anyway. "People think you're lost. After the last two days, that makes everybody jumpy."

"You found me." She smiled as best she could with her poor, swollen face, and the funny thing was, it hurt less when it was directed at him. "You always do."

Griffin stayed where he was beside her bed, like some kind of sentry, and it took her a minute to realize that he hadn't gone off somewhere to shower and change, maybe eat a big dinner, or whatever it was mighty commandos did after saving the day. He was wearing the exact same thing he'd had on out there at the barn. The same cargo pants covered with dust and dirt, and the same black T-shirt that was really more a love letter to his remarkable torso.

It made her heart flip over, imagining Griffin finishing up with the police and the federal officers—who likely had a lot of questions for the man who'd fired the bullet that had killed her abductor—and then racing right over to see her in the hospital.

Almost like he cared.

And Mariah had told him she loved him a thousand times or more by now, but she knew better than to say it just then. It was the way he stood there like he was carved from stone. Or wished he was, anyway.

He was still the most beautiful man she had ever seen. And now she knew what he could do. She'd seen it. She'd felt her abductor hit the ground right behind her, and only then had she understood that it hadn't been a bee she'd heard go by in that second before she'd been *sure* he was about to grab her.

She must have run another five steps at least before she heard the shot.

Griffin was beautiful, he was indisputably lethal, and as she gazed up at him, she knew that she had never seen another human being so lonely.

She wanted to save him the way he'd saved her. If she could have, she would have gathered him up in her arms and held him close until she melted away all those solitary walls he had put up around him.

And even lying down in her hospital bed, she could see that he was gearing himself up to lay down the law. She even had an idea of what he planned to say.

But she wasn't ready.

She just wasn't ready.

"Will you stay with me?" she asked him softly. "Just until I fall asleep?"

He wore that anguished look again, the way he had back in the barn. He was going to say no. He was going to refuse her and leave, as she had no doubt that he wanted to. She held her breath—

But he didn't.

"Sure," he said, as if the single word cost him more than she could possibly imagine. "I can stay. Until you sleep."

He lowered himself into the chair beside her bed like

it might bite him. Mariah rolled over to her side so she could look at him.

She wanted to look at him forever.

But her eyelids were heavy, and she wasn't sure she'd ever been so tired in all her life.

Just as she wasn't sure her heart was still in one piece or at all functional when he leaned forward, reached out, and pulled her hand between his.

He didn't say another word.

But his hands were so warm. His steady, intense gaze made her feel safe. And even though she fought to stay awake, to hold on to him as long as she could, as soon as the heat of his palms soaked into hers, she fell asleep.

The next time she woke up, it was morning and her IV was disconnected.

She expected Griffin to be gone, and actually caught her breath when she saw that he was still there. He'd left the chair and was standing by the window, his hands clasped behind his back in a way that struck her as profoundly military.

And even more lonely than last night.

"They're releasing you today," he told her without turning around. And Mariah had been around the Alaska Force team long enough now to know better than to ask how he'd known she was awake. "You can put on real clothes if you want. They should have your discharge papers soon."

"Shouldn't they have woken me up to discuss this?" It hurt to talk. It hurt to blink, for that matter. Mariah took a moment to catalog all the different and surprising ways she hurt, particularly when she heaved herself into a sitting position. She would have grimaced—if she wasn't sure that would hurt even more. "I'm pretty sure there's a whole law."

Griffin turned slightly from the window and raised a brow at her. "I'm very charming."

"More charming than federal law?"

"The nurse said I had to be your husband. So I told her I was."

Mariah didn't have a handy quip for that. She should have thrown something back at him, made it funny.

But instead they stared at each other for much too long. Until it got too hot and intense.

Mariah was the one who looked away first, as if the stiff hospital blankets were suddenly deeply fascinating.

"You're going to have to make a police statement. And the FBI want to talk to you, too. I could put them off another day."

"There's no need to delay anything," she said, sounding hushed. As if they were in a church instead of an antiseptic hospital room. "I'm fine."

"You're not fine, Mariah. You're beat-up. Battered. If I could—"

"For God's sake, Mariah!"

The voice from the doorway made Mariah jump. She was aware of Griffin moving, blocking her from whatever was coming.

But she didn't need to see the person at the door to recognize him.

"David?" she asked, stunned.

Her ex-husband looked the roughest she'd ever seen him when he moved into her line of sight. Which was to say, he looked as if he'd had an excellent night's sleep followed by a visit from his masseuse and a consultation with his tailor. Only the faintest hint of puffiness around his eyes and the fact that he'd left his jaw unshaven suggested that he had any more pressing affairs to attend to today than counting the family money.

"I can't believe any of this," David said, scowling at her as he advanced. "I can't believe that you would stoop so low as—"

He stopped. Abruptly. Because he ran right into Griffin's outstretched hand.

"Take one step closer to her and I'll throw you back out that door. Headfirst."

David peered up at Griffin.

And had to crane back his neck to do it.

Mariah felt dizzy all over again. She was sitting there in a hospital bed in an obnoxious hospital gown, her hair a disaster she wasn't prepared to confront, one side of her face swollen and bruised, and the full weight of everything that had happened rolling back over her in deeply unpleasant waves—

But all she could think about was the difference between the two men standing at the end of her hospital bed.

On the one side, there was David. Boyish-faced, preppy David, who kept trim on his treadmill and out on the golf course. He was in his usual uniform of khakis and a collared shirt. In peach today, which seemed to call undue attention to how smooth and soft and manicured he was.

And on the other side, there was Griffin. He looked like some kind of avenging angel, dressed like the weapon he was, all packed muscle. He towered over David. And he was so much more solid and lean, he made David look even softer than he already was.

The longer she stared at them, the calmer and more dangerous Griffin looked.

And the more agitated David became.

"You can call off your attack dog, Mariah," David snapped. He didn't wait for her to reply. He swiveled his head back around to Griffin, then nodded toward the door. "You can wait outside, brother."

Griffin snorted. "You're not a member of my family. And I'm not going to tell you again. One step closer and you're out of here."

It took David a moment to let that settle in. To accept what must have been the challenging reality that Griffin wasn't playing around. Mariah saw the very moment he understood that.

Just as she saw the next moment, when he decided to ignore Griffin, as if Griffin were nothing but a lowly member of his staff.

"You can't imagine what they're saying," David said, his tone haughty and furious. A tone Mariah knew well. "You're going to have to clean this up, and fast."

She shrugged, mostly because he'd once lectured her all the way home from a dinner party clear on the other side of Atlanta because she'd shrugged in public. He'd claimed it broadcast how low class she was. "I don't know what you're talking about."

"This is obviously some kind of revenge fantasy playing out here." David forced out an anemic chuckle. "I sympathize, I do. You're angry at me, and you want to hurt me. But you really shouldn't have dragged my father into this."

It was funny—or maybe the word she was looking for was *sad*—that she'd ever been the kind of silly girl who'd looked at David and seen him as handsome instead of weak. Charming instead of self-involved.

Her mother might have forgiven her for leaving Two Oaks with David. Mariah wasn't sure she could forgive herself.

And she discovered that the longer she looked at him, really, truly looked at this man she'd been married to for a decade, she wasn't afraid of him anymore. Somewhere along the way—maybe in the trunk of a car headed down a dirt road toward her own death—he'd lost any power he'd had over her.

She expected that to feel like a victory. Instead, it was more complicated.

Something like sorrow.

But she still didn't want anything to do with him.

"I still don't know what you're talking about," she said, trying to keep her voice as kind as she could. After all, he'd found out some nasty things about his father today, and she knew how he idolized Walton. "But I don't think you should be in here. The police are going to want to talk to me, and I don't think they'll like that you came by to . . ." She let her head drop to one side. "Why did you come by again?"

"I don't know what happened to you. Maybe you paid your goon here to rough you up. For all I know, that's what you like these days." Griffin made a sound that Mariah could only describe as a growl, and David inched away from him. Closer to the door, luckily for him. "Mariah. You need to think this through. It's your word against my father's, and I don't know who you think is going to believe you." He made that chuckling sound again. *"You."*

"They don't have to believe me," Mariah replied, trying her best to see what she'd found so appealing in him. Trying to remember when she'd believed marrying him was the happily ever after she'd hardly dared believe in before. But all she saw was an angry little man with thinning hair and a sulky mouth. Who clearly wanted nothing more than to bully her. "But I think they'll probably believe all the men he hired, none of whom are likely to waste a single second risking themselves to keep Walton Lanier out of jail."

"They're already flipping," Griffin confirmed, deadpan. Only his dark eyes glittered. "One after the next. Like ugly dominoes."

"It will never stick," David declared with great confidence. "My father is a pillar of Atlanta society. He has friends everywhere. He's not a scorned woman looking for a payout. I don't know that I believe anyone did this to you. Maybe you did it to yourself."

"In a manner of speaking, I surely did." Mariah surrendered to the full-throated glory of her real drawl. The one that David had always hated so much that she'd trained herself out of it. She sat up straighter, hoping her hair was as big and curly and messy as it felt. She smiled at him, ignoring the tugging pain on the swollen side of her face, because she knew that would irritate him, too. *Ugly women shouldn't smile,* he'd told her once. *It's plain offensive.* "I had the temerity to marry you. Your daddy told me himself how against our marriage he was. But I didn't beat myself up, David."

He started to speak, but she wasn't done.

"All I had to do was be nice to him, and when he raped me, he'd go easy. That was what he promised me." She kept her gaze trained on David, though she was aware of the way Griffin went from stone to something harder.

More terrifying. "But I wasn't that nice to him. That's why he did this to my face. And he had every intention of making it a full-body experience, then inviting all those other men to join in. That's who your father is."

Mariah had spent a lot of time coming up with scenes in her head over the years, imagining what it would be like to see David speechless.

But the reality was far better than anything she could have cooked up.

She took advantage of it and kept on. "But I'll tell you what. He was much too comfortable with his threats and his fist. That tells me that I'm not the first girl who's seen that side of your father. So I don't think it really matters if anyone believes *me*. There's going to be a line out the door behind me. You can count on it."

And it took her a moment to realize that the harsh panting wasn't hers. It was David's.

"He begged me to leave you in the gutter where I found you," David sneered. "But I thought I could make something out of you. I thought I could take a piece of crap that belonged in a toilet—"

This wasn't a new line of complaint. But this time, Griffin was here.

And he'd obviously had enough.

Mariah didn't see him move. One minute he was staring down at David like a stone carving. The next, David's arm was extended at a painful-looking angle, and Griffin was forcing him out the door, wrenching David's shoulder to bend him forward.

Mariah heard cursing from the hallway, then David's blustery shout, but he was cut off. Fast.

And when Griffin returned to the doorway, he stayed there, gazing at her from a distance.

Where he was probably more comfortable, she knew. No matter how it made her ache more.

"Thank you," she said quietly.

"The least I can do is take out the trash."

Something bright and heady swelled there between them. But Griffin turned his head, looking at a distraction out in the hall.

"Griffin . . ." Mariah began, desperate and shaky and determined to hold on to him, no matter what it took.

"The police are here," he told her, his voice too calm. Too deliberate. Too much like the way he'd talked to her so long ago, when she'd stepped off that ferry and seen him, and her world had changed forever. "It's going to be a long interview. If I were you, I'd get dressed."

He stepped into the hall, closing the door behind him. Mariah sat where she was, her hands in fists and her eyes blurry with some mixture of emotion and fury. She didn't want to move. But she was entirely too Southern not to think that a coat of armor might not be amiss if she was about to be grilled by the authorities on such a host of unpleasant subjects.

And when she came out of the bathroom some time later, she was dressed in clothes she didn't have to ask to know Griffin had found for her. She'd done what she could with her hair, washed her face, and tried her best to look less like a zombie and more like a human being. Out in her room, she found two detectives waiting for her and Isaac standing by the window, the same way Griffin had earlier.

But Griffin himself was nowhere to be found.

Twenty

Mariah talked until she was hoarse, Isaac interrupting from time to time to corroborate her story or add detail. And then she did it all over again with the FBI.

When all law enforcement officials were gone and her throat was worn out, she was poked and prodded some more by the doctors, then released.

But when the nurse rolled her out in the mandatory wheelchair, it wasn't Alaska Force she found waiting for her at the hospital entrance.

It was her family.

"Y'all sure know how to throw a homecoming party," her sister Britney drawled through the open window of her pickup truck. "I was fixing to stay mad at you for the next ten or twenty years at least. But look at you. You're much too pathetic."

"Somebody has to teach you how to make sure the other guy looks worse," her brother Justin chimed in, shaking his head as if Mariah had let down the whole family.

A position he'd taken every time any one of their relatives had gotten into a scrap, now that she considered it.

None of them hugged, because McKennas weren't huggers, save for the most dire and horrendous of circumstances—like a mother-daughter meeting up for the first time in years after having been kidnapped and hauled off to some ratty barn deep in the countryside.

But when her brother and sister packed her up into the pickup, settling her in the backseat next to Rose Ellen, Mariah had to admit it felt as good as a hug might have. Tucked up in a pickup with her family, headed down a Georgia highway toward home.

At last.

And as the days passed, Mariah expected to find it difficult to ease back into life in Two Oaks, especially when she'd been running from it all these years.

But the reality was, home was simple. It was familiar. She sank back into life in the old farmhouse like she was sinking into butter.

She met all her nieces and nephews. She caught up with Britney, Justin, and her sister Whitney. They told stories and laughed into the night around the same old bonfire out back, and when they were good and caught up on all the nuclear family scandals and disappointments—like the "misunderstanding" that had landed her brother Michael in jail—they brought in the cousins.

And as the swelling in her face went down and she got less stiff and sore with each day, Mariah found herself . . . closer to content than she remembered ever being before. She slept in that same room off the kitchen that had been hers as a girl, and some days she almost forgot that she'd been away for so long. That those years in Atlanta had even happened. She could wake up in the warm mornings, walk outside in her bare feet, and feel the Georgia dirt between her toes the way she always had.

She could breathe deeply the way she never had in Atlanta, and the way she imagined she might again someday in Alaska.

She ate her great aunt's sweet potato pie, had too many beers with her cousins, and let her drawl get thick and lazy and full-on redneck again.

The bruises on her face had gone down to little more than a few shadows by the time she'd been home for a week and a half.

Mariah walked outside after sunset on that Wednesday night, looking for lightning bugs as the sky deepened from dark blue into soft black and the stars came out. She walked away from the blazing lights of the farmhouse and the laugh track on Rose Ellen's favorite show. She picked her way across the yard, toward the woods, until she found herself at the tree line.

She stood there a moment, breathing in the rich scent of home. Jasmine and honeysuckle perfuming the night air, the rich earth, the woods and the green and, when the wind changed, the neighbor's cows.

And when she smiled, it ached a bit, but not from her injuries.

"I know you're there," she said softly. She heard an owl hoot. "I expect that means you want me to."

For a moment there was nothing but quiet. Or what passed for quiet in the country night, on a pretty spring evening in these noisy woods.

And then, where there had been only shadow a moment before, there was Griffin.

"Are you going to follow me around forever? Just hide out in the shadows for the rest of your life?"

His dark eyes glittered. "I wanted to make sure you're okay. That your ex doesn't come back to finish that conversation."

"He's got his hands full telling lies to half of Atlanta," Mariah said with a shrug. "And besides, he's not going to come back to Two Oaks. The last time he was here, look what happened."

"I dropped off your things."

The longer they stood there, the more her eyes adjusted and the more she wanted to touch him. She wanted to reach over and get her hands on him, to remind herself that no matter what he looked like out here in the dark, with only the stars to light him, he wasn't a machine. He wasn't *really* made of stone.

He was a man, flesh and blood. And so much heart, though she knew he would deny that most of all.

"Thank you." She had come home from breakfast with a selection of her aunts that morning to find her single suitcase waiting for her at the farmhouse door. Everything she'd taken on her run from Atlanta and left in Alaska was packed up inside it.

She'd carried her suitcase into her room, shut the door behind her, and cried into her pillow until she'd given herself a headache.

But she wasn't crying now.

"I'm headed back tomorrow," he told her, gruff and low. "For good."

And then they just stood there, staring at each other.

And Mariah's bruises had all but faded by now. Or the physical pain had, anyway. That ache inside her had spilled over into tears, sure—but that was this morning.

She'd walked around the past few days with the nape

of her neck prickling, fully aware that even though she couldn't see him, he was there again.

Watching over her. Keeping her safe.

Hiding, a voice in her had whispered this morning, after she'd draped a cold washcloth over her red, cried-out eyes.

She wasn't the same person who had found herself in a hospital bed after that charity event. She wasn't the girl who'd made a thousand excuses, over and over, to deny truths that had always been right there in front of her eyes.

She wasn't even the same as she'd been when she'd arrived in Grizzly Harbor.

Mariah had been forged in a different fire altogether in that barn.

"If you ever try to sacrifice yourself for me again, baby girl," Rose Ellen had told her the other night, her leg up on her coffee table and a cigarette in her hand, "you better believe that I will kick your butt. Do you hear me?"

And no matter how many years she'd spent trying to pretend otherwise, the truth was that Mariah was every inch her mother's daughter. Bad decisions, stubbornness, and deeply unimpressed with pointless sacrifices.

"So this is your version of a good-bye?" she demanded now, not surprised to find that her hands had shifted to her hips. "You're . . . what? Off to Alaska? Never to be seen again?"

"The job is complete." He gritted out the words, and she could actually hear how tight his jaw was. "I tried to tell you this was never going to be anything more than the job."

She laughed at him. She couldn't help herself. And she took his scowl as encouragement.

"You go ahead and lie to yourself all you want, Griffin. You're good at that. But don't you think for one minute that you can lie to my face. I've had enough of that to last me a lifetime."

She could feel the air crackle between them. And when he leaned closer, he looked less like stone and more like iron heated in an unforgiving fire.

"Do not compare me to your ex, princess. Ever."

"I've been beating myself up for my cowardice for longer than I care to admit." She shook her head. "But it looks like it's going around."

Then his hands were curling around her shoulders. And though she could feel his fingers and the tightness of his grip, he didn't hurt her. She knew, without the shadow of a doubt, that he never would. That he would hurt himself first.

At least if they were talking about his hands.

"You know exactly what I do. You've watched me do it. I can't be the man you want me to be, Mariah. I don't *want* to be the man you want me to be."

"You mean you don't know how," she threw back at him.

"I can't do this." His voice was lower, harsher. And it broke her heart. "I spent my entire adult life making sure that I was without vulnerabilities. Without weaknesses. Anything less than total commitment to the job and I'm a danger to myself. To my brothers." She could see the emotions all over his face. Emotions she knew he would deny having. "I should never have touched you. That's on me. I knew better and I did it anyway."

"I was there, too," she whispered fiercely. "You can tell yourself any story you have to, I guess. But don't tell me it wasn't magic."

His breath left him then, as if she'd landed a blow to the gut. Or lower still.

"I'm not the man you think I am," he insisted after a long moment. "I'm not a man at all. You might not believe me now, but I'm doing you a favor."

She let out another laugh, but this time it was hollow and dark. "You can't let yourself have anything unless it's a hair shirt, can you? You pride yourself on it. But love isn't about pride, Griffin."

He made a sound that seemed to be ripped from inside him, as if he'd been hurt fatally, bleeding out from within.

"You don't love me," he growled at her, and his grip on her shoulders tightened. "It doesn't matter how many times you say it. It doesn't make it true."

"Fine," Mariah threw at him. "Then I'll show you."

She surged against him, out there in the dark. She pressed her mouth to his, and they were far, far past that achingly sweet kiss that had melted her and broken her heart when he'd caught her after she'd escaped the barn.

This was heat. Fire.

Pain, and proof of the depth of her feelings for him, whether he wanted to believe it or not.

This time, they were the ones who exploded, as surely as that Mercedes had.

Their hands moved against each other in the dark as Griffin angled his head and took control.

Mariah wrapped herself around him, lifting herself up and knowing without a doubt that he would hold her when she climbed him like he was another one of the trees that rimmed the property.

He kissed her and she kissed him, scalding and impossible kisses, tasting of magic and mourning, all wrapped up in the wild, insane heat that grew and grew between them with every sweep of his mouth against hers.

One moment they were standing, and Griffin was holding her against him. The next they were on the ground, and he was pressing her down into the sweet, fragrant grass.

Mariah didn't wait for an invitation. She pushed him until he rolled, and then she sat astride him, reaching down to the hem of the dress she'd borrowed from her sister. She pulled it up and over her head, then dropped it beside them.

He muttered a curse. His big, hard hands slid around to her back, pressing her until she arched toward him and he could take her nipple in his mouth.

It was better than she remembered. It was better than anything.

Her hands were clumsy and her mouth fell open, because she couldn't keep all those greedy noises inside. She reached between them, struggling with his fly.

He lifted his hips and she pulled his jeans down, then lifted him free, panting as if she were running again.

She was wild with greed, pure and simple.

And for a moment, slick and hot and breathless, she caressed his hard satiny strength, like a kind of prayer.

But she wanted more. She wanted everything.

Mariah flowed over him in the dark, the stars washing over her like a benediction. She leaned forward, found his mouth with hers, and settled the core of her against the hardest part of him.

Then twisted her hips and took him deep inside her.

She exploded instantly, shaking and shuddering. And she heard him mutter yet another curse—or maybe it was a prayer—there against her mouth.

But he didn't wait for her to come down. Instead, he started to move.

She shook and she shook, and the way he stroked in and out of her threw her from one fire deep into the next.

Mariah was sure she would die if he made her wait the way he had before. If he played those games.

But this was too intense. Too wild. Neither one of them was playing.

Griffin wrapped his arms around her, holding her as close as he possibly could, and then everything went white hot.

There was no finesse. There were no games.

Just the sheer, glorious madness of the endless fire between them.

And Mariah knew then.

She finally knew what he looked like when he was as out of control as she was, as lost and as wrecked.

Griffin pounded into her and she met him, thrust for thrust, until they were both hurtling over that edge together.

This was love. Mariah knew that with every fiber of her being.

But as they lay there together afterward, wrapped so tightly around each other that it was like they were one, she also knew that she deserved better than another fight she couldn't win.

She was the one who disengaged, then felt around until she found her dress. She stood and pulled it on. And when she tugged her head through, he'd stood, too, and was already finished buttoning himself up.

And maybe she'd had too much of that dangerous hope in her heart. Maybe she'd imagined that this would make a difference.

But she could already see the way he went still as he faced her. The way his face changed into armor.

And all the distance he put between them without having to move away.

"I love you, Griffin," she told him, and she didn't care if she sounded husky. If her voice shook. Or even if she did. "It's not going to fade away when the adrenaline wears off. But I'm not going to spend one more second of my life begging a man to love me. Wondering if I'm worthy of it. Tying myself into knots in the hopes that if I work hard enough, I'll deserve him someday. I won't do it." She swallowed. "Not even for you."

And the crack in her voice on that last word was louder than the shot he'd taken to save her.

When he spoke, he sounded as wrecked as she did, and all she could wonder was what it cost him. "I never asked you to do anything for me."

"Believe me, I know." She felt as if he'd taken one of those stones he was made out of and heaved it onto her chest. Then strapped it to her, leaving her to figure out how to breathe. "That's part of the problem."

And Mariah had done too many hard things to count recently.

But the hardest thing, the absolute hardest thing she had ever done in her life, was make herself turn her back on Griffin when she could still feel him all over her like a brand.

And then walk away.

Leaving him there in the dark, because one way or another—with him or alone—she was heading for the light.

Twenty-one

"I'm fine," Griffin growled at Templeton.

For the nine hundredth time. That morning.

It had been two months since that night in the Georgia dirt, surrounded by the woods and the war inside him he knew he'd lost. Two months since Mariah had left him with the taste of her on his mouth and nothing but emptiness inside.

A man could get used to the emptiness. He kept telling himself he could. Any day now. All he had to do was commit to it.

He'd spent years swept clean of emotion. He'd turned himself into a machine years ago, then had gone even deeper into it after he'd left Arizona. He didn't know why it was taking so long to get there this time.

Rory had come back to work and workouts after the first month, still pissed some loser had gotten the drop on him, but even more coldly determined to prove himself. Earning Jonas's high opinion of him, as far as everyone else was concerned.

Everything and everyone was *fine*.

"News flash, brother," Templeton barked at him, half a shout and half that booming laughter of his. "You're not fine."

They were out on a partner sandbag carry after an early morning session of hand-to-hand combat and grappling that had left everyone bruised and amped up. Griffin and Templeton were sharing the weight of a two-hundred-pound sandbag along a nasty mile-long loop down by the water. Every time one of them dropped the bag, they had to bang out ten burpees before they could continue.

"The workout sucks," Griffin bit out while the bag crushed his chest. "I don't have to like it, but I will survive it, and yeah, that makes me perfectly fine."

Templeton made no attempt to hide his skepticism, making Griffin wish he'd hit him harder during the hand-to-hand drills. "If you say so."

The carry went on forever, because a measly little mile was never longer than when a man was staggering beneath extra weight for the length of it.

Worse than the physical discomfort, which Griffin was good at ignoring, was the time and space the mile gave him to note all the ways he was a failure to himself.

He couldn't find his breath. He couldn't lose himself in the workout the way he liked to. And as much as he pretended otherwise when anyone asked, he couldn't seem to build back up all those compartments inside him.

He compensated for it by reinforcing the boundaries around him instead, hoping that if he armored up, it would all work out the same. That he could fake it until he made it.

But so far, all it had done was make everything worse.

After the workout, he went back to his cabin, showered, and found himself staring off into space, the way he often did these days.

It was that weakness, he knew. It was taking him over.

Griffin couldn't tell anymore if there was anything left in him but that weakness.

He was late to the morning briefing, and he knew that he was in for it when no one said a word. They all just exchanged glances, like he'd accidentally stumbled into a lunchroom filled with teenage girls to discover they'd all been sitting around talking about him. *Terrific.*

But no one approached him to get in his face about anything, not even after the meeting.

Griffin told himself he wasn't the least bit let down. That he didn't *want* to pick a fight with anyone.

He pushed his way out onto the lodge's wide porch, pulling in a deep, settling breath—like that might work this time, when it hadn't in two months. He paused when he saw he wasn't alone in the crisp morning.

Everly was out there, crooning sweet nothings to Isaac's dog, Horatio, as the moody cloud cover surrendered to the sunshine out over the far mountains. And Horatio was smarter than most humans, so he didn't bother to turn around and look at Griffin. He leaned in to Everly's hands instead, his tongue lolling out.

She was the one who straightened and smiled. And didn't stop when he stared back at her.

"Come on, Griffin," she said, mildly enough. "We're friends, right? You can smile back at me."

"I don't . . ." He stopped. He considered the fact that

this woman made Blue happy. He'd never really under-stood that before, and he didn't want to think too much about it now, but it made him feel a kind of grudging gratitude. "I don't dislike you. Particularly."

Her smile widened. "High praise indeed."

At her feet, half of his butt on those strange bright slippers she called shoes, Horatio straightened. Then whined slightly.

That was how Griffin knew that Isaac had appeared behind him. Without making a sound.

"Since we're friends," Everly said, in her warm, ir-reverent way—maybe it was just *friendliness*, now that he considered it—"I wanted to give you advance warn-ing. The way friends do."

"What do I need to be warned about?" Griffin asked coolly.

But he already knew.

Because there was only one topic he could imagine Blue's woman would think she needed to consult him about. Much less *warn* him about.

He tried to feel the emptiness. He reached for it, want-ing to clear out all of the things that made him distress-ingly human before they were the end of him, but all he could find were memories of hot, sweet nights and a drawl like honey and fire.

"I have a friend coming into town," Everly said. And it was the fact that her voice was so kind that bothered him the most. He wasn't some child who needed news broken to him gently. "I guess I'm neck-deep in friends these days. Anyway, she's visiting. She'll be here awhile. A week. I thought you should know."

He didn't insult them both by pretending to wonder who was visiting.

"I don't know why you think I need that information."

Everly opened her hands wide. "Maybe you don't. My bad."

Griffin didn't watch her as she walked away, headed back toward the cabin she shared with Blue. He was too busy waiting for whatever sucker punch was coming at him from behind, as surely as night followed day, even in the light-soaked Alaskan summer. Eventually.

"You can relax, brother," Isaac said in that low, easy way that only made wise men more tense.

Griffin wheeled around. "But I can't relax, can I? Not with all of you clucking around me like a bunch of hens. *I'm fine.*"

"Clearly."

"If you doubt that, fire me."

He hadn't known he'd meant to say that. But once he did, it was out there. Done.

And thrown down between them like a challenge.

When Isaac wasn't the kind of man a sane person challenged. Ever.

But Griffin didn't back down.

Isaac stared at him, a hint of his legendary temper—the one he kept under wraps for obvious reasons, such as everyone else's safety—in his gray eyes.

But then he shook his head slowly.

"You're bound and determined to cut off your nose to spite your face. What's that going to get you?"

"There seems to be some concern that my performance is slipping." Griffin sounded like the machine he'd always tried so hard to become. Stiff. Distant. But he didn't feel clear inside. At all. "You want that rectified, say the word. I'll be gone within the hour."

Again, that flash of temper, and a whine from Horatio to underscore it, in case Griffin might have missed the danger he was in.

"First of all, dumbass, no one is concerned about your performance." This time when Isaac shook his head, it looked a lot like he did it to keep from reaching out with his fists. "I don't know what the word *brother* means to you, but I know what it means to me. And to everyone else. When we say family, we mean it."

"Now you're defining words for me?"

"You're not right, Griffin," Isaac threw at him, almost as vicious as his punch. "I have no doubt that you can and do perform in the field at one hundred percent capacity. If I had any doubt about that, you wouldn't set foot in the field, and you know it. What I'm worried about is off the field."

"I am—"

"If you tell me you're fine one more time, I'll kick your ass myself."

It wasn't an empty threat.

They glared at each other. Griffin could feel his blood kicking through him, the way he did much too often these days. Wild. Ungovernable.

Out of control. Still.

"You? Or you and your entire personal army?" Griffin demanded, because it turned out that maybe he really did have a death wish. "Maybe look at yourself, *brother*. I'm not the one tangled up into some crazy knot over a woman. For years."

He expected Isaac to deck him. Maybe he wanted it to happen.

Instead, the other man laughed. "Aren't you?"

"No," Griffin growled. "I get that you and everyone else wants me to feel something. But I don't. I'm not built that way."

Isaac was quiet. The moment stretched out. Isaac reached down to scratch Horatio's ears and took his time doing it. But when he looked up again, his gray eyes were intense.

"You can't carry all the weight all the time, Griffin. Sometimes you have to put it down."

"You don't—"

"Don't tell me I don't understand."

And maybe if he'd said that with any heat, Griffin could have used it. He could have gotten angrier, meaner. Tried even harder to blow this up so he could fight it with his fists. But Isaac had been so quiet. Calm, even. With entirely too much understanding in his gray gaze.

"There's a reason I decided a long time ago that it was much, much better to be a machine than a man," Griffin heard himself say, as if from far away. He shifted his gaze to the water. The mountains. What was left of the morning fog. Anything but Isaac or the conversation they were having. "Not only for my sake. For everyone around me, too."

"Funny thing about that," Isaac said in that same quiet, devastating way. "You can call yourself a machine all you want. But no matter what you do, no matter how good you are at cutting yourself off or pretending you don't feel anything, you can't get away from the fact that you're a man. Flesh and blood, brother. Whether you like it or not."

And he didn't stick around to hammer in that point any further, which only meant Griffin was left to do it himself.

He threw himself into work instead. There were mission parameters to plot out, and current active situations to run support on. There were always logistical issues that needed sorting, and the Alaska Force arsenal to practice with and master.

Griffin reminded himself—repeatedly, and ferociously—that he loved his life.

This was the life he had built, the one that gave no quarter to anyone else and didn't require him to put on his civilian costume, even for a day.

He was a man of routine. Of competence, accuracy, and focus in all things.

He had never needed or wanted anything else.

Griffin had spent the two months since he left Georgia—since Mariah had walked away from him in the soft darkness, leaving him there without a single glance back—reveling in his life. *Glorying* in it, in fact.

He knew exactly who he was. He knew precisely what he needed. He wasn't built for softness. Of any kind. If Mariah had taught him anything, it was that he needed to make more of an effort to tend to his body's needs over time, so he wasn't tempted to confuse sex for something else ever again.

And sure, as he hiked back to his cabin in the brightness that evenings offered at this time of year—at the end of the long week since Everly had told him Mariah had returned to Grizzly Harbor and he'd restricted himself to Fool's Cove *for work reasons*—he might have been slightly stressed out about all the ways he had betrayed himself with a client. He needed to find a way to repair what Mariah had broken. What he'd let her break. He needed to patch up all those walls and compartments, and reorder himself so that he made sense again.

And maybe he continued to be surprised that it was a whole lot harder to do than it had seemed when he'd created those spaces inside him in the first place.

He got to his cabin, and it was cold and gloomy and empty, exactly as he'd left it. Exactly as it always was.

Griffin pushed his way inside but didn't switch on the generator and start his lights. He stayed where he was. Frozen in the gloom, the quiet.

The emptiness.

And there, when no one could see him and he could barely see himself, he faced the uncomfortable truth that he'd been avoiding for days.

The fact that she was here, a simple boat ride away, was killing him.

Killing him.

And it was more than that.

He knew when she'd arrived on the ferry. He knew when she'd checked into Blue Bear Inn again. He knew that she'd spent her week here the way she'd spent her days before, only without an Alaska Force escort this time. And he'd kept himself on alert, waiting for the inevitable attempt she'd make to reach out to him—

But she didn't.

Mariah had made no effort whatsoever to see him, and Griffin didn't know what the hell to do with that.

Especially now that her whole week here had passed.

And she was leaving on the morning ferry.

She was *killing* him.

She'd told him back in Georgia that she wasn't going to chase him. She wasn't going to beg him for anything. She deserved better.

Griffin would have sworn up and down that he didn't want any of this. That it was all for the best that he hadn't seen her, and better still that she was leaving without any kind of confrontation between them. But here in the precarious summer evening light, nothing around him but the silent forest and the ruthless mountains, he could admit, at last, that it was eating him alive that she hadn't tried.

"You hypocrite," he muttered at himself. Then swore at himself in his family's Spanish, the French he'd learned in high school, and the Arabic he'd learned in the service to really nail the point home.

It was as if, once he admitted any kind of feeling to himself—any hint of an emotion at all—the floodgates opened.

But that was a lie, too. They were already wide open.

Mariah had taken a sledgehammer to every barrier and every wall that made him who he was, and Griffin had no idea how to put them back together.

How to put *him* back together.

And he could fool himself, with all his lectures about how fine he was and how he was getting along with renovating himself from the inside out—

But she was here.

She was right here in Grizzly Harbor, happily living a life that didn't include him, and he wasn't sure he could bear it.

He braced his hands against the counter in his kitchen, like that might keep the wild storm locked away inside him.

He knew how to control his heartbeat, but he had never felt it like this before, storming at him and taking him over.

He knew the power of stillness, of waiting, of fierce and total focus, but he had never allowed himself to free-fall the way he was now, with nothing to hold on to and no idea where he was going.

Griffin remembered his tours with the Marines, and the necessary steps he'd taken to make sure he could live with the man the Corps had made him. Some walls protected not just him, after all, but anyone unlucky enough to be around him.

He didn't need to bring a war zone home to his family. He didn't need to bludgeon the people he loved with the reality of what he'd seen. He had been called to serve, and part of that service was holding weight that civilians couldn't. And shouldn't. That service didn't end when he left the Marines. If anything, it was more crucial as a veteran.

But as he stood there in the gloom of his cabin, what Isaac had said about putting down weight and what Mariah had said about the masks both he and she wore felt tangled up inside him.

Do you carry the weight of that life? she'd asked him while he'd held her. And she'd put her hand on his heart, not his shoulders.

Because it was one thing to hold fast to his honor and carry what he could. That was the vow he had taken when he'd chosen to become a soldier. But it was something else entirely to fashion the mask he'd worn from the moment he'd come back from the Marines and spend all these years hiding behind it.

Griffin had thought it was because he was too different. Too alien. Incapable of interacting with humans and unfit for relationships beyond that one week a year he spent in Tucson practicing his smile for his family.

He'd told himself that he was doing everyone a favor

when he'd coldly walked away from the life he'd had there.

But it had taken him all these years to understand that he'd been lying to himself all along.

It wasn't civilians or civilian life in general that wasn't for him. It was *that life*. That particular life.

He hadn't loved Gabrielle. Not with any kind of intensity or intimacy. He hadn't shown her the truth about himself, and he'd had no intention of ever doing so.

There in his silent cabin, it was as if he'd ripped off his own skin. He felt stripped naked and vulnerable, and he hated it. God, how he hated it.

But hating it didn't make it any less true.

He hadn't felt even a fraction for Gabrielle, the girl he'd asked to marry him, what he felt for Mariah—the woman who'd walked away from him. It wasn't any kind of contest. It wasn't even close.

In the end, as Mariah had told him in Georgia and he'd denied to himself ever since, this had always and ever been about his pride.

Gabrielle had wounded his pride, never him. And Griffin had built himself a glorious temple made entirely of walls to keep the world away, the better to nurture that pride. He had abandoned his family, walked away from his life, and done it all with his self-righteousness dressed up like concern for others.

He had never been a machine. He was good at what he did, but that didn't make him inhuman.

The sad truth was that all this time, he'd been hiding from himself. From the simple, uncomfortable reality that his ex had embarrassed him. With his best friend. And instead of dealing with that, he'd locked any feelings he had about it away and told himself he didn't feel anything at all.

Ever.

When it was actually a lot messier. He shouldn't have asked Gabrielle to marry him when what he'd really wanted was the idea of somebody waiting for him. And he should have let her go the moment he'd understood that he cared more about the Marines than he did about her. That what she'd really been to him was one more way to make it clear he couldn't and wouldn't follow in his father's footsteps.

Instead, it had been a lot easier to wrap himself up in all his lofty talk of compartments and ice.

And all it had taken was one blue-eyed blonde with a drawl like honey, and he'd been exposed for the liar he was.

No wonder he felt like he was falling apart. He was finally seeing the truth about himself, and it was jarring.

And she was here.

She was here.

Griffin had always prided himself on never surrendering, to anything—

But it seemed to him as he stood in his lonely cabin, in the remote and stark life he'd built to exalt the lies he preferred to tell himself, that he had finally run out of alternatives.

He could keep trying to pretend that he didn't feel the things he did, but that was going to ruin what he truly loved about his place in Alaska Force. His brothers would only take so much. And one of these days, if he kept on the way he was, he was going to dare Isaac to fire him, and Isaac was going to rise to that challenge.

And that might truly kill him.

He knew it would.

Griffin also knew exactly whose fault it was that he was in this situation in the first place.

And she was here until morning.

Twenty-two

Mariah left the Fairweather with a smile on her face, pushing through the door and out into the long, still-bright Alaskan evening. It was ten o'clock at night and yet light outside, and that simple reality was so . . . exhilarating.

Just like the fact that she could walk herself back to her hotel room. All alone and perfectly safe.

It had been a lovely week. Grizzly Harbor was exactly as she remembered it and possibly even better, now that no one was chasing her. Now that there were no questionable shadows or strangers at her door in the middle of the night. The charming town looked even more like a postcard in the sunnier weather of almost-summer. And it was still filled with interesting people, quirky and strange in all the right ways, and most of them surprisingly accepting of an Alaska Force client turned tourist.

Well. The tourism was a side benefit. The real reason she was here, as she reminded herself daily, was because she'd decided to make a career out of the one thing she was good at—investing money and making more of it—and Everly was her very first client.

"It's like I started a trend," Everly had said during one of their lunches at Caradine's, where the grumpiest restaurant owner in the world had allowed as how she, too, might not mind Mariah's services, either—not that it made them friends or anything. "I think everyone's wondering how many Alaska Force clients will decide they want to come live here."

Mariah hadn't told her that she doubted very much she was going to pack up and move here anytime soon, no matter how much she liked breathing in the fresh air here, where there was no Southern humidity and no McKennas to deal with.

She'd moved her few remaining things out of her apartment in Atlanta. Even with Walton under the watchful eye of the police—and better yet, now that he was out on bail, the pointed attention of the news media—she knew she could never feel safe there. More than that, she was done with Atlanta. The whole city felt tainted to her now. And there was a whole world out there, filled with cities her ex-husband—and David was legally her ex now, thanks to Georgia's no-fault divorce option, which Mariah had been happy to run with because she wanted it over, so she could cut him that check he hadn't been expecting—had no sway in whatsoever.

Maybe she'd start spending some of her money seeing each and every one of them.

When Everly had emailed her in need of a financial advisor, Mariah had jumped on it. It was an opportunity to create an actual *career*, when as far as she knew, there wasn't a McKenna alive who'd ever had more than a series of jobs. It was exactly the sort of thing David had always told her she was much too stupid to do—which was maybe why she'd never told him about her experiments with the stock market.

Becoming a kind of financial advisor for friends didn't feel like work. It felt fun.

And Mariah was all about having fun these days. It had been good to spend a couple of months back home in Two Oaks. She'd reconnected with all her family members. There'd been some hard conversations, certainly, but in the end, they'd all ended up on the same page. And there had been a lot of laughter to go with it. She'd careened around the countryside in beat-up old pickups. She'd gone fishing in quiet rivers and had taken hikes through the woods. She'd danced in questionable bars, partaken of a small McKenna cure or two, and eaten her mama's biscuits and gravy to make it through a few painful morning-afters.

But two months in—as much as she loved her family, and as much as she loved being able to appreciate her hometown and her people in a way she hadn't growing up—the truth of the matter was that she still didn't want to live there.

Everly's email had seemed like a godsend. First, the idea that she could be any kind of financial advisor to anyone would never have occurred to her on her own. There was still too much David in her head.

But mostly, she wanted to go back to Alaska. She needed to go back to the place she'd been taken from. She needed to stay there, then leave under her own power. Mariah wasn't sure how she knew this was what she needed, only that it was necessary.

Crucial, even.

She'd been back in Grizzly Harbor a week now, she was leaving on the morning ferry without any interference from horrible men who wanted to abduct her, and she liked it as much as she had before that awful man had forced her back to Georgia with him. She liked coffee with Caradine and self-defense classes with Blue. She liked laughter with new friends in the Fairweather or quiet evenings with her books. She liked the way summer took ever more of a hold, most evident in the light that wore on later and later into the night.

But she would have been lying if she'd tried to tell herself that it was the same as it had been before that man had appeared at her door with a wig and all those vile threats.

It wasn't. Of course it wasn't.

Because everywhere she went in this town, she saw Griffin.

At first she thought that maybe he was following her around again, and her heart had leaped at the notion— but he wasn't.

Or if he was, he had no intention of revealing himself this time.

And either way, she was left with an emptiness that she knew was going to sit there forever. It was the precise shape and size of how much she missed him. And how much she wished she'd made a different choice that night out behind her mother's old farmhouse.

But after everything that had happened, after her whole life up to this point, Mariah refused to allow herself to run after him. She refused to go back on the promise she'd made to the both of them that night.

She deserved more.

Even if she would never feel whole again, she deserved more.

And so did he.

It was better to feel less than whole alone than with him. Because if she knew anything, it was how quickly relationships that were unbalanced in that way ended up crushing the person who felt more.

She'd already lived it once. She wasn't doing it again—and certainly not with Griffin, who made her feel so much more than David ever had that she might have laughed about it. If it didn't hurt.

It was a cool night tonight. Much warmer than when she'd been in town before, and yet so much colder than Two Oaks. She shoved her hands in the pockets of her cargo pants, the ones she admitted only to herself that she'd bought because they reminded her of the kinds of things the Alaska Force men wore.

But that was one more thing she kept between her and her grieving heart.

She wandered up the street, nodding at the people who were also outside, soaking in the weather now that summer was almost here. This week was the Grizzly Harbor Music Festival. As far as Mariah could tell, it was an opportunity for every local person who'd ever built their own instruments or whiled away the winter singing songs to themselves to come on out, sit somewhere on the docks or outside the various shops along the boardwalks, and perform for their friends.

She skirted around a man playing a handmade ukulele who was engaged in a duet with a woman whose soprano singing voice sent chills down Mariah's spine. Then she headed for her last night in Blue Bear Inn.

She'd asked for her same room and had been surprised how easy it was to sleep in it, despite the memory of the man who'd shoved his way in through the door.

"If I'd seen him take you out of here, I'd have shot him myself," Madeleine had told her when she'd checked back in, so stern and serious her red beehive shook as she spoke.

"I'd have appreciated that," Mariah had said, and smiled so the other woman knew there was no blame there.

She didn't blame anyone but Walton for the things his minions had done. And would have found a way to do, sooner or later, no matter if Griffin and his Alaska Force buddies had locked her in a cage for her own protection.

The street was clear between the singers and the inn, and Mariah smiled down at her feet as she walked, pleased that she didn't have to worry about the cold or the possibility of icy patches that could take her down without warning. Grizzly Harbor felt like a different town in all this light and relative warmth.

She'd packed her things before she'd met Everly and Caradine in the Fairweather for a farewell drink, on the off chance she succumbed to tequila again. But she didn't go into the inn and to her room to sleep through her last hours here. At the last moment she followed an urge, turning to follow the stairs chopped into the side of the hill that led up to a lookout point Caradine had showed her. It was set high above the town, a gorgeous spot with a sweeping view out over the harbor, toward the sea.

Mariah made the steep climb and then sat on the cleared landing at the top, gazing out at this place that still felt to her like a spot of real magic tucked away at the edge of the world.

She tipped her head back. She stared up at the sky, still light at this hour, as if she could see where the stars ought to be if she looked hard enough.

When she lowered her head again, her heart felt lighter.

This was what she'd needed, this quiet moment on the side of a mountain, to leave this place again and finally find her own way in the world.

She picked her way down the stairs again, and as she went she started to feel a prickle on the back of her neck. Mariah told herself it was that stiff breeze, kicking down from the mountains and always colder than the sea air. She went down a few more steps, but it was still there. And stronger.

Finally she stopped. Her head fell forward, and she found her hands on her hips, gripping herself a lot harder than he ever had.

"No," she said, very distinctly, and she didn't care that she would look like a crazy person if anyone happened by. Standing there, talking to the trees. "You do not get to follow me around like you're doing surveillance. Not anymore."

There was a whisper of sound, though she couldn't have said where it came from, and then a shadow between two trees turned into a man.

A man she would have recognized even if it was as dark as it should have been at this hour. A man she would know if she were blind.

"If I had you under surveillance," Griffin said coolly, "you wouldn't know I was here."

And Mariah could have blamed the fact that she'd been in the Fairweather, but in reality, she'd had only one drink over the course of the couple of hours she and

Everly had sat there watching Caradine beat a group of fishermen at pool. She wasn't the least bit drunk.

She only felt that way when she looked at him.

As if everything in the world spun around and around, the mountains and the sea and the Alaskan sky, leaving only him. Only Griffin.

"Nothing's changed," she told him, as evenly as she could.

"That's where you're wrong," he said, and it took her a moment to realize that he didn't sound like himself. He sounded furious. "Everything's changed."

She studied his features, hard and beautiful, his dark eyes glinting in the late evening light. And she ignored her traitorous heart and the things it whispered.

"Not for me, sugar," she drawled. "I'm still in love with you. I still think you're an idiot. And if you think that this is an opportunity for you to storm around doing your robot impersonation—"

"You've ruined me," he told her, and she'd never heard that particular tone from him before. As if he wasn't entirely in control of himself. "You might as well have set a charge and detonated it yourself."

In that moment, she realized it wasn't temper on his face, or nothing that simple. It was something else. Something pure and raw.

He looked the way she felt.

And deep inside her, all those broken pieces that she would simply have to learn how to live with seemed to hum. While the whispers from her heart grew louder and more insistent.

"Griffin," she began, as calmly as she could, when she wanted to scream. When she wanted to do all the things she'd promised herself—and him—she wouldn't ever do. Beg. Cry. Bend herself into whatever shape would allow her to touch him again.

But she couldn't do that. She knew she couldn't.

"I don't know what you came here for," he told her, in that same strange tone of voice that made her shiver. And made her wonder why she'd imagined she'd wanted to see the fury of such a patient man in the first place. There was a whole proverb about how foolish that was. "Was it to torture me? Was it to rub salt in the wound?"

"Of course not."

"You told me you wouldn't beg. You wouldn't chase after me. You told me you knew what you deserved."

But she hadn't told him how much it hurt. "I do. I finally do."

Griffin shook his head once. Then again. He took a step toward her, and it wasn't the way he usually moved. It wasn't smooth like silk. It was jerky, as if he didn't know how to operate his own body. And then he lifted his hands in the air as if he was . . .

But no. That was impossible.

Griffin Cisneros did not *surrender* to anything or anyone. And certainly not to her.

"Tell me what that is, Mariah," he threw at her, his voice as unsteady as the rest of him. "Tell me what you deserve. I don't know how to do any of this. I don't know how to give anyone anything. I think you deserve a man who can give you everything you want. Need. Dream about. And I don't—" He stopped himself, then pulled in a harsh breath, his gaze even darker than usual. "I don't know if that man is me. I don't know if I'm built that way."

"Griffin." And this time Mariah stepped toward him, aching when he stiffened as if a single touch from her might break him. Because that was the last thing she wanted. "I don't need you to be anything that you're not. I love you, not some made-up version of who I think you could be, maybe, someday. That's exactly what I don't want. I've already lived that way once already, and you had a front row seat to how that ended."

"The only other person who ever loved me came to hate me, in the end," Griffin told her, as if he were delivering his own indictment. "Because I could never love her the way she needed."

"The difference is that you already love me the way I need," Mariah said quietly. Softly. "You just don't want to."

He broke then. She watched it happen. This big strong man made of so much steel and lethal intent, wracked from the inside out because of what she'd said.

Because you told him the truth, a voice inside her countered.

"You've destroyed me," he told her, anguished and furious. Wide open and clearly not happy about it. "I can function in any war zone I'm dropped in, and always have. Nothing affects me. Nothing gets through. Except you."

"It's okay to love me back, Griffin," she said softly, letting her treacherous heart take over. Because she had the distinct impression that was what he'd done, right here in front of her. "I promise you, it won't really ruin you. It only feels that way at first."

He was breathing hard, as if he were running—or as if he was someone else running, someone in far less stellar physical condition than he was.

"You deserve the world, but all I have to give you is a man who spent the better part of his adult life trying to strip himself down to parts," Griffin thundered at her, as if he wanted to use himself as a weapon. "Half the time I think I'm not trying to be a machine, I'm trying to be a man. And I fail miserably at it."

Mariah sighed, blinking back the tears threatening to spill over. She leaned closer, then slid her hands over his chest, soaking in his heat. His strength.

And the heartbeat that told her exactly how human he was.

"It's the trying that matters," she told him, tipping her face up to his.

"That's nothing but a pathetic excuse." He belted the words out as if he were hitting something. Himself, maybe. "That's what people tell themselves, but it's a lie. It's failure dressed up in pretty words."

She didn't think there was any arguing with that bleak look on his face, so she didn't try. Mariah slid one palm over his heart and held it there, the way she had once before.

He remembered it, too. She felt the way he tensed— and better still, the way his heart kicked at her.

"Your heart is safe with me, Griffin," she whispered. "I promise."

He frowned at her like her words didn't make any sense, his beautiful dark eyes still so troubled. But less bleak, maybe, when he reached out and slowly took a chunk of her hair in his hand, testing the curl around his fingers.

"If I could keep you safe, you never would have been taken. You never would have ended up in the trunk of a car. You never would have gotten beaten up in a barn in Georgia." He didn't look bleak then. He looked tortured. "And then had to run for your life with that animal on your heels."

Mariah only laughed, arching into him, knowing as she did it that he would catch her.

And he did.

He always did.

"You silly man," she told him, reveling in the way his hands wrapped around her upper arms like he'd been made to hold her. "I wasn't running for my life. I was running to you."

She watched the storm move across his face, and moved even closer.

"They're not the same thing. One is fear, and the other is hope."

"I can't be anyone's hope," Griffin threw out.

Mariah shrugged, liking the way he gripped her harder when she did. "Too late, sugar."

He stared down at her as if she were a ghost. As if she were torment and disaster, and Mariah couldn't say she minded it much. Not if he would keep on doing it. There were worse fates than being the thing that brought a tough man to his knees.

"I want you to stay," he told her gruffly, as if it hurt. As if all of this hurt. "I don't know if I can be the man you deserve, but I want to try. And I don't usually fail."

He bent down to pick her up, and then held her steady as she wrapped herself around him. Mariah gazed down into his face as he looked up at her, his strong arms around her as if that was all the wall either one of them would ever need.

"I want to make you smile," Griffin told her, and she was overwhelmed by his heat against her. Her heart was flipping over and over, and his words sounded less like pain and more like vows. Just him and her and the trees all around them. "I want to feel that dirty laugh of yours pour over me like honey. I like you drunk and I like you sober and I like you here, Mariah. I like you wrapped all around me, day and night, and I never thought my life was empty until you left me in it all alone." He shifted so she was flush against him. "Don't go. Please."

"I love you, too," she murmured.

And then she kissed him, the two of them wrapped up in the light of a long Alaskan evening.

No shadows, no fear.

He held her, strong like stone but made of flesh and blood, and he kissed her with all the need and desperation she felt inside her, too.

He kissed her and he kissed her, this beautiful man who believed he was less than perfectly human.

Mariah knew better. And she wanted nothing more than to show him.

"Give me a year," he told her, there against her mouth. "And I'll give you everything I have."

"I have a better idea," she replied. "Just give me you. I'll do the same in return. And we'll see where we end up."

He pulled back to look at her then, like he was drinking her in. Tattooing her deep into his skin.

"If you give me the chance," he told her, this man who lived by his vows and would, she knew, die by them if necessary, "I'll give you forever."

And as she had so many other times—whether it was running across that field in Georgia or right here, right now, on the edge of the world in the beginning of this brand-new life they could forge together—Mariah believed him.

She trusted him. She loved him.

So she threw herself straight off into that forever he'd promised, knowing he would catch her.

Epilogue

SIX MONTHS LATER

Griffin waited for Mariah outside a lawyer's office in Atlanta, watching her handle herself with her usual grace through the glass wall of the meeting room. He was fully prepared to haul her out of there if she looked the slightest bit upset.

They had left Grizzly Harbor the week before, sneaking out ahead of a nasty storm that would have kept them landlocked for a few days. Griffin wouldn't have minded all that much. Before.

But now he was more concerned with keeping Mariah happy than he was with succumbing to his own impulses to hole up and act like a hermit.

That was how they'd ended up spending Thanksgiving with Griffin's family in Arizona. Griffin had been humbled by how excited his family was that he had finally stepped outside the usual strict boundaries of his relationship with them. He'd allowed them not only the extra holiday, but more access to him—and it had made his mother cry.

Which had made him feel like a jackass.

"Happy tears are a good thing," Mariah had assured him on a walk through the neighborhood that had once felt like a noose around his neck. And now was simply . . . pretty. "Happy tears mean you're doing it right. I promise."

The crazy thing was, he believed her.

Mariah changed him more and more every day, and he'd stopped fighting it. He'd surrendered to his feelings for her up on that hill overlooking Grizzly Harbor, which felt a whole lot like winning. That wasn't to say he didn't kick back into his old robot habits from time to time, but she handled conflict the way she handled everything else.

Usually by laughing at him until he got over himself.

He was slowly learning to do it right back.

And if it wasn't solved in laughter, there were other ways. More deliberate ways that had more to do with flashes of temper, and far more satisfying ways to let those flames burn through the both of them.

Over and over again.

At first Griffin had been afraid that losing his distance and objectivity and all those walls would ruin his ability to do his job. He was sure he would be unable to do what he needed to do and find himself sidelined without having to challenge Isaac to fire him.

But instead, life with Mariah made him realize that he could pick and choose the kind of compartments he needed. That it wasn't all or nothing. That he could pour himself into his work and pour himself into her, in turn.

He'd had no idea, in all those years that he'd prided himself on being so sharp and cold and removed from petty concerns, that he'd been living only half a life. Closed down, cut off.

He'd been nothing but black and white, and Mariah was color.

Bright. Haunting.

And stunningly beautiful, all the time.

He studied her, dressed like a princess, through the glass. His princess. Her blond hair was smooth, her clothes were sleek, and she was every inch the Atlanta society queen she'd been in her previous life.

The one she'd shrugged off when she'd come to Alaska.

David Lanier and his father might attempt to paint Mariah as grasping, gold-digging trash who'd plotted out her own abduction, but the jury was more likely to see Grace Kelly.

Who also happened to be a financial whiz in her spare time—more interested in gold digging from financial markets than from her ex-husband.

Griffin was the lucky man who got all those sides of her, all the time.

All his.

"Okay?" he asked her when she finally left the deposition and came to him.

The way she would always come to him, he thought with a rush of possessiveness he'd learned to revel in. Especially when she was just as possessive in turn.

"Of course," she replied, smiling up at him.

Her real smile. Not the one she used as a weapon, especially here.

He took her hand and walked with her to the elevator,

then outside into a beautiful winter's day in Atlanta that did a fabulous impression of a perfect high-summer day in Alaska. Only brighter. Softer. And faintly perfumed with flowers, even in the middle of the concrete of downtown.

They stood there on Peachtree Street, the Atlanta skyscrapers looming around them like urban mountains, and for no reason at all, found themselves grinning at each other.

"I love you," Griffin said.

As if there had ever been any doubt.

He said it, and didn't understand why it had been so hard to say. He'd been so sure that he was too broken to mean it the way she needed to hear it. He didn't think he could ever love her or trust her the way she did him, but he wanted to. God, how he wanted to.

It had been such a hard thing for all these months, and yet in the end, it was easy.

The easiest thing he'd ever said in his life.

He said it a few more times, to make sure.

Right here in this city where they'd come to put demons to rest, one by one.

Her blue eyes gleamed, bright with tears he was sure were the happy kind. "It's because I'm all dressed up like the kind of society princess you pretend to hate, isn't it?"

"It's because you're you." He took both her hands in his and didn't care if the whole city ground to a halt around them. "It's because if I asked you to marry me now, you'd say no. This time. Because I think you're going to take a long while to come back around on that, and I'm willing to wait. It's because I know you love me something crazy. I can see it every time you look at me. It's because I've given you a thousand reasons to leave me, and no doubt will again, but you're not going anywhere."

She didn't like his cabin—or the mile-long hike to get to it, especially in bad weather—though she'd tried her best. Mariah, though not the princess he'd originally imagined her, wasn't exactly an outdoor woman, either. He planned to surprise her when they got back to Grizzly Harbor with the little house he'd bought for them in town, where she could keep up that routine she loved so much, and he could commute by boat to Fool's Cove. He'd even made sure they could finally have their own little library.

It amazed him how much he loved to make her happy.

"No," she whispered now, and there was so much emotion in her gaze that he was surprised it didn't hurt. But then, he imagined there was the same kind of emotion in his. And if she had taught him anything, it was that feeling all these things was worth it. More than worth it. It was everything. "I'm not going anywhere."

"I love you when you talk like a princess, and I love you when your drawl comes out with your family, your accent so thick and rich I can't understand a word you're saying." He lifted her hands to his mouth and kissed each one in turn. "I want to spend the rest of my life learning each and every one of all those imperfections that make you *you*. And I will."

"I love you, Griffin," she whispered, and her tears weren't staying put any longer.

He reached over and dashed them away.

Because this was it.

This woman would marry him, sooner or later. She would have his babies, now that she'd been checked out by a real doctor and her fertility wasn't in doubt any longer. They would build a life together, and it wouldn't be a labyrinth of walled-off compartments. It wouldn't be dark or bleak.

It would be bright lights, shining so beautiful and wild that if they let it, it would light up even the relentless dark of an Alaskan winter.

And best of all, they would do it together.

"Mariah," he said, as if this were their wedding, right here on a busy city street on a random workday. As if these were the vows that mattered, and everything else would be an afterthought. "I love you. I will always love you."

And that smile spread over her face, crooked and wicked and the most beautiful thing he'd ever seen. Or ever would.

The happy tears were a bonus.

"Oh, sugar," she murmured, that accent just the way he liked it, thick as honey and twice as sweet. And better still, forever his. "I know you will."

And then she kissed him, like something right out of the fairy tales both of them would have sworn up and down they didn't believe in.

Until now.

Keep reading for an excerpt from the next
book in the Alaska Force series

SERGEANT'S
CHRISTMAS SIEGE

Available in Fall 2019

The man she was supposed to meet was late.

Deliberately, she assumed.

Investigator Kate Holiday of the Alaska State Troopers noted the time, then sat straighter in the chair she'd chosen specifically because it faced the door of the only café she'd found open here in tiny Grizzly Harbor, one of Southeast Alaska's rugged fishing villages that was accessible only by personal boat, ferry—which, at this time of year, seldom ran—or air.

Another minute passed. Five minutes. Ten.

This was not a particularly auspicious beginning to her investigation into the strange goings-on in and around this remote town, tucked away on one of the thousand or so islands along the state's southeastern coast. Kate took a dim view of strange goings-on in general, but particularly when they consistently involved a band of ex–military operatives running around and calling themselves Alaska Force.

Of all things.

Kate was not impressed with groups of armed, dangerous, unsupervised men in general. Much less with those who gave themselves cute names, seemed to expend entirely too much energy attempting to keep the bulk of their activities off the official radar, and yet kept turning up in the middle of all kinds of trouble. Which they then lied about.

She had been unimpressed the moment she'd read the file that carefully detailed the list of potential transgressions her department at the Alaska Bureau of Investigations believed the members of Alaska Force had committed. But then, Kate had a thing about the men up here, on this island and all over the state, who seemed to think that the law did not apply to them. It was a time-honored part of the Alaskan frontier spirit, and Kate had hated it pretty much all her life.

But this was not the time to think about her unpleasant childhood. What mattered was that Kate had grown up. She had escaped from the armed, dangerous, and unsupervised men who had run roughshod over her early years, helped put them away, and had thereafter dedicated herself to upholding the rule of law in the most defiantly, gleefully lawless place in the United States.

This introductory interview with the supposed public relations point person of Alaska Force was only the opening shot. Kate was unamused that the group—who secreted themselves away on the near-inaccessible backside of the island, and when had anything good come from groups of dangerous men with hideouts?—considered it necessary to have a public relations point person in the first place.

She had every intention of taking them down if they

were responsible for the escalating series of disturbances that had culminated in the latest act of arson two days ago, which had amped up her department's interest in what was happening out here in Grizzly Harbor. Because she had no tolerance whatsoever for people who imagined themselves above the law.

Much less people who thought it was entertaining to blow up fishing boats in the sounds and inlets that made up so much of Southeast Alaska, where summer brought cruise ships filled with tourists. This time there had been no one on board, likely because it was the first week of a dark December.

But it wouldn't always be December.

The door to the café opened then, letting in a blast of frigid air from outside, where the temperature hovered at a relatively balmy thirty-three degrees.

Kate glanced up, expecting the usual local in typical winter clothes.

But the man who sauntered in from the cold was more like a mountain.

She sat at attention as if she couldn't help herself, as if her body was responding unconsciously to the authority and command the man exuded the way the many deadly wild animals who roamed these islands threw off scent. And she loathed herself for the silly, embarrassingly feminine part of her that wanted to flutter about and straighten her blue uniform. She refrained.

The man before her was dressed for the cold and the coming dark, which should have made him look bulky and misshapen. But it didn't, because all of his gear was very clearly tactical. He was big. Very big. She put him at about six four, and that wasn't taking into account the width of his shoulders or the way he held himself, as if he fully expected anyone looking at him to either cower in fear or applaud. Possibly both.

Kate did neither.

It was December on an Alaskan island, a bit of steep, rugged land made from the top of a submerged mountain and covered in dense evergreen trees, perched there in the treacherous northern Pacific with glaciers all around. One of the most beautiful if inhospitable parts of the world. There were only about one hundred and fifty year-round residents of this particular village, and Kate was the only person in the café besides the distinctly unfriendly owner, who had provided her a cup of coffee without comment, then disappeared into the kitchen.

Meaning she was, for all intents and purposes, alone with a man who made her feel as instantly on edge as she would if she'd come face to face with a grizzly.

Kate didn't speak as she eyed the new arrival. She'd joined the Troopers after college, and had been on the job ever since, helping her fellow Alaskans in all parts of this great state. And sometimes providing that help had involved finding herself in all kinds of questionable situations. The man standing before her radiated power, but Kate knew a thing or two about it herself.

She watched, expressionless, as he stuffed his hat and gloves in the arm of his jacket like a normal person when he wasn't, then hung it up on one of the hooks near the door, all with what seemed to Kate to be entirely too much languid indifference for a man who was clearly well aware he was nothing less than a loaded weapon.

He looked around the café, as if he expected to see a crowd on this dreary, cold Friday afternoon in the darkest stretch of the year. Then he finally looked straight at Kate.

For a moment, she felt wildly, bizarrely dizzy. As if

the chair she was in had started to spin. She went to sit down, then realized three things, one on top of the next. One, she was already sitting down. Two, the man might have made a big show of looking around, but he'd taken in every single detail about her before he'd fully crossed the threshold. She knew it. She could tell.

And three, the man in front of her wasn't only big and powerful—and incredibly dangerous if the file on him was even partially correct—he was also beautiful.

Shockingly, astonishingly, absurdly beautiful, in a way that struck her as too masculine, too physical, and too carnal, all at once.

He had thick black hair that didn't look the least bit military, and he made no attempt to smooth it now that he'd pulled his hat off. His eyebrows were arched and distinctly wicked. His eyes were as dark as strong coffee, his mouth was implausibly distracting, and his cheekbones were like weapons. He looked the way Kate imagined a Hawaiian god might.

Which was a fanciful notion that she couldn't believe she'd just entertained about a person of interest in a recurring series of questionable events.

His gaze was locked to hers, and she wondered if people mistook all that inarguable male beauty for softness, when she could see the gravity in those dark eyes. And a certain sternness in his expression.

But in the next second he smiled, big and wide, and Kate was almost . . . dazzled.

"You must be Alaska State Trooper Kate Holiday," he said in a booming voice. "Come all the way out to Grizzly Harbor to sniff around Alaska Force. I'm Templeton Cross, at your service."

And when he moved, it was liquid and easy, two strides

to get across the floor and extend his hand to Kate as if he were welcoming her to his home like some cheerful, oversized patriarch. As if he weren't on the wrong side of an interview with law enforcement.

As if he wasn't very likely responsible for—or complicit in—a string of disturbances, hospitalizations, explosions, and other dubious events as far away as Juneau, but mostly concentrated here in Grizzly Harbor, going back years. With a noted and concerning uptick over the past year.

But being a Trooper wasn't like other kinds of policing, or so Kate gathered from watching police shows based in the Lower 48. Alaska State Troopers had to get used to roles that defied proper job descriptions, because anything could and would happen in the course of a shift when that shift took place somewhere out in the Last Frontier. Kate knew how to play her part. She stood, smiled nonthreateningly, and took his hand.

And told herself that she was cataloguing how hard and big it was, that was all. How it wrapped around hers. How Templeton Cross, whose military record stated he had been an Army Ranger until he'd moved off into something too classified to name, made no attempt to overpower her. He didn't shake too hard. He didn't try to crush the bones in her hand, to let her know who was boss. There was no he-man, Neanderthal moment, the way there too often was in situations like these.

He shook her hand like a good man might, and she filed that away because she suspected he wasn't a good man at all. And a man who could fake it was exponentially more dangerous than one who oozed his evil everywhere like a fuel leak.

She angled her head toward the table she'd claimed,

removing her hand from his and waving it in invitation. Because she could act like this was her home, too. No matter that the hand he'd shaken . . . tingled. "Please. Sit down."

"Right to business," Templeton said, with a big laugh that jolted through Kate. She told herself it was an unpleasant sensation, especially the way it wound around and around inside her like it was heating her up from within.

She smiled at him as he threw himself down into the seat across from her, taking up more than his fair share of space. As if his big arms, clad in a tight henley that showed her exactly how seriously he took his physique and suggested he dedicated a huge amount of energy to maintaining it, couldn't help but sprawl out on either side of him of their own accord.

"Do you think this will make you seem more approachable?" she asked.

He belted out another laugh. "Do I seem approachable? I must be slipping."

And for a moment they both smiled at each other, like it was a competition to see who could be more pleasant.

"You must know that I'm here after the rash of incidents that seemed to stem entirely from your little group," Kate said, folding her hands on the table and watching his face. His expression didn't change at all. "You've chosen to show up for this conversation late, then engage in what I imagine you think is charming small talk. Your military record goes to great lengths not to say what sort of classified things you engaged in after you were a Ranger, but I'm going to guess it was Delta Force."

"I don't like that name," Templeton said, almost helpfully. "It's so dramatic, don't you think?"

"Now you're being funny," Kate observed. "Which suggests you find yourself entertaining. What interests me, Mr. Cross, is that you think comedy is the appropriate way to handle the situation you find yourself in."

She knew a lot of things about Templeton Cross. Among them, that he'd achieved the rank of Master Sergeant—but unlike many people with military backgrounds she'd encountered, he didn't correct her when he failed to address him by his rank.

"And what situation is that?" he asked instead. "I'm having a cup of coffee with a law enforcement officer. As a former soldier myself, I have nothing but respect for a badge. I didn't realize there was an expectation that this conversation stay grumpy. But we can do that, too."

"Fascinating," Kate murmured, as if he were answering her questions with these evasions. "Why don't we start with you explaining to me what Alaska Force is."

Templeton leaned back, his big body looking as if it might splinter the chair beneath him if he moved wrong. Then again, this was Alaska, where everything was necessarily hardy. Even chairs in an otherwise empty café in a town so sleepy this time of year that Kate hadn't seen a single person on her walk from the sea plane she'd flown here from Juneau. She'd felt eyes on her when she'd walked through the residential part of town, and had heard music from inside the local dive bar, but she hadn't actually *seen* a soul.

"Alaska Force isn't anything but a group of combat vets who run a little business together," Templeton said genially. "It's all apple pie and Uncle Sam around here, I promise."

"Mercenaries, in other words."

"Not quite mercenaries," Templeton said, and she thought she saw something in his gaze then, some flash of heat, but it was gone almost as soon as she identified it. "I can't say I like that word."

"Is there a better word to describe what you do?"

"We like to consider ourselves problem solvers," Templeton said, sounding friendly and at his ease. He looked it, too. Yet Kate didn't believe he was either of those things. "You start throwing around words like 'mercenary,' and people think we're straight-up soldiers of fortune. Soulless men who whore themselves out to the highest bidder. That's not us."

"And yet Alaska Force has, to my count, been involved in no less than six disturbing incidents in the past six months," Kate replied in the same friendly tone he'd used. She even sat back a little, mirroring his ease and supposed laziness right back at him. "There was a member of your own team who presented at the hospital in Juneau with injuries consistent with being beaten over the head and forcibly restrained. He claimed he tripped and fell."

"Green Berets are notoriously clumsy," Templeton replied blandly.

"Right around that time, an individual known to be a self-styled doomsday preacher, who Alaska Force interfered with years back—"

"If you mean we made sure he couldn't hurt the women and children he was terrorizing."

"—stole a boat and then rendezvoused with your team this past spring. And with you, if I'm not mistaken." Kate knew she was not mistaken about anything involving this case.

"His story changes every hour on the hour." Templeton's smile struck her as more edgy than before, his eyes more narrow. "We happened to be in place to contain a potentially far more threatening incident. You're welcome."

"Since then there have been four more incidents involving property damage in and around this island and the surrounding area. Culminating in what happened two nights ago when a boat that shouldn't have been in the harbor in the first place blew up within sight of the ferry terminal. The anonymous tip that we received suggested Alaska Force was responsible."

Templeton looked unconcerned. "We're not."

"That's it? That's the whole defense you intend to mount?"

"I'm not going to waste my time defending something we didn't do," Templeton said in that amiable, friendly, excessively mild way that was beginning to grate on Kate's nerves. "A reasonable person might ask herself why Alaska Force would blow things up right here in our own backyard. If we were the kind of mercenaries you seem to think we are, that would only draw unwanted attention. Like this meeting."

It was the first hint of anything other than excessive friendliness in his voice. Kate was delighted she was finally getting somewhere.

"You claim you're not that kind of mercenary," she said. "So what kind of mercenary are you? The kind who thinks it's fun to blow things up, maybe? Just because you can?"